Southern   DD-GR

Prairie Schooner Book Prize in Fiction EDITOR Hilda Raz

For Dave & Ress—
All my good wishes
for your own writing!
Cheers,
Kenny

Last Call

K. L. COOK

K L Cook

University of Nebraska Press
Lincoln and London

Library of Congress
Cataloging-in-Publication Data
Cook, K. L.
Last call / K. L. Cook.
p. cm. — (Prairie schooner book
prize in fiction)
ISBN 0-8032-1540-1 (cloth : alk. paper)
1. Texas, West—Fiction.   2. Missing
persons—Fiction.   3. Loss (Psychol-
ogy)—Fiction.   I. Title.   II. Series.
PS3603.O572L37 2004
813'.6—dc22
2004003458

Set in Quadraat by Kim Essman.
Designed by A. Shahan.
Printed by Thomson-Shore, Inc.

FOR CHARISSA

Contents

Acknowledgments

I wish to extend my thanks to the following: College of Charleston, Warren Wilson College, and Prescott College for professional support; The MacDowell Colony, The Vermont Studio Center, The Corporation of Yaddo, Blue Mountain Center, and Dave and Lisa Hanna for the time and space to complete this manuscript; the Arizona Commission on the Arts for a fellowship in fiction; Joan Silber, Jean Thompson, Robert Boswell, and Richard Russo, mentors extraordinaire; the many friends and editors who read these stories and provided insight, encouragement, and criticism; my agent, Jennifer Cayea, and the staffs of *Prairie Schooner* and the University of Nebraska Press; Melanie Bishop, Wayne Regina, Gret Antilla, Sheila Sanderson, Susan Lang, Bret Lott, Mike Thomason, and Joe Schuster for their support and friendship; and my family, especially my children and my wife, Charissa Menefee, who inspire me daily.

Earlier versions of the stories in this collection originally appeared in the following publications: "Easter Weekend" in *Post Road*; "Nature's Way" in *Witness*; "Gone" in *Santa Fe Writers Project*; "Texas Moon" in *Denver Quarterly*; "Last Call" in *Puerto del Sol*; "Knock Down, Drag Out" in *Shenandoah*; "Costa Rica" in *Threepenny Review*; "Breaking Glass" (as "Mother Rejects Her Lover") in *New Laurel Review*; "Marty" in *Colorado Review*; "Pool Boy" in *Writers' Forum*; and "Penance" in *American Short Fiction*. "Texas Moon" and "Last Call" won the grand prize in the 2002 Santa Fe Writers Project Literary Arts Series under the title "Last Call: The Texas Moon Stories."

I have learned that neither kindness nor cruelty by themselves, independent of each other, creates any effect beyond themselves; and I have learned that the two combined, together, at the same time, are the teaching emotion.   **Edward Albee** *Zoo Story*

Last Call

Nature's Way

Easter Weekend

Their family had two dogs back then, mongrel collie mixes —
Fay Wray, the older female, and Greta, the only pup from Fay's
last litter that they hadn't been able to give away. Greta had some
breed mixed in that made her jumpy and snappy around anybody
but the family. Laura's father named her after Greta Garbo, who
he thought was the best-looking woman he'd ever seen until he
met Laura's mother. He'd always wink and smile when he said
that. Mrs. Tate wouldn't look at him. She'd just knead the bread
dough or fold the laundry or read Rich and Gene a story, but
Laura could see her lips turn upward in the slightest smile and a
pink flush spread over her neck.

In heat, Fay would attract all the neighboring hounds and
mutts and alley rovers, who would howl and paw and try to jump
the rusting metal fence to get in the backyard, and sometimes
they would succeed. Laura and her brothers would watch in fas-
cination as the dogs nipped and bit at each other, the males with
their extended pink penises, like flayed lizards, obscene, raw,

vulnerable. If a dog got in the pen, Mr. or Mrs. Tate would be out with a broomstick or a rake, beating the dog or shooing it away until it jumped back over the fence, sometimes with its tail between its legs, sometimes snarling at the thwarted opportunity. If Laura's parents were not there, then Manny or, before she eloped, Gloria would fight off the dogs. But on occasion they would all just watch the males tie up with Fay, panting, their tongues lolling wetly from the sides of their mouths, the other males barking and whining and pacing back and forth in the alley next to the fence, Greta either hiding in her shed or barking madly at the coupled animals.

Laura and her brothers and sometimes the gang of freckled fools Manny ran around with would watch the dogs' ritual, laughing at first, the boys wisecracking — *Get 'er, stud! Stick it in 'er!* — but then they would quiet down and stare with a charged stillness as the dogs labored with a persistence that seemed both grotesque and fascinating. They weren't dumb. They knew litters resulted from these incidents, and that they themselves were the result of their parents' similar activities, but it was not pleasant for them to make the connection in their heads. Laura had never been able to adequately imagine her mother and father tied up, tongues dripping, grunting mindlessly like this. To think too much about it, which she sometimes did when seeing the dogs, always made her feel nauseous and sad and strangely frightened.

When Greta first came into heat, two weeks before Easter, rather than wait for the males to jump over the fence, she dug a hole underneath and was gone. The whole family searched down alleys and gravel roads, at the pound, in the fields and parks, on the two highways leading out of Charnelle. They were sure she was lost forever, maybe dead, or had run off with a pack of coyotes. Gene and Rich cried.

"There's nothing we can do," Mrs. Tate said, looking out the window, her arms folded across her chest. It was dark outside, so the light reflected off the glass like a mirror. From the big chair Laura could see her mother's face in the glass.

Mr. Tate knelt down beside the couch, where the boys were sitting. "Maybe she'll come back."

Laura's mother turned toward them. "Maybe she won't," she said flatly.

He gave her a sharp look. "We don't know," he said.

"Exactly. We don't know. She was difficult and a misfit, and she didn't want to be here. It's just as well that she's gone."

"We're responsible for her," he said.

"No, we're not."

"She's ours. She belongs to us."

"She doesn't belong to anyone, Zeeke."

There was a pocket of painful silence. He rose from the couch and squared his shoulders. "She's ours," he said again.

Laura's mother looked at him for a moment, then turned back to the window and stared into the dark yard. She didn't say anything else.

Laura noticed that her mother seemed quieter than usual. Laura believed she was the only one who had noticed. Her father had been very busy, working long hours, taking jobs in nearby towns some weeks, leaving for Amarillo before sunrise and often not returning until after midnight, so he wasn't around much that spring. When they did see him, he was often too tired for talk, slipping into a doze at the kitchen table or in his chair in the living room. Manny was fifteen and a half, just a year older than Laura, and in high school now. He paid little attention to what was going on with the family. He'd gotten a job at a filling station after school and on Saturdays, and he seemed to spend most of the time he was home primping in the bathroom, greasing his hair and combing it into a meticulously groomed duck's ass — probably to impress some girl at school. Gene, who was eight, and Rich, who was only four, weren't old enough to know when people acted differently. They just wanted to have food fixed when they were hungry and be tucked in bed at night. But Laura did notice what seemed to be happening with her mother. She knew her mother had been hurt when Gloria eloped, before Gloria even graduated from high school, but that had been a while now, almost a year, long enough to get used to. As Laura watched her mother go about her chores, fixing meals, washing clothes, bathing children, she worried that she didn't smile much, that she didn't say much, that she did everything and did it right, but that something was gone that had been there before.

Her mother was also more easily angered and strict, quick to punish the younger boys for the least little thing. Laura found herself walking on eggshells when she was home, not starting any arguments, doing her chores before she was asked, even offering to help with the dishes or cooking or laundry when it wasn't her turn. She had been a little sick throughout the winter and into early spring, feeling feverish, never quite able to shake the sniffles and the itchiness in her nose and throat and eyes. Even school, which she liked — especially geography and English — seemed to limp sluggishly toward the end of the year, like a wounded soldier.

She was relieved that everyone seemed to cheer up when they decided to visit Aunt Velma for Easter. The whole house brightened and straightened into shape, like a clean, snapped-out sheet. Laura's sinuses cleared — ah, how wonderful to breathe normally again. Her father sang bits and pieces of old songs in the shower, and her mother seemed more tender and tolerant with them all, even softly whistling while she hung the wet clothes on the line.

They left for Aunt Velma's shortly after lunch on Good Friday, when Mr. Tate got off work. Mrs. Tate had already packed the suitcases and wrapped the ham she planned to cook for Easter dinner. Fay—who'd been moping since Greta had run off—jumped around like an excited pup as they readied themselves for the trip. She hopped in and out of the truck bed, barking. She was ready to go, right now, let's get on the road and head to the farm—now, now, come on people, get moving.

Except for Mr. Tate, none of the family had been out of town since last Thanksgiving. Laura didn't realize how good it felt to leave until they were on the highway, driving away—Gene, Manny, Fay, and her in the back of the pickup with the luggage and the food, the sky white and breezy and cool, Charnelle dissolving behind them.

They arrived just after three in the afternoon. Aunt Velma was waiting in the yard, her strawberry-print apron over her dress, her large mop of gray hair pinned in a loose bun that fluttered in the breeze. She hugged and kissed them all. When Laura embraced her, she could smell baked cinnamon apples.

Aunt Velma said, "You're just in time to feed the chickens," and she whacked Gene and Rich's butts playfully with a broom and sent them off to the barn, where they scattered the grain and imitated the clucking, head-bobbing, selfish strutting of the six hens and the rooster.

After a few minutes, Rich ran back up. "I wanna ride Ginger."

"That's fine, honey," Aunt Velma crooned, "but you better ask your parents."

He was off in a waddling run to the house, where he retrieved Manny and his father, who saddled and bridled the older horse, Ginger. Manny rode with Rich, while Gene and Laura took turns riding the younger mare, Hayworth. Later, Laura and Manny galloped the two horses beyond the pasture, through the peach and apple orchards, to the open land that bordered the new highway.

"Hi-yaaa!" Manny yelled, heeling Ginger into a run.

Though nervous — Laura'd almost been thrown from Hayworth the previous Thanksgiving — she tightened her grip on the reins, clamped her legs against the mare's sides, clicked her tongue, and pressed her heels into the rear flanks. The horse galloped faster, and Laura said, "Come on, girl," then shouted like Manny, and the horse, as if a current of electricity had suddenly jolted through her, snapped into a run, whiplashing Laura's head.

She nearly fell off, but righted herself, leaned forward, and clasped the reins more securely. The air whished by, and her hair swirled around her face like a nest of blonde spiders. Too scared to let go, she shook her head until her hair streaked behind her, and she let the horse run for a while before she started to relax, to ease her body into the rhythm of the horse's gait, to let the rippling of Hayworth's muscles flow through rather than against her own.

Manny had stopped a hundred or so yards ahead, and Ginger was drinking from a freshwater pond. Laura tugged to the right and circled in a fat arc toward Manny. She slapped the horse's side with the reins so Hayworth wouldn't slow down. Laura wanted to prolong this feeling, this wide-open, fast-galloping looseness. She closed her eyes, took a deep breath, and could feel at the core of her body a kind of bobbing.

Then, just as she opened her eyes, Hayworth jumped at something and the blue sky tilted. Her head bumped the horse's neck. She lost her balance and could feel herself falling, slowly, like dripping molasses off the side of the running horse. She clung to the reins, but they were slipping, slipping, slipping, a hot burn of leather on her palms, and she knew, absolutely knew, in those split seconds when she was perpendicular to the horse, like a spear in its side, that she was going to hit the ground, head first and hard. The horse would trample her, and she would be dead, gone for good.

"Are you okay?" Manny kept repeating. "Are you okay?" His hand cradled her skull, and around his darkened face was a corona of sunlight that blinded her into a rapid blink.

"What happened?" she asked.

"I was watching you, but then I turned away for a second, and when I looked again, you were on the ground."

"How long have I been here?"

"A few minutes. I thought you were dead at first. You feel okay?"

"I think so."

She sat up and felt a sharp, dizzying spike in her forehead, like when she ate ice cream too fast, but that pain left quickly, and Manny lifted her up and helped spank the grass and dirt from her hair and body. Her back and right arm ached, but not enough to gripe about — just stingers that would go away if she didn't dwell on them.

"Don't tell anyone about this," she said.

"Are you sure you're all right?"

"They might not let me ride again."

"Maybe you *shouldn't* ride again."

"I just got her going too fast."

"You shouldn't have chased after me."

"You wanted me to."

"That's not the point."

"It was fun until I lost hold."

The horses were drinking at the pond. She and Manny sat down on the bank, broke off a couple of cattails and absently fingered them. The water was smooth, just a ripple from the horses' mouths, every now and again a light wrinkle across the surface from the breeze. A half-mile in the distance, trucks rolled across the highway, and she believed she could smell faintly the diesel in the air, though the horses' sweat was closer, more pungent. The sun had turned from hot white to a liquid red at the horizon, and after it dipped below, she and Manny climbed back up on the horses. She was a little nervous at first, afraid she might fall again. She clasped her thighs tightly against the horse's flanks, and they started back to the barn in a slow canter.

They tethered the horses in the stall, and when they exited the barn, darkness had fallen quickblack over the sky.

Aunt Velma wasn't really anybody's aunt. She was Mrs. Tate's cousin by marriage. Uncle Unser, who was really Mrs. Tate's cousin, died in 1953. During World War II, when he'd served as a captain in the infantry, he lost the vision in his left eye and both his arms up to the elbows when a grenade exploded in his hands as he withdrew the pin. He had metal hands attached at the V.A. hospital and tried to return to normal life, but he couldn't do the farm work very efficiently nor, of course, the fiddle making, which he'd been known for in the Panhandle before he joined the military. He and Aunt Velma had never had children, so they had always treated Laura's family like their own. During the war he'd sent them odd war remnants — pieces of shrapnel constructed into beautiful, strange collages, bullet casings with Italian or Russian lettering on the side, an Italian military sash for Mr. Tate, a German baby blanket for Laura. And even after he returned from the hospital, he seemed extraordinarily good natured, letting the kids touch his purple-striated stumps or even play with his metal hands as he sat on a stool or in his big leather chair, smiling serenely.

Mrs. Tate always referred to him as her uncle, as both a term of endearment and because he was almost twenty years older than she was. He'd always been, as she put it, a naturally happy man, quick with a joke or a tease. So they were all shocked when Uncle Unser hanged himself in the barn. No note, no nothing. Aunt Velma found him swinging from the rafters one morning in May. Laura was sure there were explanations, but neither his death nor its possible causes were discussed with the kids. Manny told Laura that he thought Uncle Unser was an alcoholic. Gloria said that was a big fat lie, that he was just depressed, cumulatively depressed from the war and from his inability to do what he loved most. He just didn't want to live anymore. It was that simple.

But it wasn't so simple to Laura. She could never quite wrap her mind around that notion — not wanting to live — particularly since he seemed so obviously happy. There was some mysterious chasm between the man she had known and the man who had dangled from the rafters, like a secret self had taken over. It had troubled her for nearly a year — she even dreamed of it horribly, this demonic second self rising out of Uncle Unser's body and knotting the rope, draping it over his neck — but then she had suddenly stopped thinking and dreaming about it altogether. As she grew older it seemed more and more difficult to remember him very clearly, though every once in a while, especially when visiting Aunt Velma's, a charged memory would swim to the surface and overwhelm her for a few seconds — how his sun-tanned face looked like a sculpture, bronzed and creviced in the sunlight, or the singsong way in which he sometimes spoke, or a snippet of one of his jokes, or his deadpan, teasing manner, his glass eye rolling loosely to one side while his good eye stared straight at you.

For supper Aunt Velma and Mrs. Tate fixed catfish, okra, black-eyed peas, two pans of cornbread, and an apple cobbler for dessert. The kitchen smelled warm, buttery, sweet, and greasy. After Manny and Laura washed up, they all sat at the table, held hands, and Aunt Velma said an extended grace. The Tates weren't religious, though they sometimes attended the Charnelle Methodist Church. But Aunt Velma claimed that the church had saved her after Uncle Unser died, literally saved both her physical and spiritual lives, and she had devoted herself to volunteer work and intensive study sessions with other members of the congregation, particularly those who'd lost spouses, parents, children, brothers, or sisters. Though Manny made fun of Aunt Velma's devotion, and Mr. and Mrs. Tate seemed to tolerate it respectfully, Laura was fascinated and often moved by Aunt Velma's fervor. Regardless of whether you believed what she believed, it was clear, to Laura at least, that it had changed Aunt Velma for the better — not like religion did for some people. It made her generous and forgiving and sustained her as she grew old, lit her from within rather than turning her cynical and ossified, as Laura could see easily happening to someone else in Aunt Velma's shoes. When your husband kills himself . . . well, no telling what could happen to you.

Aunt Velma reminded them that today, of all days, is what they must be grateful for, and she painted a vivid portrait of the frail Messiah, nearly naked, thorns digging into His skull, blood and sweat and dirt streaming into His eyes, which He could barely keep open, the spikes being driven through His hands and tender feet, and how the rabble of the town came to watch Him suffer, to throw stones and rotted vegetables, and as He faded into unconsciousness and death the sky blackened. It was a day of torment and abject humiliation, but in this suffering was planted the seeds of the world's salvation.

"Amen," Mr. Tate said, and the rest of them, on cue, chimed in with their amens. Manny looked at Laura and rolled his eyes, smiling, and she smiled too, but felt bad about it, as if she was conspiring against Aunt Velma.

Then the plates and silverware began to clatter as they all helped themselves. The food was delicious. Laura hadn't realized how hungry she was, or how the events of the day had made her ravenous. She ate two heaping platefuls and had a huge piece of cobbler, and afterward, lying on the floor near the unlit fireplace, a pillow under her head, her eyes closed, she listened to the radio — The Hollywood Star Gazer and then a special Good Friday musical special featuring the New York City Boys' Choir — as her brothers and parents and Aunt Velma sang and chattered and played Chinese checkers around her. She felt sated and pleasantly warm, a tingly buzz on her skin. Truly relaxed and well for the first time in months.

It seemed as if the drop from the horse had shaken whatever was bad or festering out of her, that those few minutes of deadness had made way for this sense of pleasure she now felt. She smiled to think of what Aunt Velma would make of this. In fact, she wondered if she was starting to think like Aunt

Velma. She wouldn't say anything to Manny—he'd just make fun of her—or to anyone for that matter. It was just a fleeting thought anyway, but maybe that's how people like Aunt Velma find themselves, through these odd connected moments, ripened with mystery, like beads on a string—leaving town, falling off a horse, brooding over the dead, eating until you're stuffed—and *poof!* Through some magical alchemy, you're crazy for Jesus.

"Good night, Laura," her mother said.

She opened her eyes as her mother draped a blanket over her. The windows were dark, and no one else was in the room. "What time is it?" she asked.

"Late," her mother said and leaned over and kissed her.

"I love you," Laura whispered.

"I love you too."

Saturday afternoon Mr. Tate took them all to see *The Ten Commandments*, a special event since they had never, as a family, been to an indoor movie theater before. Several times each summer, especially before Rich was born, they all went to the Charnelle Drive-in. Mr. Tate would park the truck with the bed facing the screen, and they'd sit on cushions in the back, Manny lying atop the cab, Gloria down front in the grassy area with her girlfriends or later in some beat-up jalopy with another girl and two pimply-faced boys. A sweaty jug of iced lemonade and a huge paper bag full of buttered popcorn (which they'd spent the afternoon popping at home) were wedged beside the wheel hump. Laura's father would clamp the speakers to each side of the truck and turn the volume up high, even though it wasn't necessary because the sound from the two hundred other speakers in the drive-in could easily be heard. But that was okay with Laura. She loved the sensation, strange, almost dreamlike, of hearing the same private conversation being carried on simultaneously all around her while the film flickered on the monstrous, bug-spattered screen. It was both communal and intimate — the smell of food, the collective smacking and munching and swallowing, the stars twinkling overhead like a Hollywood effect. If the movie were boring, she would look around or head off to the bathroom. Sometimes she would spy couples kissing in cars and trucks, ponytails smashed against the windows, and other vehicles parked way in the back, windows fogged over, rocking slightly. It often seemed to her like permissible eavesdropping, a public display of secrets.

The Paladian Theater in Amarillo, however, possessed its own special exoticism. It had just opened its doors, and Mr. Tate wanted to see a movie there because he had supervised a portion of the construction the previous fall. They arrived a good half hour before the film began, bought their tickets, and Mr. Tate spoke with the manager and then gave them all a tour of the theater, which seemed as thrillingly majestic as an English palace with its tall, red, crushed-velvet curtains, and the gold and black rococo curlicues on the facing of the balcony, and the screen towering impressively above them, protected and veiled rather than exposed, like the drive-in screen, to the elements and insects and beer-swigging vandalism of adolescent boys.

Dressed sharply in a white shirt, jeans, and boots, Mr. Tate spoke to and laughed with the manager like they were old friends, and then he strode about the empty theater like he owned it, pointing to the inlaid design of the balcony, explaining the joist work of the three pillars and steel-framed balcony support that he himself had welded, rattling off the cost of the seats and the curtains and the screen, which indicated (Laura couldn't quite tell from her father's tone) either magnanimous wealth or a waste of money. At his insistence, Manny, Gene, and Laura clambered up the carpeted spiral stairs to the balcony and leaned over the ledge, waving down to Rich, who stood smiling like a munchkin before the massive screen.

They took their seats as other people filed in. Mr. Tate gave Manny and Laura three dollars and told them — in a clownish, mock-hick voice that made everybody laugh — to "oversee the movie vittles." They bought lemonade for their parents, Velma, and Rich, and root beer for themselves and Gene, a brick of Hershey's chocolate for everybody to share, as well as two big bags of popcorn scooped from the reservoir of orange-yellow fluff.

The glass-covered lightbulbs dimmed. The red curtain parted as the music from the first short, a Disney cartoon, trumpeted. Unlike at the drive-in, the sound was not loud, but it was clear, the picture sharp, brighter without the crackles and lines and burn holes Laura had learned to ignore on the outdoor screen.

A trailer for a black and white John Wayne western, and then a newsreel, and then the movie itself. Laura hadn't quite known what to expect — a Technicolor sermon? — but soon she was enthralled by the grand panoramic majesty of it all. It made her want to read the Bible. Who knew it was that romantic, that dramatic?

When they had arrived in early afternoon it had been hot and cloudless, but when they emerged from the theater over four hours later, the sun had slipped beneath the horizon. The sidewalk and grass glistened with rain, the sky milky purple, as swollen and variegated as a two-day bruise. Laura felt disoriented. It was like falling asleep in the middle of the afternoon and waking in the night, not sure what had happened or even what day it was. Time seemed to evaporate or be kidnapped. She didn't know if she liked this feeling — thick, narcotic, as palpable as an overripe melon.

Aunt Velma loved the movie, though she thought it a little racy for kids. Rich had fallen asleep. Manny loved the fights and the special effects, and Gene's favorite part was when Moses seemed to be walking around in a burning bush–induced glaze, his face red, his hair suddenly white. Mr. Tate thought it was way too long and had twice stepped outside to smoke a cigarette. Mrs. Tate liked the Exodus — the joy on all those people's faces when they finally left Egypt.

"What did you think, Laura?" Aunt Velma asked.

"I loved it."

"And your favorite part?"

"All of it," she said, but felt her answer disappointed everyone. They had given specifics, but she still felt too stunned by the experience to talk about it.

Easter Sunday. They rose before dawn and went to the sunrise service at Aunt Velma's church, where the preacher recounted the old familiar story of the Crucifixion, the days of darkness, the stone mysteriously moved from the tomb, Jesus appearing to the women who loved Him and then later to His disciples, who needed testing, a hand in the holes of His body, and the final glorious ascension, hallelujah, hallelujah, amen.

Laura listened absently. She'd heard this story many times, and while on Friday, during Aunt Velma's dinner blessing, it had seemed vividly alive, it now had lost its power to hold her attention. It seemed, in fact, hackneyed compared to the movie they'd watched yesterday. She bent her head, as if in prayer, closed her eyes and tried to unfurl the movie in her mind. The most distinct images weren't the ones she would have thought — the Red Sea parting, Pharaoh's army stopped by the pillar of fire. She saw, instead, the more intimate moments. The princess playing that crazy game, called Hounds and Jackals, with the pharaoh. (It stunned her to think of biblical figures playing board games.) The gold dress "spun from the beards of shellfish." Moses in chains in the dungeon, the princess prostrate before him. The dark shine of his sweaty body, half-naked and caked in mud, in the immaculate throne room before his father, who turned away from him, who forbade the name of Moses to be mentioned again. Yul Brynner with that black snake of hair coiled exotically out of the side of his bald head.

Everyone suddenly stood and shuffled the hymnals. She opened her eyes and stood up too, out of habit, and pretended to sing, "He arose, He arose, He arose," while a bright flicker of shame goosed over her because she'd been thinking about the movie, particularly Moses' sweat-glistened chest, instead of being thankful for Jesus dying to take away her sins.

After church they rode Ginger and Hayworth again, played several matches of horseshoes, and then Mr. Tate took them fishing at the pond, but no one caught anything except Gene, who nabbed a little white perch. Aunt Velma, Mrs. Tate, and Laura made the dinner, and everyone played dominoes and Canasta, ate watermelon, and then listened to a special Easter radio program from the Grand Ole Opry.

After cleaning the kitchen, Laura's mother wiped her hands and said, "I'm taking Fay for a walk."

Gene said, "I want to go." Both Manny and Laura looked on expectantly, like they too could use a walk before the trip home.

"No, you stay here," she said and was out the screen door before anyone could answer.

"Aw, come on," Gene said, moving toward the door.

Aunt Velma caught his arm. "You come sit with me, honey."

"But I want to go."

"Come sit here in this chair with me. Let your mother have a little time to herself."

By eight Laura's mother still hadn't returned. Mr. Tate, Manny, and Gene were loading the truck for the return trip. Laura helped Aunt Velma dry the last of the dishes and wrap the leftovers they were taking back to Charnelle.

Mr. Tate came in and asked Laura, "Where's your mother?"

"I don't know."

"Well, go find her and tell her it's time to go."

She dried her hands, put on her sweater, and walked across the dark meadow, calling for her mother and Fay. She walked to the orchard where the light from the barn crept to the edge of the trees, but she didn't go into the grove, not at night. She heard rustling off in the branched shadows. She called again. A flurry of indistinct movement, then some animal, a coyote maybe, scrambled out of the panoply of trees. She sucked in her breath and backpedaled quickly, thinking the animal was charging toward her. But when she glanced again, she saw it lope in the opposite direction, as afraid as she was, moonlight skittering across the edge of its neck and head. It disappeared over a hill.

She felt apprehensive, jumpy, so she walked swiftly, calling again. The evening had cooled; her breath misted in front of her. A twig snapped, and she broke into a run toward the faint light of the barn, where the chickens chastised her as she entered. Ingrid, the Holstein, mooed loudly, and in the midst of this animal chorus, she felt suddenly ridiculous. She laughed nervously, then heard the familiar wheezing of a dog, and said, "Fay? Mom?"

The one-bulb light of the barn was creepy. From the hay-strewn corner, Fay emerged surprisingly, as if passing through a watery membrane separating darkness from light, and walked up to Laura and licked her hand. She bent down and rubbed the dog's chin, and Fay immediately lay down on her back and exposed her belly for more scratching.

"Where's Momma?" she asked the dog, who closed her eyes and lifted her paws. Laura peered into the darkness and could vaguely make out a still, human shape. A quick shuddering dread whipped through her.

"Momma, is that you?"

"Yes."

Laura walked toward her and could see her sitting against a bale of hay. Why hadn't she answered her calls or said anything? She wondered how long her mother had been here. Had her mother watched her running into the barn? It frightened Laura, this strange silence. In the shadows, her mother's cheeks shimmered, shiny and wet.

"Are you okay?" Laura asked.

Her mother didn't answer.

"Momma, are you okay?"

"Yes, Laura."

"Why are you crying?"

"I didn't realize it'd gotten so late. Is it time to go?" She wiped her face with her sleeve and rose and walked into the light.

"You're bleeding!" Laura shouted.

Her mother's yellow blouse was ripped below her left ribs. A blot of darkened blood encircled the ragged hole. Laura reached out and touched the stain.

"Oww!" her mother said, pulling back sharply. "Don't do that."

"What happened?" The blood felt warm and greasy on her fingers.

"I caught it on some barbed wire. Dumb. It's nothing. We better get going. Come on, Fay."

The dog stood sleepily, hay clinging to her back, and fell in step at Mrs. Tate's heels.

"You too, Laura."

"But Mom —"

Her mother was already through the barn gate, though, striding across the meadow toward the distant light of the house. Laura followed, but her mother moved fast, dissolving into the darkness until both she and the dog seemed merely gold-lined silhouettes.

On the drive home, Manny, Gene, and Laura wore their wool caps and mufflers and huddled together with Fay under the two afghans Aunt Velma had given them. Gene fell asleep, and Manny and Laura watched the shifting stars as the truck hummed north along the highway back to Charnelle. With the wind and the sound of the truck's tires on the asphalt, it was too loud for talk, which suited her just fine because she liked this time without words. Lying flat in the bed, she could see the headlights from passing cars and trucks shining over them like spotlights. The sky had cleared, and she delighted in identifying the constellations she knew and searching for her own patterns, which she gave foolish names she soon forgot.

She could tell they were close to Charnelle at least ten minutes before they arrived. The traffic going the other way increased, and the sky brightened from the lights. She sat up and peered through the cab window. The tip of her father's cigarette glowed orange and brightened when he inhaled. Rich was asleep in Mrs. Tate's lap, and Laura's mother had her head turned toward the side window to the low dark hills that rose and toppled as they sped along. Laura rubbed her fingers together. Though she couldn't see them, she knew they were still stained with her mother's blood. In the scramble to get going, she had forgotten to wash it off. She put her fingers to her nose but smelled nothing.

What was her mother thinking about? Laura wondered. She seemed so secretive, ever since Gloria left, almost a year ago, or perhaps before that—yes, definitely before. Laura wished she could get inside her mother's head for just a few minutes and see what was going on in there, but she knew that was impossible, just as she sensed that others would probably never be able to clearly know what she thought and felt.

Through both the cab window and the front window, she could see the lights of Charnelle spread across the plains like a long prairie fire, flickering, blinking, calling them home. Tomorrow she'd be back in school, back to the routines of classes and chores and the chattery, joking banter with her friends. That would be good, but she wasn't there yet, and the weekend itself, the reason they'd gone, the fun they'd had, was over, and there was only this between time of traveling in the dark.

A wave of sadness swept through her. She didn't know if it was the weekend ending, or worries about her mother, or just tiredness. She was prone to these quick spells of sadness or confusion. She often felt a strange, conflicting pull to either give in to the spells — "wallow in it," as her father said — or to resist, shake them off, get up and do something, anything, which did seem to work. Motion triumphing over mood.

Gene and Manny, asleep on either side of her now, turned at the same moment and tugged the afghans from her, sending a whistling chill through her bones. She pulled the covers back and nestled against Fay. She absently stroked the dog's warm fur as she watched the sky lighten from behind, the town seeming to curl over the cab into the truck bed.

After pulling into the gravel driveway, her father turned off the truck, which rattled and shook Gene and Manny awake. The silence after the drive seemed cottony and thick. Her father said something to her, but she couldn't understand and had to yawn several times to unplug her ears. Gene wobbled sleepily, and Laura helped him to bed. Her father put Rich in his crib, and after helping unload everything into the living room, Laura slipped into her nightgown.

She expected her mother to say goodnight, but she didn't utter a sound, just retreated to the bathroom and then her bedroom, the door closing abruptly behind her. *Another sign,* Laura thought, *but of what?* Falling asleep, the sadness from before was replaced now by a grateful warmth, the familiar pleasure of the journey finally ended, of returning home, of being home. Still, she felt unsettled, as if this weekend had been trying to warn her of something but she had not been listening carefully. She tried to recall all that had happened. Greta gone, the fall from the horse, the movie, which seemed, now that she thought about it, all about exile and return. Her mother's disappearance to the barn where Uncle Unser still seemed to reside, her mother crying in the shadows with the dog, the sense of there being invisible barriers between her mother and the rest of the family. Laura sensed darkness, glass, and a quietly hostile silence that no one else seemed to register. She felt she was on the verge of understanding something, as if she could almost grasp how a puzzle fit together. But the darkness and the breathing of her brothers in the room enveloped her, pressing down, and the sculpted contours of her mattress held her like a soft hand and urged her to sleep.

Nature's Way

APRIL – MAY 1958

A few days after Easter, as she was going out to feed Fay, Laura found Greta whimpering by the fence, her fur matted, filthy, cockleburred. Deep, coagulated wounds were gouged in her nose and back right foot. The end of her tail and chunks from her left ear were missing. Laura, her brothers, and her mother fed and bathed the dog, tried to nurse her wounds. She bared her teeth and snapped, put marks in Manny's boots. Mrs. Tate poured some sweet rum inside a butter cake and fed it to Greta to calm her down. Then Manny stroked her coat gently as Mrs. Tate muzzled her with a leather belt so that they could finish tending to her wounds. The dog shook at first, as with a palsy, then relinquished her fear and let herself be cared for.

When Mr. Tate returned home, he removed the muzzle and sat outside with Greta for a full two hours, stroking her, feeling for broken bones, inspecting the wounds and bandages, redoing most of it, soothing the dog with his voice. He palmed her belly, and she snapped again, but he stayed calm, told her everything was okay, not to worry. He fed her crumbled strips of jerky from his hand, held water up to her mouth, stroked her until she fell asleep. When he came inside he scrubbed his hands with the gritty rectangle of soap he sandpapered himself with after work. Then he ran his fingers through his pomaded hair and announced, "I think that dog's pregnant."

"Zeeke, she's too young," Mrs. Tate said.

"I guess not."

"We can't let her. She's not ready."

"We ain't got a choice."

"We do too."

He shook his head.

Mrs. Tate stared down at the knotholes on the floor for the longest time as if they held secrets that the family was waiting for her to decode. Then she shook her head and stared at her husband. "This is gonna turn out bad, Zeeke. I'm telling you."

"It might calm her down," he said.

"Mark my words," she said.

Weeks passed. Greta's wounds healed until she was well enough to eat by herself and to get on her feet. There was something darkly troubling about the dog, and Laura found herself studying Greta, afraid both of and for her. Her teeth had yellowed. She bared them constantly. Her eyes were bloodshot. Fay tried to help Greta, mothering her, licking her wounds, nuzzling her when she was ill, but once Greta grew stronger, she attacked the older dog, biting at her neck, drawing blood, sending Fay whimpering off. Mr. Tate put up a new pen to isolate Greta, who lay in her shed, panting, shifting her head suspiciously from side to side, awaiting intruders. Except for Mr. Tate, she wouldn't let anyone approach her, not even to give her food or water. During the day she'd gnaw at the hair on her stomach, welting herself. During the warmer afternoons, when she was able, she'd pace frantically in her pen, burning the grass, her belly with its load and the dark, thick, extended teats swaying below her.

At first, Mrs. Tate wouldn't have anything to do with the dog, wouldn't even acknowledge her, was short-tempered with the kids and silent and sullen when Mr. Tate was home. But as Greta began to heal from her wounds and progressed in her pregnancy, Laura's mother began watching the dog from the kitchen window. When she was outside, while doing the laundry or preparing the garden, she'd eye Greta curiously as the dog lay huddled in her shed, half in light, half in shadow, panting, watching the woman in return.

On a Friday morning in early May, a month before they thought Greta was due, Laura was sick and home from school. She sat at the kitchen table, sipping hot cider, nibbling on buttered toast, watching Rich play as Mrs. Tate did chores in the backyard: hanging up the laundry on the lines, sweeping dried mud from the porch, wiping off the dust from the canned tomatoes and peaches that were in the storm cellar, hoeing the weeds in the garden, which had been recently seeded. It was an exceptionally warm day. The kitchen window was open for the fresh air. Laura heard her mother whistling songs, Bob Wills's and Hank Williams's tunes that were always playing on the radio. Fay was loose, nosing her way along the edges of the alley fence, sniffing and pissing where the strays had entered her territory. At first Greta stayed in her shed, as usual, though her eyes were open. She seldom slept. After a while she stood and cautiously inched out of the shed toward her water and food bowls, all the while watching Mrs. Tate and Fay. Greta drank from her bowl, then looked up and barked.

Mrs. Tate turned to her quickly from the clothesline and arched her eyebrow. "What is it, girl?"

The dog barked again. Fay ambled over to the edge of Greta's pen and cautiously sniffed.

"You don't like my whistling?"

Both dogs looked at her, then cocked their heads quizzically. Greta barked again, followed by Fay. Laura's mother laughed and walked over to the pen with a sheet and some clothespins in her hands. Inside the house, Laura smiled, sipped her cider.

"You out of water?" Mrs. Tate said. She went over to the hose in the garden, which was dripping in the dirt, and pulled it to the bowl and let it fill up. Greta looked at the hose and at the woman and back at the hose in something like a gesture of gratitude. Mrs. Tate tossed the sheet in the laundry basket and sat on the flat stump across from Greta. The clothespins, like two tiny wooden beaks, dangled from her mouth. She watched the dog drink. Greta ignored her, though Fay kept nuzzling under her apron, and Mrs. Tate scratched the older dog's head.

She took some jerky from her apron pocket and let Fay eat it from her palm. Greta looked up, put her face through the chain link of the pen, and sniffed.

"You want some of this, girl?"

Greta stuck her nose farther through the chain link. Mrs. Tate shooed the older dog away, stood up, and slowly approached the pen. Greta withdrew her snout and began retreating with her head low, her ears back.

"It's okay. Calm down now, girl."

Mrs. Tate dangled the jerky and bent toward the bowl. Greta growled low and deep without opening her mouth. Mrs. Tate took one of the clothespins wedged in her mouth, fingered the wood, and opened and closed it methodically. The dog's lips quivered. She growled again, her yellow teeth showing this time.

Fay barked.

"Hush up, you!" Mrs. Tate turned back to the younger dog and spoke to her soothingly, a whispery litany on the theme of "I'm not gonna hurt you." She crouched close to the fence and slowly inched the jerky through the holes, encouraging, "Come on, girl. Come here and get it. It's good."

Suddenly, Greta charged the fence and leapt not at the jerky strip but at Mrs. Tate's face, mouth open, her teeth possessing a malevolent propulsion of their own. Laura's mother sprawled back. The fence rattled. Greta yelped and then, miraculously, stuck there on the fence, her back paws dangling above her water bowl. The wires were stuck between her teeth, and the whole fence bowed with the weight of the wailing dog. Fay commenced a full-scale bark at her daughter. Greta's bloodshot eyes rolled in her head. She seemed to be searching for some way out, expecting something terrible to happen.

Jumping up from the table, Laura knocked off her cider cup. It smashed on the hardwood floor, green ceramic shards splashing. She felt spikes in her feet, but she hopped to the door and out on the porch, where she saw her mother back-sprawled on the ground, Greta still hanging on the fence.

"Are you okay?" Laura shouted. Fay barked crazily. Greta's wails were high pitched and hurt Laura's ears.

"Shut up, Fay!" Mrs. Tate shouted. "Shut up!"

"Momma!" Laura called.

"Fay, shut up! Now!"

"Are you okay?"

"Yeah."

"What are you going to do?"

"I don't know. Fay, hush!"

Her mother rose and inspected the caught dog. She grabbed the fence above Greta's face and shook it to free her, but the shaking only served to flop the dog's body in a way that left her shoulder now flush against the fence and her head twisted sideways. Greta whimpered now, exhausted.

Laura swiped at her feet. There was blood, nothing serious.

"Laura, go fetch me your father's toolbox. Hurry now."

Rich had followed Laura. She picked him up and put him in his crib. She grabbed the toolbox from the closet and ran out to the backyard. The steel wire had somehow slipped between the back molars and was caught between her teeth and gums. How the wire got there without breaking the teeth was amazing, like a magician Laura had once seen pull a cloth from a fully set table without displacing the settings.

Her mother took the long flathead screwdriver and wedged it into Greta's mouth, between the tooth and the fence. "Hand me those pliers, Laura. Now hold on to this screwdriver while I work the wire out."

It must have taken only a few minutes to dislodge the dog, but it seemed interminable, with Greta whimpering shrilly, her bloody fangs poking through the fence, Fay jumping around, barking, Rich inside screaming. Mrs. Tate was able to wriggle the wire free from one side. Greta let out a muted wail and hung there now by the two molars on the left side of her face. The leverage was against them. Finally, Mrs. Tate jerked the wire through the other teeth. They broke, tiny enamel missiles flying past Laura's face. The dog fell to the ground, lay in shock for several minutes, and then passed out. Mrs. Tate sat down on the stump across from the pen and stared at the dog, then sent Laura inside to check on Rich.

She rescued him from his crib, calmed him down, swept up the broken cup, tossed it in the trash, then sat down on the back porch and watched her mother stroke Fay. Greta got up and staggered back to her shed. Blood was matted on her chin. She yelped in pain every few seconds.

"What should we do?" Laura asked.

"You go back in, honey. I'll take care of this."

Mrs. Tate stayed there on the stump for the rest of the afternoon, just staring, not saying a word and not coming in, just opening and closing the wooden pins in her hands. *Something's happening*, Laura sensed, *there's something more to this*, but she didn't know how to say it because it was at once impossible to articulate and yet so obvious, hovering in the air like an unacknowledged ghost.

Later, after the excitement had waned, Laura felt weak and feverish again, but she was afraid to disturb her mother. She put Rich down for his nap and then lay down herself. Drifting in and out of a shivering daytime sleep, she replayed what had happened, what it meant. It had been the same way, she suddenly thought, a year ago when Gloria eloped with Jerome. Gloria didn't say a word about it to Laura, even though they shared a bed. Laura knew her sister was in love with the lieutenant. She'd read some of their letters, hidden in a small brown box at the back of Gloria's bottom drawer, beneath her underwear, and Laura figured they might get married soon enough, after Gloria turned eighteen, but the whole family was shocked to find her gone one morning, leaving only a note saying she and Jerome had eloped to Mexico and that she would write later.

Laura's father was in a furious rant for months, then seemed to resign himself to the fact of her absence. Her mother stayed silent, as if she knew more about what had happened with Gloria than she was willing to tell. Not until a week after Gloria's eighteenth birthday did they receive a postcard from Switzerland saying that she and Jerome were stationed in West Germany and would be moving to Greece soon. It wasn't clear to any of them if she was ever coming back.

"There are no secrets," Laura's mother said mysteriously after the family read the postcard, shaking her head as if indeed there were secrets, and you needed to be clairvoyant to understand them.

It had amazed Laura that her sister could do such a thing. At the time it had seemed, like what Greta had done, violent and inexplicable. But the more she brooded over it, the more she retraced her conversations in bed at night with Gloria, the more she recalled her sister's behavior leading up to the elopement — the secret letters, Gloria working extra jobs and hoarding her money, the way she seemed distracted and worried but also jovial, manic even — the more it all made sense, as her mother had said, like a clear and obvious path leading backward in time from this one moment. It made her a believer, though she wouldn't have known how to say it at the time, that there were always seeds of the future in the present, growing, preparing for the blossom.

In mid-May Mr. Tate went to Amarillo for four days to work on a construction job for the new downtown bank. They didn't expect Greta's puppies for a couple of weeks, but Mr. Tate had already built the whelping pen, an open-topped plywood box, with one side partially cut away and a pull-out chicken wire gate over the opening. He nailed down old scraps of carpet he'd salvaged. Greta had been relatively docile since falling from the fence. She paced less, didn't growl as much. But she still favored Mr. Tate.

He made a small door in the fence so that Manny could feed her without having to go into the pen, and the hose could be draped, as usual, through the chain link into her water bowl. He told the family not to worry about her. She still had plenty of time.

The third day he was gone, however, Greta started her labor. By dusk she'd begun turning in circles, clawing at the old scraps of carpet in her shed. Fay lay in her own shed with her head on her paws and watched quietly.

"We've got to get her into the whelping pen," Mrs. Tate said. "If she stays in the shed, we won't be able to help her."

When they opened the gate, Greta barked wildly. The hair on the back of her neck bristled. Then she hunkered into her shed and growled, her teeth glowing in the evening light. Mrs. Tate sent Manny to the back of the shed and had him bang on it to get her out, but she just barked until he slipped his stick between two boards and prodded her. She snapped at it, then skittered out. Mrs. Tate stood by the door, and after Greta ran through the opening, she guided the dog with the rake into the whelping pen and dropped the gate. Manny then boarded up the opening of her shed with a piece of plywood.

"Should we muzzle her?" Manny asked.

"I don't know if we could if we wanted to. Besides, we got to let her pant. We'll just wait here and see what happens. Gene, go get the newspapers."

Gene brought the stack of old newspapers they'd been saving. Mrs. Tate and Manny dumped the paper in the pen and moved back. Greta clawed at the paper, bunched it together in a pile, sat on it, rose, turned several more circles, and clawed again. She sat back down and began breathing in short, shallow breaths, her belly rising and falling quickly. Mrs. Tate slipped the garden hose through the links and filled the water bowl. Greta lapped at it, but she still eyed them all as if they were to blame for her misery.

"It's okay now, girl," Mrs. Tate said. "Don't you worry."

Laura turned the porch light on, and Manny clamped a floodlight to the pen. It had been surprisingly hot for this time of year, though when nightfall came it cooled off, so everyone put on old sweaters. Greta's eyes were bloodshot and watery from labor, with black droplets, like candle wax, in the corners near her nose.

Around eight, after Rich was in bed, the dogs down the alley started barking and howling, aggravating Fay, then Greta, who both barked back. Greta paced the pen rapidly, panting, then turned in tighter and tighter circles. Suddenly, she let out a whimpering growl, squatted, and out slithered a watery black sack the size of Laura's cupped palms. When Fay had litters, she'd always torn the dark-veined sack immediately, bit at the cord, and licked at the face until the nose and mouth were clear. Greta sniffed at the twisting sack, pushed it over with her paw, sniffed again, but didn't break the thin membrane. Then she walked to the other side of the pen, indifferent.

"Laura, quick, bring me the sewing kit and washcloths," Mrs. Tate shouted. Laura ran inside and got the kit from the counter and warmed the cloths that her mother had set out.

When she returned, the puppy still lay in the corner in its sack. Manny and Mrs. Tate had entered the whelping pen and were blocking the dog with the stick and rake. Mrs. Tate reached down and grabbed the puppy, then backed out of the pen with Manny following. She sat down on the ground and broke the sack with her finger. Mucousy fluid dribbled down her arm and onto her sweater. She laid the slick pup on her lap. It didn't seem to be breathing.

"Manny, get me some thread from the kit. Laura, take one of those cloths and wipe its nose and mouth. Hurry now. But be gentle."

As Laura wiped, her mother knotted the small end of the cord and then took the cloth and finished cleaning the pup's face.

"It's not breathing," Laura said.

Her mother turned it over and patted it firmly on the back, then reached into its mouth with her finger and pulled out a thimbleful of blackish-green gum. The pup whimpered. Fay barked, followed by Greta. Mrs. Tate leaned over the fence and set the pup down on the papers in front of Greta. The dog eyed her warily, then sniffed at the wet bundle. Greta reached out and pawed the pup, knocking it on its back. It rolled over and shook its tiny head quickly, rooting. With her hind leg, Greta kicked it across the carpet until it lay against the wall with shreds of newspaper stuck to its wet fur. Fay barked sharply three times. Greta seemed spooked. She turned and growled.

"It's okay, Greta," Mrs. Tate soothed.

But Greta growled again, and then, in a rapid dart, she lunged toward the pup, snapped viciously twice, then raised it over her head and shook it. Blood spewed over Greta's face.

Gene and Laura screamed.

"Oh, my God!" yelled Manny. "She's killing it, she's killing it!"

"Stop her, Momma!" Gene hollered.

Mrs. Tate, who had fallen back stunned, clutched at the rake, knocked it over, then grabbed it again in the shadows and whacked Greta three times on the head with the base of the handle until the dog dropped the puppy. Greta bit at the iron brace. They all heard the click of teeth on metal, and then she leapt back in the far corner and crouched into a snarling coil. Mrs. Tate kept her in the corner with the rake's splayed end. Wet, black-red spots darkened the dog's white and tan coat.

"Manny, get in there and get the puppy."

"I can't go in there."

"Yes, you can. I'll hold her here. Take your stick."

"But—"

"Do it!"

Manny crawled in. Greta barked savagely, growling, throwing herself against the rake, letting herself be stabbed by the tines, but Mrs. Tate held her in the corner while Manny grabbed the puppy and jumped back out of the pen. Greta snapped at the rake again as Mrs. Tate dropped the gate over the opening.

In the floodlight, they inspected the puppy. The back of its neck had been severed almost clean through. The head was barely connected to the body. Gene staggered backward and vomited on the stump. Laura took one of the warm, wet cloths and wiped her brother's face. Manny went inside and brought back a small paper lunch sack. Mrs. Tate placed the pup in it, twisted the top, and sent Manny to the other end of the yard to bury it. Then she went inside and washed her hands, held Gene until he stopped shaking, and put him to bed. She finally came back outside.

"Why'd she do that?" Laura asked.

"Because I touched it, I think," her mother said. "She smelled me on the pup."

"Is she gonna have more?" Gene asked.

"Yes. I think so."

"What are we gonna do?" Laura asked.

Her mother shook her head and stared at Greta, who lay panting in her whelping pen with her eyes half shut.

"Manny, let's put Fay in the pen with her. Fay will show her what to do."

"She'll attack her," Manny said.

"No, I don't think so. It's me she objects to."

They let Fay into the pen. Greta barked and growled at her at first, but Fay paced the pen away from Greta, then sat down and watched the younger dog until Greta calmed down. Then Fay went to Greta and began licking her face and the still half-torn ear. Greta snapped at her, but not with the viciousness from before. Finally, she let Fay stay with her.

Within a half hour, Greta began whimpering again. She turned tighter and tighter circles, and then she squatted. Out came another sack. Greta sniffed it, pawed at it, and then, as before, ignored it. Fay nosed her way to the sack, broke it open with her teeth, and began licking the mucus from the pup's face until it squealed. Then Fay ate the sack. The pup was lighter colored than the last one, tan with white and black marks, and bigger. Fay nosed the pup toward Greta, who lay in the far corner, recovering. Greta immediately stood up and walked away. Fay lay down next to the pup to keep it warm.

By midnight Greta had delivered five more puppies and lay in the corner of the pen, exhausted and alone. From what the family could tell, at least four of the puppies were alive. One puppy never moved or made a sound. Although Fay kept them warm, they were squealing from hunger, but Greta wouldn't do anything. Manny brought a saucer of warm milk. They let Greta out of the whelping pen, and then Mrs. Tate pulled each pup from the pen and finger-fed it. They waited another hour, but Greta seemed to be through with the births. She licked herself, eyeing Fay every once in a while, growling at Mrs. Tate and the kids whenever they spoke.

By two in the morning, Mrs. Tate told Manny and Laura to go on to bed.

"What's going to happen?" Laura asked.

"It'll be all right. Dogs have been having puppies for years without our help. They don't need us."

"But she's ignoring them," Laura said.

"It just may take her longer to figure out what to do. Besides, whatever happens will happen. I'll stay here a while. Fay will help her. Laura, check on Rich and Gene, and then you and Manny go on to bed yourselves. You got school tomorrow."

"Let me stay and help, Momma," Manny said.

"There ain't nothing else to do."

"What if she goes crazy again?"

"I said I'd take care of it. Go on to bed."

"But — "

"Don't 'but' me, Manny. I said go on! I don't want any back talk now. I want you all in bed!"

"Yes, ma'am," Manny and Laura said in unison.

"And stay there," she said, pursing her lips. They nodded. "If I need you, I'll come and get you."

Manny and Laura went into the house, washed up, then nodded off. About an hour later Laura heard her mother open the back door and go into her room. Shortly after that Fay and Greta began barking. Mrs. Tate got up again, then went back to bed, even though the dogs' noise intensified. There were growls, snarling, and biting. And then more terrible sounds.

Manny and Laura went to their mother in her bed, pleaded with her to do something, but without opening her eyes, she said, "There ain't nothing we can do. Now go on to sleep."

In bed they listened intently to the squeals and yelps, the snarling, the growling, and that other sound, the sound they couldn't identify but understood the next day. And then, still worse, the black silence afterward. *How can she sleep through that?* Laura thought, astonished. That must be what being an adult was about, being able to sleep through suffering, to adjust yourself so it doesn't matter, or matters less, hardening yourself like the way roast gets when you cook it too long. From tender to rock.

The next morning the puppies were gone. Greta had jumped from the whelping pen and lay with her face pointed inside the shed, asleep. They could see her belly, bloated, dried black blood streaked and speckled over her coat. Fay lay in the whelping pen, whimpering, two claw rips across her left shoulder and one above her eye. Her head was on her paws, her eyes closed. The shredded newspaper was dark and wet. Laura was sure she saw small pieces of bloody fur scattered in the pen.

When her father returned home that evening, her mother explained that there was nothing to do but let it happen.

"Nature's way," she said, an edgy irony in her voice.

Mr. Tate shook his head in confusion, then quickly a thin hard shadow congealed over his face, and without a word, just in one long dreamlike sweeping motion, he fetched his gun from the top of his closet, opened the back door, and strode to Greta's shed. From inside the house they heard the shot, like a thunderclap on a cloudless day, and then a second shot, which seemed even more of a jolt. Mrs. Tate sent Manny out, and he and Mr. Tate put Greta in a potato sack, tossed her in the back of the pickup like a load of grain, and they drove away to bury her.

Gone

MAY 1958

Laura watched the thunderstorm from the living room window. The clouds bloated and darkened, common in the Panhandle in the late afternoons, and then it poured — a gusty, whipsaw wind driving the rain sideways against the house. The rain hardened into thick, white pellets of hail, which soon sheeted the yard. Gene and Rich joined her at the window, and their mother stopped cooking in the kitchen and stood behind them, drying her hands on a cloth.

The boys soon tired of the show, but Laura and her mother continued to stare at the white pellets pouring down — dumped, it seemed, from a huge bucket in the clouds. Lightning crinkled the gray sky, and to gauge the distance, Laura counted slowly until she heard the thunder. One, two, three, four, BOOM! The time between the light and the sound shortened, and then in an instant the hail stopped, the sky opened up, and a bright beam of sunlight shone on the street. They squinted.

A moment later, simultaneous thunder and a flash of silver heat cracked in their yard. The house shook as if bulldozed. Rich screamed. Laura was blinded for a few seconds. Her body vibrated, jangled, and her teeth kept clicking, as if she was sending a signal in code.

Her mother stood in front of the window, frozen, her face cut by the sudden shadows after the light. Gene led Laura to the couch.

"Are you okay?" he asked.

"The tree," Laura stuttered, "the tree."

Her mother opened the door and went outside. The old oak was split in half, a bright black burn down the center, the leaves and branches strewn across the white-pelleted lawn and porch. The ends touched the door.

"My God," Mrs. Tate said, shuffling through the melting hail. She touched the dark center of the trunk. "It's hot," she said. "It's still hot."

Laura moved to the door, the muscles in her thighs and calves quivering, the joints of her knees still vibrating. Her teeth wouldn't stop clicking. Small lines of blinking silver crosshatched her vision. The sky darkened again. She and her brothers stood on the porch, afraid to move into the yard.

Their mother touched the trunk, the branches, the leaves, as if searching for a heartbeat. "So hot," she muttered, "so hot."

The next morning the destroyed oak lay about most of the yard like a huge, stricken animal. Mr. Tate and Manny had cleared away some of the debris that night, but the large job of cutting the heavy branches and uprooting the burnt base of the trunk would take longer and would require special equipment. Leaving for school, they had to maneuver carefully around the fallen branches and the blackened husk of the split trunk. It was a mess.

Coming home on her bicycle later, Laura rounded the curve, saw the tree, and felt again the lightning in her body. Faint silver lines again blurred her vision. Her teeth involuntarily clicked. All this triggered, miraculously, by the presence of the tree.

She got off her bike in the front yard and wheeled it around to the side of the house. The front door was slightly ajar, and she pushed it open.

"I'm home." No one answered. "Momma? Rich?"

Still no answer. She went through the kitchen and opened the back door, expecting them to be in the backyard. But all she saw was Fay scratching around the fences.

"Where's everybody?" she called.

Fay trotted over. Laura patted the old dog's coat and head, careful around the wounds that Greta had gouged in her face. Fay licked Laura's wrists and cheek with her bad breath. Inside, on the kitchen table, Laura found the note, quickly scrawled, in her mother's crooked handwriting: "Rich is at Mrs. Ambling's."

"Where did my mother go?" Laura asked Mrs. Ambling.

"I was wondering the same question. She just asked me if I would watch Rich until all of you kids got home. She seemed in a hurry. She headed down the road with a suitcase."

"A suitcase?"

"Yes, a brown one. Not that big."

"Where's your mother?" Mr. Tate asked when he and Gene got home.

"We thought you were going to tell us," Manny said.

"Huh?"

"Mrs. Ambling said that she left Rich with her and told her we would pick him up when we got home. Laura found the note. Give it to him, Laura."

"Where did she go?" he asked, glancing at the paper, turning it over as if there had to be more to it.

"We don't know," Manny said.

"She took a suitcase," Laura said.

"A suitcase? She walked to town with a suitcase?" he asked.

"That's what Mrs. Ambling said."

Mr. Tate went into his room, searched his dresser and night-stands. He opened the closet and grabbed the empty hangers and dropped them to the floor. The hangers bounced. He pulled the covers from the bed, looked under the pillows, threw them on the floor. The kids watched him warily from the doorway. His lips twitched. His forehead was stitched into a wrinkled frown. He eyed them as if he was going to say something but then didn't. Suddenly, he slammed his hand down on the top of the dresser, and they all jumped. Rich grabbed Laura's leg. Her father whipped the drawers from out of the dresser, overturned the contents onto the bed and floor. Laura and her brothers continued to watch from the hallway, not crossing the threshold.

"Damn it!" their father shouted. And then he struck the lamp by his bed. It crashed against the headboard.

He looked at them as if they were to blame. Then he shook his head, sighed heavily, and brushed past them into the living room. "Stay here," he said, then opened the front door and slammed it behind him. They ran to the window and watched him walk to Mrs. Ambling's house, kicking the dead branches from the oak aside. They did not follow him.

Mrs. Ambling answered her door, and with his arms folded across his chest and his forehead still furrowed, he asked her questions they couldn't hear. She nodded and shook her head. They spoke for a few moments, and then he looked up and saw Laura and her brothers at the window. Mrs. Ambling turned and looked at them too, and then he went inside her house, his arms still crossed.

"What did she say?" Manny asked.

Mr. Tate didn't answer. He hurriedly grabbed his keys. "I'll be back later."

"Where are you going?"

"To look for your mother."

"Where is she?"

"That's what I aim to find out."

They ran to the porch as he started the truck and backed out, shooting gravel. They all jumped down and skirted the tree and stood at the edge of the road and watched him drive away, his tires squealing.

By midnight, he hadn't returned. Laura made Rich go to bed. The child was cranky, unsettled, and had been crying off and on in jags, saying, "Where's Momma? Where did Momma go?"

Laura said, "She'll be back soon. Don't worry." She lay down with him on her bed and rubbed his back and sang songs quietly until he nodded off, and then she went back in the living room. "Gene, you should go to bed too," she said. Skinny Gene, the most frail of them all, just stood at the window, looking out. "We have school tomorrow."

"No," he said.

"It's after midnight. You'll be exhausted."

"I'm not going to school tomorrow."

"Yes, you are."

Manny said, "Give it a break, Laura. None of us are going to school tomorrow."

"We don't have a choice."

"We goddamn sure do," he said.

"Momma won't stand for it."

"She's not here, you idiot! And she ain't coming back either. Can't you see that?"

"Dad's going to find her."

"Fat chance! Are you blind? She's gone. Just like Gloria. Long gone."

"You're wrong," Laura said.

Gene sat down on their father's chair, covered his ears, and began to cry.

"Quit yelling," she said to Manny. "See what you've done?" She bent down to comfort Gene.

"Who gives a shit?" Manny said.

"Shhh. You'll wake Rich."

"He might as well be up," Manny said.

"It's okay, Gene," Laura said, stroking his head.

"No, it's not," Manny said. "It's not okay."

"Will you just shut up," she said.

"You fucking shut up!" Manny shouted and lurched toward her, his face red. She put her arm up to ward off his blow, but he stopped himself. Still, he hovered over the chair.

Gene yelled, through his tears, "Stop it, stop it, stop it!" The intensity of his voice startled both of them.

Rich screamed shrilly, then called, "Momma!"

Laura shook her head and grimaced at Manny. "What is the matter with you? It's not our fault."

"Laura!"

"Rich, I'm right here," she said. She went in the bedroom and made him lie back down. "I'll check on you in a minute."

"Don't leave," he cried.

"I'm just in the living room."

"Stay with me."

She lay down on the bed next to him and rubbed his back again. She thought he was asleep several times, but each time she moved, he startled awake, clutching her.

"I'm right here," she said.

She remained as still as possible and closed her eyes and tried not to think. Gene and Manny spoke in hushed whispers in the living room, and then they opened the front door and went outside. Their father wasn't home, though. She hadn't heard his truck. She relaxed for a second, nodded off, and then woke, startled, afraid that she'd slept too long. She looked at the clock. Only twenty minutes had passed, but she felt groggy, disoriented. Rich was deeply asleep now.

She grabbed her sweater and slipped on her shoes and went outside, where Gene and Manny sat on the ground in the debris of the halved oak. She turned on the porch light, left the front door open in case Rich woke again, and then sat down with them.

"I'm sorry," Manny said.

"It's okay," she said. "Let's go on to bed. He'll be back soon, and we'll wake up then."

"You two go on," Manny said. "I'll wait here."

"I'll wait too," Gene said.

"No, you come on to bed with me," she said. "We'll get up when he comes home."

"Go on, Gene," Manny said. "She's right."

"I don't want—"

"I don't care what you want," Manny said. "Go on with Laura."

Gene and Laura slipped into the house, and then into bed, without changing into pajamas. Gene slept fitfully. Laura heard him tossing throughout the night. Rich wouldn't stay on one side of the bed, but he kept waking when she moved him. Finally, she sat in the chair by the window and watched Manny, standing now in the split of the tree, staring down the dark street. Waiting.

Mr. Tate did not show up the next morning, and so they did not go to school. Laura tried to busy herself and Gene and Rich with chores — making breakfast and lunch, washing some laundry and hanging it on the line, pulling weeds from the garden. She fed Fay, who had lost her appetite and moped about, as if she also knew what was going on. Then they watched television, but nothing good was on — no baseball game, just a silly soap opera. So they played Crazy Eights, but Gene started crying in the middle of the game, and that set off Rich, and then soon she was crying as well.

Manny left on his bike right after lunch, said he couldn't just wait around. He was going to try and find their father, and maybe figure out what in the hell happened. Around three in the afternoon, he rode back up.

"Did you find him?" Laura asked.

"No. The man at the bus station said he came by last night, asking questions."

"Did the man know anything about Momma?"

"He said she caught the bus yesterday."

"Where?"

"He couldn't remember. Maybe Amarillo, maybe Denver."

"Where is Dad?"

"Gone looking for her, I guess." After a few moments of silence, he added, "She left us."

"Why would she do that?"

"How the hell do I know? She hates us, I guess."

"It's my fault," Gene said.

"No, it's not," Laura said.

"Yeah, it is. On Sunday I stole two quarters from her dresser, and she caught me and whipped me."

"It's not your fault," she said again. "Besides, Dad will find her."

Manny was conspicuously silent.

Mr. Tate didn't come back home until early Friday morning, close to dawn. His truck rolled into the driveway, and they all jumped from their beds. He'd not called. Laura had started to wonder if perhaps neither of her parents was coming back. She ran to the window.

He was alone. She felt her stomach drop. She and her brothers all stood at the window now, staring at him. He had turned the ignition off, but he didn't get out. He laid his head on the steering wheel. She wondered if he had not slept the entire time he'd been gone, and now, exhausted, home, he didn't have the energy or will to even get out of the truck. He was there for five, then ten, then fifteen minutes.

"I'm gonna get him," Manny finally said.

"Maybe you should just let him stay there a little longer," she suggested.

He ignored her and opened the door. She, Gene, and Rich stood on the porch and watched as Manny walked cautiously to the truck.

"Dad," he said, but their father didn't stir. Manny placed his hand on his shoulder, shook him. "Dad!"

He lifted his head slowly. His sagging face was grizzled with black and white stubble.

"It's almost six," Manny said. "You fell asleep."

Mr. Tate opened the truck door and eased out. He didn't speak. He started for the porch but stopped by the debris of the oak.

"What happened?" Manny asked him.

He didn't respond. It was as if their father didn't even register their presence. He moved among the branches of the tree. He crouched down at the base and put his hand on the black charred wood.

"Dad," Manny said, "tell us what happened."

Their father rubbed his fingers over the dead wood and then smelled the burn on his fingers. He put his face down to the tree. When he lifted back up, his cheeks and nose were blackened. Manny's body stiffened. He inhaled deeply and then waded quickly through the branches and closed in on his father. Gene, Rich, and Laura moved instinctively down a step toward the yard.

"*Damn it*," Manny shouted, "what in the *hell* happened?" He grabbed his father's arm.

The man whirled and, quick and vicious as lightning, slapped Manny across the face. Manny fell among the branches. He did not rise. Black finger marks were streaked across his cheek. He lay on the branches and started to cry. Even though he was fifteen, he seemed like a small boy, crumpled there. Mr. Tate looked down at him for a few seconds, and then he crouched next to him and placed his hand on Manny's head. He began to cry too. Laura had never seen her father cry before, not even when Gloria eloped.

Rich and Gene sat down on the porch, and first Gene and then Rich began to cry. Laura breathed deeply and looked up at the sky.

It was cloudy and pink. The light spilled over their house, but the sun was blocked from view. The street was empty. She stood on the lawn, her two younger brothers on the porch, crying; her father and Manny, huddled by the tree, crying.

She stared at the horizon. It seemed right there, but so far. She thought of that bus, disappearing over the edge, rolling away from them, her mother not looking back.

Thrumming

AUGUST 1958

It was a Saturday night in early August of that year, and Laura baked pork chops and fried potatoes, her father's favorite meal. Manny was camping with his buddies that weekend, so she made less than usual, just enough for her father, Gene, Rich, and herself. As she took out the last batch of potatoes, the grease popping and splattering in the pan, her father waltzed into the kitchen, smelling of Old Spice and hair oil, dressed up in his red short-sleeved, snap-button shirt, jeans, and stitched boots.

"Mmmm-mmm," he said, and then leaned over and kissed her on the forehead. "I'm starving."

"When will you be back?" she asked.

"I don't know. Late, probably."

"What band is playing?"

"The Pick Wickers maybe."

She nodded.

Gene and Rich chattered through dinner, and her father

53

told them jokes. They kept laughing and spluttering with their mouths full. She watched silently.

He hadn't been dancing in a long time. She remembered that he used to take her mother dancing years ago. But he'd gone out only a couple of times in the last few weeks — for drinks with his welding buddies and fishing once with the Cransburgh brothers. She wanted to believe his going out was a good sign — that he was returning to his old self, back to his normal life, that he could still find ways to enjoy himself even though her mother had disappeared less than three months ago. But she also felt uneasy whenever he left the house. She couldn't shake the unspoken belief that he was somehow responsible for her leaving. He'd done something to drive her away, maybe they all had, but he seemed more responsible than the rest of them because he was her husband and their father, and it was too soon (wasn't it?) to be having a good time.

A shameful heat spread up her neck and over her chin and cheeks. She was as bad as those idiot deacons at the church, "old shitheads who didn't know their mouths from their assholes," as Manny said. It wasn't fair to her father, not at all. He was the one still here. Not her mother. She had disappeared. Not him. Right?

"I don't see why we have to go over to Mrs. Ambling's," she said.

"I told you, I don't know when I'll be back. I may play some cards after."

"I always watch the boys anyway. Why not tonight?"

"I just don't feel right you being here alone at night without me or Manny."

"I'm not a kid," she said. "Manny's just a year older, and you let him do anything he wants."

She didn't like being treated like the younger boys. Yet she also felt somewhat relieved because she hadn't been in the house at night without her father or Manny since her mother left, and she *was* a little afraid. She also wondered if he thought she needed watching. Maybe because Gloria had eloped and her mother had left a year later, he wasn't going to take any chances with the last female in the house.

"We already settled this, Laura," he said. "You and the boys clean up, then go on over. I'll get you in the morning."

"Yes, sir," she said, ambivalent.

"You mind your sister now. You hear?"

"Yes, sir," Gene said.

"And be good for Mrs. Ambling."

Rich had potatoes and ketchup in his mouth, but he nodded.

While they finished their meals, she started clearing the table. Her father suddenly stood up and sang "Your Cheatin' Heart," hamming it up until Rich and Gene spluttered again with laughter.

"Hey, good lookin', whatcha got cookin'?"

He pulled her away from the sink, hugging her close to him, and they twirled quickly on the small kitchen floor. "Sing for me, boys."

Gene and Rich sang along and pounded the table. She and her father two-stepped, ended with an extravagant twirl, then he held her close and dipped her dramatically like Fred Astaire did with Ginger Rogers. Gene and Rich cheered. She laughed and tried to push him away, but he picked her up and twirled her around the kitchen once again, almost knocking over the skillet full of still-warm grease. When he put her down, little sweat beads trickled along both their hairlines. It was hot outside, and despite the windows being open, it seemed even hotter in the kitchen.

He sat down. "Whoa! I need some more tea. Your sister's done worn me out."

He poured himself another tall glass from the pitcher on the table, and they all watched him lift his head and the tea drain down his throat, his big Adam's apple bobbing. When he finished he shook his head vigorously a couple of times, which made the boys laugh but sent a dark, cold shiver across the back of Laura's neck. The image reminded her, for some reason, of Greta and her puppies.

He reached out his hand to her, and she took it, and he gently pulled her into his lap and said, "Boys, your sister is our little sweetie. Don't you ever forget it." He nuzzled his clean-shaven chin into her throat and kissed her cheek. It felt rough. Quickly, he was up, putting on his watch, patting the boys' heads. Then he was gone.

Watching him rumble down the road in his truck, leaving a gray-white plume of dust behind him, she felt empty. The word *forlorn* popped into her head.

"Gene, why don't you do the dishes."

"It ain't my turn."

"I don't care," she snapped. "Just do it."

On the front porch she sat on the metal chair her father had welded and listened to the loud buzzing of the cicadas. The evening sun was still hot and bright. She looked at the hole where their old oak tree had been uprooted after it had been struck by lightning the day before her mother disappeared. Her father had not refilled the hole, and it looked like a robbed grave.

She slipped inside and helped Gene dry the plates. The three of them went to the backyard, and Rich played in the sandbox while she and Gene pulled the laundry off the line.

She checked Fay's food bowl. Still full. The dog hadn't eaten much in the past few months. Although her father said it was because of the heat more than anything else, Laura still believed it was because of what happened with Greta, followed by the disappearance of their mother. He said that was foolishness. She stroked Fay's side and neck and rubbed her belly. Despite what her father said, she knew why Fay was upset.

She helped bathe Rich, and they all grabbed their pillows and sleeping bags and went next door. Mrs. Ambling answered the door in her nightgown. Her face looked blotchy, her eyes watery, her nose red and runny. She had a tissue in her hand.

"Oh, Lord," she said. "I meant to call. I took some medicine, and it's made me a little dopey."

"What's wrong?" Laura asked.

"I've come down with something. I don't know what. I've got a fever. Has your father already left?"

"Yes, ma'am," she said.

"Well, I suppose you all can just come on in. I hope you don't catch what I've got, though."

"We can stay at our house."

"Your father said he'd be out late."

"It's okay. I watch the boys all the time."

"But Daddy said — " Gene began.

"It's okay, really," Laura said. "You don't feel good. We'll be right next door. We can come over if there's a problem."

"Are you sure?"

"I'm sure."

She left her father a note on the kitchen table, explaining about Mrs. Ambling, so he wouldn't be angry. The three of them listened to a baseball game on the radio. Later, after Gene and

Rich went to bed, she pulled out the letter she'd received from Gloria just this week. In it she'd included a picture of herself, her husband, the air force pilot she married, and their new baby girl, Julie. In the background was the Mediterranean Sea with craggy cliffs rising dramatically in the distance. Gloria didn't know about their mother yet; they didn't know how to reach Gloria, and even if they could have, their father didn't like to talk about either her mother or Gloria. Her sister looked happy in the picture. Laura wished she could be with her, though she knew that if she were with her, then Gloria would have to know about their mother, and part of what made Gloria seem happy was the fact that she didn't know. Laura missed her, but she didn't feel sad anymore that she was gone. Just a kind of sweet longing to be with her again. It was more complicated with her mother.

She picked up *The Hollywood Gazette*, which she'd bought with babysitting money. But the bright, thickly textured pictures of Janet Leigh and Deborah Kerr agitated her. She was only four-teen and felt she was still too boyish looking, nothing like these glamorous, curvy women. They reminded her, strangely, of her mother, whose body had been made thick in the middle by hard work and children, but she was still womanly enough, and her face had not yet been too hardened by age or the West Texas cli-mate. No movie star, but she was pretty with large, dark brown eyes and a thin, perfect nose, and sometimes, when she was free from worry and her ash blonde hair was loose around her face, she seemed radiant to Laura.

She didn't like to think about her mother too much, especially when she was alone, but sometimes she couldn't help it. The thoughts or images would be there in her mind and wouldn't go away. Her mother was like a ghost who might return at any time, but if she did, what would happen then? Laura tried to imagine where she was now, what she was doing, but without any context, it all seemed like that huge hole in the yard, with nothing very distinguishable. Laura feared she might forget what her mother looked like. She wished she had a photograph.

She got up, turned the radio to a music station, and sang along quietly to Patsy Cline and a Weavers' song and Bob Wills, always Bob Wills, and danced around the room. She closed her eyes and imagined herself with Charlton Heston, and then with her father on the sawdust dance floor of the Armory, the smoky, sweaty, sweet-smelling perfume of the couples, the skirts billowing out, the two-stepping, waltzing, fast-twirling, double-dipping couples. She couldn't wait until she was able to go dancing there herself. In less than a month, she'd be starting high school, and she could go if someone asked her. She'd already picked out the dress she wanted to buy — a green and white striped linen one with small white satin bows on the sleeves and waist. She was saving her babysitting money to get it.

She spun one last time before plopping down on the couch, sweaty again because it was so hot inside, even with the breeze blowing in. She sat there and listened to the radio until it signed off, and the house seemed eerily quiet, except for the cicadas and the occasional bark or lonely howl of a dog down the alley.

In bed, trying to will herself to sleep, she could hear the late summer breeze whistling in the trees. She wondered if her mother had lain awake at night, preparing herself to leave, to not have to think about what would be left behind, toughening her spirit. Had she been planning it for a long time? It seemed so sudden, without warning. Mrs. Ambling said she just walked out to the road, carrying that brown suitcase. And now she was gone, but of course she wasn't. How could she be completely gone when she was here right now in Laura's mind?

She opened her eyes, tried to keep them open for thirty seconds — one Mississippi, two Mississippi, three Mississippi — which Gloria had told her was the secret to washing away bad thoughts or dreams. Then she closed her eyes again and told herself, *fall asleep, fall asleep, fall asleep, fall asleep* until the phrase seemed funny. So strange that word *falling*, like going over an embankment, standing on the unrailed precipice at Palo Duro Canyon, the vertigo of below, trying to stop the silly crazy foolish impulse to jump, jump, jump. Just an inch — no, not even that much — separating ground from air.

And then falling into where? Into air, into nothing. Like being asleep is the fall itself, not the landing. You don't fall *from* or *into* or *onto* sleep. You just fall asleep. Like disappearing. Like her mother. She'd fallen. But fallen where? No. Fallen away — away *from* them, but *to* what? *Into* what? Or maybe it was like sleep, after all, neither away from nor to anything. It was the thing itself.

And then Laura was asleep, solidly, without thought or dream.

When she woke, it was to the sound of something being knocked over in another room. Gene lay curled on the corner of his and Manny's bed. Rich was stretched out with his feet hanging through the bars because he was too big for the crib.

She heard a laugh, then muffled whispers. She grabbed the pocketknife from her dresser and crept toward the hallway.

The lights were out, but the moon filtered through the sheer curtains. Her father's door was slightly ajar. She heard laughter, more whispering, and she knew then that her father was in the room with a woman. She hesitated in the hallway with the knife in her hand. She felt stupid. She started to return to bed and sleep, but then she heard a little high-pitched yelp, and she stopped and sat down, her back against the wall. The darkness of the house enveloped her. She scooted close to her father's door and sat there on her knees. She closed her eyes. Outside, the cicadas buzzed. The bed squeaked, rocking back and forth. She imagined a small canoe swaying in the troughs of waves. She squeezed her eyes tightly and thought she could hear their lips against each other. Her father's breathing seemed labored and deep and rhythmic, and the woman's voice swelled between his, higher pitched and sharp, almost whistling.

She moved her face closer to the door. Her heart beat in her chest and neck and temples. She felt paralyzed by their laboring. She thought of Fay when she was in heat, the male dogs panting, their tongues dripping. Laura's stomach dropped, but she pressed her face next to the cracked door. She closed one eye and with the other tried to see into the room. It was dark except for a faint light from the open-shuttered window, which cast a slatted splash of yellow over her father's bare moving back and made a silhouette of the woman. The sheets and covers clung to the edges of the bed.

When her eyes adjusted, she saw the outline of her father's body pressing down onto the woman. The bed did seem to roll, though not with the sea wildness she had imagined. The springs continued to squeak. Their breathing increased in intensity. She could see the woman's white thighs spread wide, like phosphorescent wings perpendicular to his hips, but the rest of her body seemed trapped beneath his, swallowed in the sagging, lumpy mattress and under his long broad body. The woman's arm was slung back against the pillow, crooked over her face, her mouth pinched at the corners in a grimace as his shoulders rubbed against her cheeks. He moved forcefully over her, and his breathing turned to muffled groans. He rocked and pressed so that her body disappeared into the bed.

Is this why my mother disappeared? The question caught in her mind like a hook.

The woman shook her head and let out what sounded like a painful moan, and Laura felt sickened by it and unsure if she should open the door and let herself be seen. She wanted to stop this, wanted her father off this woman, wanted him to quit pressing and breathing in this way. But she could not bring herself to do it. She closed her eyes, but the sounds overwhelmed her. She heard the mocking drone of the cicadas outside.

When she opened her eyes again, her heart leapt into her throat because the woman's arm was no longer over her face, and she stared directly at Laura. Could she see Laura there? Surely not. But there the woman was; she just kept staring, her eyes distinct and luminous in the dark. Laura stared back and could see that the face was not womanish but girlish, with chubby white cheeks and a soft puckerish mouth. She felt a panic billow inside her as her father made more noise, and the bed rocked against the wall, and the woman-girl let out a small groan, muffled by her father's shoulder.

Laura jerked back. She felt dizzy in the hall and closed her eyes, but all the noise — those crazy cicadas, her father's breathing, the bedsprings — thundered in her head. She felt turned, as if she was being held upside down, and when she opened her eyes, she was surprised to find herself still sitting upright in the hall. She crawled toward her room, shut the door, and slipped into her bed. She put her face into the pillow and covered her ears so she couldn't hear anything except the rush of blood in her temples, which after a few minutes diminished to a steady throb.

She tried to sleep but couldn't. And then she heard a rustling in the hallway. The bathroom door opened and closed. Water ran. The toilet flushed. A minute later the door opened again, and then there were footsteps outside her own door. It creaked. She kept her eyes closed, fearing what she would see when she opened them. She knew someone was in the room, her father certainly, though the presence seemed lighter, and she could also smell something sweet, like warmed buttermilk, so she didn't move. She held her breath and felt a slight pressure by the side of her bed, a rustle, and then the door closed. Feet padded to her father's room, then his door shut.

She opened her eyes. Beside her on the small bed was the knife. It seemed puny and foolish there. She swallowed hard, her throat scratchy, raw. She reached out and grabbed the knife handle. It was moist. She opened it and pressed her finger against the dull blade. It did not cut her. She closed it again, slipped it between the mattress and foundation, and lay there in the dark listening. After a while there was rustling in the other room, the click of her father's door, the sound of feet over the hardwood floor, her father whispering. Finally, the front door creaked open and shut. Her father's truck rumbled to life.

She tiptoed to the window and watched the truck back out, crunching the gravel of the driveway, the beams from the head-lights making small, yellow circles in the dark street. She felt the hot summer air through the bug screen, could smell the dust from the road, the ragweed twitching her nostrils, could hear the cicadas still at it.

The night was barely lit now by the clouded moon. She waited until she no longer heard the truck. She didn't return to her own bed, but checked on Gene and Rich in the beds beside hers. Even though Manny was gone for the night, Gene was huddled close to his edge, a habit of deferring to his older brother even in his absence. Though only six years older than Gene, she felt sorry for him, and angry too, that life had already taught him to expect so little. She reached out and stroked his head, but he didn't stir. Even his breathing was shallow, as if he was afraid to take too much air from the world. Rich, by contrast, was stretched out in the crib, a space hog, a thrasher, someone who demanded his due without even knowing it. It was just part of his nature.

And what was *her* nature? What did she look like when she slept? What would she think if she could see herself clearly? The fact that she could not know, that she remained partially blind to herself, bewildered her. Eyes always looking out and then in, but not *at*. She reached over the crib and straightened Rich, tugged the sheet from beneath him, covered him up. There was no real reason with the heat, but it was a habit of hers, this need to be covered and to cover others at night.

She glided out of the bedroom, into the hallway, and then into her father's room, where the windows were open. She pulled the lamp cord, and a white harsh glow splashed the room, forced her to squint. The covers and sheets lay tangled around the mattress. There was a pocket in the middle of the bed where the woman-girl had been. She placed one hand out and down, ran it just a few inches over the top of the sheets, feeling the heat still present from their bodies. She was hesitant at first to touch, to disturb. The heat radiated the entire length of the mattress, from the foot to the pillows, and she floated both hands above the bed and was surprised by the invisible warmth. She reached down to the center, where their hips met, and she touched the sheet. It was hot and slightly damp, but she pressed one palm down flat, her fingers spread, and ran her hand back and forth and then around in a circle. She reached out with her other hand and could imagine the two of them in here, not even a half hour ago, and the quiet stillness of the room was like the buzzing sound you hear in the silence after thunder.

She smelled them here, too, and took a calm pleasure in isolating the scents. Her father's hair oil and Old Spice, the woman-girl's too-sweet perfume, like that buttermilk smell drifting into her room. There was a faint whiff of the rum her father liked and spearmint gum and something else, something sharp, pungent, the smell of sex, she figured, and lingering above and below and swirling through was the dank, tangy odor of sweat.

She searched for her mother's own particular smell, the talcum powder like a fine dust on her body, but it wasn't here anymore, not even a trace. She felt saddened by that loss, a kind of betrayal, but Laura wasn't sure now who was being betrayed.

She opened her eyes, tugged on the lamp cord, and slipped her feet purposefully over the hardwood floor so she could hear the callused *shwoosh* of her feet, out of her father's room, through the narrow hallway that seemed like a tunnel to her — she'd never noticed this before — and then to the living room. It too held the smell of her father and the woman-girl in it, and she followed slowly, could trace it to the door, which she opened. She stepped outside to the porch, and even there she could smell them, as if they'd left a vaporous trail. Then the odors dissipated and were gone.

She sat down on the porch, feeling very calm, very *awake*. She let the breeze brush through her nightgown. It was still hot. She then stood up on her tiptoes, pulled her gown over her head, and reaching high, stretched out her body, which seemed dangerous, thrilling. She hadn't been outside with so little on since she was a child; she remembered the last time, running around naked in the summery yard, chasing Fay and some of her puppies before they gave them away.

It was dark out, not quite sunrise yet and no cars, not even the far away sound of trucks from the highway. She liked this feeling, like a shedding, like an opening up. She thought of the way the rattlers and bull snakes sometimes left long papery casings in the night for her brothers and her to find the next day. She imagined the snakes slipping away, the new skin wet and vulnerable and free.

She walked over the lawn, skirting the place where the old oak had been, and on out to the middle of the road, where she stood and stared down one end of the street and then the other. Both ends extended farther than she could see at night with only this thin moon and cloud-tangled stars. The ends of the road turned away, bent out of sight, away, away, away into darkness. She stood there and looked at the row of houses on either side of the street and then at her own small house, where inside her brothers and father and she slept, ate, argued, sulked, laughed, dreamed. Where that woman-girl stared at her from her mother's bed. Where her mother was before she disappeared. No, *not disappeared. Before she left.*

It seemed so small, this place, too small to contain all their lives. She thought about the other houses with their own lives cramped too tightly inside. And the road extended into darkness, the black night high above, the cicadas buzzing.

She felt no fear, not even the cold threat of being caught.

Who cares?

She closed her eyes and, with her arms out, started to spin slowly, then faster and faster until she staggered and fell on the dusty road. It didn't hurt, and she just stayed there for a while with the acrid taste of dust in her mouth. Then she stretched out on her back and felt the still-warm gravel beneath, sticking like shards into her body, but even that didn't hurt. She stared up at the black sky, traced the constellations with her fingers, and just as the first light of sunrise began its promise, she heard — or rather felt — a sound emanating from her body, a low vibrating whistle that seemed in tune with the cicadas and the wind and the breathing of the night and the warm road.

She closed her eyes and listened, stayed calmly there as she heard and could almost taste a deep, pressured thrumming inside her head. A tingly heat spread through her neck and chest and stomach and arms and down through her thighs and calves and toes. It seemed as if a shade was slowly being lifted over her closed eyelids.

She opened her eyes and could see headlights, like two pale animals loping toward the curve. It was her father's truck, she knew, and she wondered, without worry or fear, what he would do if she stayed right where she was.

Will he see me in time? Will he run over me?

It made her smile to think about it. She imagined that anxious twitch he got around the corners of his mouth when he was confused or worried or sad. She didn't feel afraid, just curious, as the truck zigzagged slowly down the street, still pretty far in the distance. She wished he was gone, would disappear himself for a while, let her stay here like this and let the sun rise fully on her, transforming the world and the house and everything she could smell and hear and see and feel and taste into light and blistering heat. She didn't want to share this feeling. She didn't want to have to explain herself to him or to anyone, just as now she didn't want explanations *from* him.

As the beams closed in, she rose quickly and felt again that she was gliding as she grabbed her gown. She slipped through the door, into bed, and pulled the sheet up and over her face so that it floated for a couple of seconds before shrouding her. The dust from her body created a layer of fine grit on the bottom sheet.

She closed her eyes and tried to recall the thrumming, coax it back. She breathed slowly, listening to her breath, her heartbeat. She heard her father's truck crunch in the driveway, the rattle of the engine as it died, the front door creak open, then click shut.

Almost there, yes, close, just out of reach.

Her father opened her door. He paused before whispering, "Laura, honey, was that you?"

She didn't answer. She was far away now, far away. She could almost feel it again, the thrum and radiating heat, and she wanted to let it spread through her body. Was this what her mother had felt as she left, this buzz and heat, this pulsing in her own body? Was this what had pulled her, like a compulsion, from the house and to the bus station and away from them forever? Did she find a small, private part of herself where there wasn't room for anyone else? Laura could almost understand that. It seemed sad and mysterious — and even beautiful.

"Are you awake?" her father whispered worriedly, nudging her shoulder. "Why aren't you at Mrs. Ambling's?"

She could smell the cigarettes and sweet rum on his breath. Her eyes blurred hotly. Her throat constricted. Still she didn't answer. That feeling, that thrumming, was slipping from her now, drifting too quickly away. She could almost see it, like a brightly colored balloon — rising, rising, and then riding on the wind, growing smaller and smaller until it was barely visible, merely a colored dot in the distance, insignificant.

And then not even there.

"Last Call

Texas Moon

1978

The band had just begun the Cotton-Eyed Joe, and I could see from under the table the legs of the dancers, like spokes of a wheel, stomping around on the dance floor, everybody chanting,

> One, two, three. BULL-SHIT!
> What'd you say? BULL-SHIT!

I had never seen the Cotton-Eyed Joe from this angle. It was quite a sight. All the skirts swirling, legs rubbing against each other to the whine of the fiddle. About that time two big boots and a pair of denim jeans appeared at the table. I could tell without a word spoken that it was Rich, my brother.

"Did you lose your keys again or are you out of chewing tobacco?"

It was an embarrassing situation, me under the table in the sawdust at the Texas Moon. I was trying to hide from Angie, my wife, who I'd glimpsed just moments earlier. Trapped in the corner of the bar, there was no place for me to go but under.

Rich stuck his head down to get a better look. A white skirt fluttered between his bowed legs. He'd already had a few drinks, I could tell. His blond beard looked too curly, like a girl had fingered it, and his eyes were glassy.

"I've got some Red Man, Gene. You don't have to chew sawdust." He pulled the pouch from his pocket and offered it to me. He loved to rile me. I scooped up a small handful of sawdust and poured it in his open pouch.

That silly bastard mixed it up with his index finger, pinched off a big wad, and stuck it in the front of his lip. He didn't even flinch, just kept playing along, like it was the sweetest-tasting thing he had ever sucked on. It must have been a pretty ridiculous sight, us carrying on a conversation, me under the table, him chewing sawdust, his butt facing the dance floor.

Rich was semi-crazy, that was for sure. And the luckiest man I ever knew. When he was twenty he bought himself a '76 red Nova with two bright purple stripes down the hood. The second day he had it his brakes locked as we raced down Adirondack Street, and he plowed right into a huge sycamore tree. I jumped out of my Skylark, thinking he was dead for sure, but when the firemen wedged the door open, Rich crawled out with only a few scratches on his arm. He'd get into a fight every other week or so, come home bloody, but never disfigured. He'd had pool cues busted over his head, bats cracked across his kneecaps, beer bottles practically shoved down his throat. He claimed he'd even been swimming with sharks when he rigged offshore. He had come through it all laughing like the blessed idiot he was. Eating sawdust wasn't any big deal.

"You care to have any, Gene?" He held the pouch out to me, grinning. "It sure is tasty."

"I'll pass, thank you."

"Suit yourself. By the way, Angie's here," he said. "She's over by the pool tables with Shelly Denison. She looks mighty good."

I got out from under the table. The Texas Moon used to be a roller skating rink back when Rich and I were growing up, but it had been converted into a country and western club a few years back, so now there was a large dance floor where the rink used to be, three bars, a stage big enough for a six-piece band, pool tables in one corner and in the other a mechanical bull on which I had seen just a few months earlier a man break his neck. Rich and I had been coming here more often since our sister Gloria and her son Travis started working here. Gloria's husband and oldest son had died in a car accident earlier in the year, and while they waited for the lawyers to bicker over the insurance settlement, they had been working — she as a waitress, he as an underage helper for the bartenders. I felt bad for them and visited them whenever I could. Since they'd been working here, they both seemed in better spirits. It was that kind of place. The good band music, the lively crowds, the dancing, and the silliness of the mechanical bull could cheer you up.

Across the dance floor, Angie leaned over the green felt on the center pool table, a cue stick in her hand, studying her shot. She looked wonderful, wearing the blue cotton captain's shirt I'd bought her last summer at South Padre Island, her thick black hair done up in a French braid, the way I liked it. It's a strange thing to see a woman you love and have lived with after not seeing her for four months. It makes you wonder, for one thing, what the hell you are doing piddling around on the floor of the Texas Moon.

We'd been separated for about six months, the longest we'd ever been apart. I hadn't seen her at all in four months because we hadn't broken up on the best of terms, and she said she was going to file for divorce this time. I felt sure she was bluffing. We'd always been together, and except for a few intervals, I was sure we always would be. At the moment, though, I had about ten good reasons for not wanting to see her, the most important of which was that I owed her money.

"Does she know I'm here?" I asked Rich.

"She didn't ask."

"Did you volunteer the information?"

"She ain't dumb, Gene."

"You son of a bitch."

"What the hell are you so scared of?" he asked.

"It's not a matter of being scared." He was awfully stupid sometimes.

He'd never been married himself, though he'd been dating a girl named Babs for about a year, and there were things I couldn't seem to explain to him. "She doesn't want to see me, does she?" I asked.

"I'm not one to tell you what you can and can't do. I gotta get back to the pool table. I have a game coming up."

"Go on then," I said.

"Could you loan me a twenty?" he asked, but changed his request when he saw my face. "Ten? I lost some money to a little Mexican runt, and I want a chance to win it back."

I had just been paid, so I had a little more than a hundred with me. I handed Rich a twenty. "I'm going home," I said.

"You can't hide from her forever," he called over his shoulder from the middle of the dance floor. He didn't even wait for an answer, just laughed and walked toward the pool tables, sawdust bulging in his lower lip. Crazy bastard.

Angie finished her game and, heading back to her table, caught my eye. I couldn't tell if seeing me made her happy, but I knew I couldn't get away clean. To tell you the truth, she looked so damn good at that moment that I didn't entirely want to. I waved, picked up my Colorado Bulldog, and headed for her table.

I chose the most direct path, across the dance floor. Unfortunately, it was full of two-stepping couples who kept bumping into me. By the time I reached Angie, half my drink had sloshed onto the floor. I left a trail behind me that, given my luck, would cause some poor couple to slip and break their necks and sue me for the few possessions I still owned: a twin bed, a portable stereo, a black and white TV, and a green, cat-clawed couch my older brother, Manny, had given me — all of it stored in the same depressing efficiency I always rented when Angie and I separated.

"Mind if I sit down?"

"What's the matter, grace?" Shelly said. "Crawled under a table 'cause you couldn't find anyone to dance with?"

Shelly was a smart-ass. She had a permanent smirk nestled in the corner of her mouth, as if everything she said was a joke you would never be privy to. She worked with Angie in the Skagg's-Albertson's bakery as chief cake decorator. She looked to be about mine and Angie's age but she had a son who had started high school, and she'd been married at least three times, so I couldn't tell for sure.

"Better than dancing with you, Olive Oyl," I said.

"You could do worse," she told me.

"I have," I said, smiling. I should have shot myself then. I hadn't meant to insult Angie.

Shelly turned to her, and it was clear that she'd either drunk a few too many of whatever she was having, or she was between spouses and felt obliged to take her anger out on the closest errant husband she could find.

"Jesus, no wonder you ditched the lout," she said.

"I didn't mean anything by that."

Angie nodded to let me know she understood, but she still didn't say anything, which unsettled me a little. I'd forgotten how white and even her teeth were and how her green and brown-speckled eyes could look through you and the five men standing in line behind you. I wished Shelly would have the decency to go break her neck on the mechanical bull.

"Are you sure you don't want me to give him one right in the kisser?" Shelly said, so loudly that four or five people looked up from their conversations. She swallowed some of her drink.

"We'll let him off the hook this time," Angie said, and her voice surprised me a little since I'd not heard it in a long time. My throat went dry, and I could feel beads of sweat running down the side of my ribs. The band started the first few notes of an old Bob Wills and the Texas Playboys' song, "Ida Red," one of my favorites.

"You're too easy on him," Shelly went on. She finished off her drink in a gulp and turned to me with that bony face of hers. "I've seen this all too often. You smack the little woman around, mope about your house like a mangy dog with its ear gnawed off, forget a couple of alimony checks, and when you see her at a honky-tonk, you say, 'I'm sorry, honeybabysugarsweetie.'"

"Shelly, please," Angie said.

It was clear that Angie had told Shelly everything about us. "Then they look at you all googly eyed and want to stick it in you," Shelly continued.

I cocked an eyebrow at Angie, then stared right back at Shelly.

It would have felt really good to slap that silly smile off Shelly's face. Instead, I leaned in close so that I could see, even in the dark of the Texas Moon, crows' feet at the corners of her eyes.

"Shelly, you like to pretend you're a real bitch, don't you?" I said.

She grinned, then leaned back in her chair and laughed like somebody who thinks she knows more about you than you know yourself. She popped an ice cube in her mouth and chomped on it a couple of times, and I felt this was another private joke of hers.

"Look here, slick. I don't have to pretend."

I turned my chair to Angie, but she ignored me, just watched the dancers.

I felt my coming over had been a big mistake. They had obviously been huddling in the employee room in Skagg's, sipping on Diet Cokes, Angie summarizing our marriage, Shelly dishing out the wisdom about divorce and husbands. I sure wasn't in any mood for Shelly's particular brand of persecution.

Fortunately, Rich came over. "I see you're making your usual headway with the women," he said.

Angie smiled at him and let him kiss her on the cheek. I envied him being able to kiss her like that. They had always gotten along. He was just a kid when we first married, and we used to play three-day games of Monopoly on my odd shifts with Santa Fe. Then later we'd all play poker and party together at Gloria's house. I felt suddenly nostalgic for those days, now that Angie and I were separated and Gloria's husband and my nephew had died.

He dipped around and pulled out Shelly's chair. "Your turn to shoot some pool," he said.

"I don't shoot pool," she groaned.

"I'll teach you." He steered her toward an empty table as he motioned us to the dance floor. "You two go dance," he said.

The band had just started "Crazy" and the woman singing sounded pretty close to Patsy Cline, a croon dipped in honey. "We gotta dance to Patsy," I said. "It's a sacrilege not to."

In the first couple of years of our marriage, we used to come to the Texas Moon whenever I'd return from seven- and eight-day railroad runs. I'd be desperate and horny after those long layovers and anxious to get back not just to the lovemaking, but to the dancing that, for us, was akin to lovemaking. I'd pick her up from Skagg's when she got off at ten, taking along a blouse and a fresh pair of Wranglers. She'd change in the backseat of the car, and I'd watch in the rearview mirror, whistle, and offer lewd remarks. When we got on the floor, we'd dance every song.

"I really don't want to, Gene. Not now."

I fiddled with the swizzle stick in my drink. The floor was full. The woman singing was doing a wonderful job. When she got to the line, "What in the world did I do," she stretched the "do" out for a long time, so that the "ooh-ooh-ooh" sounded bluesy and painful. Over at the bar I could see Travis, who smiled and waved to me. I waved, and he went back to washing glasses. Gloria was at a table, chatting up some couple. She looked up and saw me sitting with Angie. She blew us a kiss and gave me a thumbs-up.

"How are they doing?" Angie asked.

"As well as can be expected," I said. "They like working here."

"I miss 'em," she said.

"You don't have to. They're around. You're family."

"It's not the same anymore."

"Sure it is."

"No, it isn't, Gene. You know that."

At the pool table Shelly knocked the cue ball off the felt, then turned around and jabbed Rich in the gut with the chalky end of her cue stick before tottering off to the bathroom.

"What's her problem?" I said, for something to say.

"Her son got expelled when the principal found cocaine in his locker. She's up to her neck in social workers and school counselors and a lot of other crap. The father said it's not his problem."

"So shouldn't she be home, taking away his needles or something?" Angie and I didn't have any kids, so it was easy to moralize.

"He's in a detox center for a week," she said. "She wanted to get out of her house, so she and Janey and I decided to come here."

"Where's Janey?" I asked.

"She was here earlier. She went with some other friends to the Caravan for a little while."

"You're stranded?"

"She won't be gone long."

"Nice friends you've got," I said.

Her jaws clenched. She shook her head. Finally she said, "I don't understand you sometimes. Why do you have to have this attitude, Gene? You haven't given much of a damn for four months. Why should you care now?"

"Who said I didn't care? I just don't see why Shelly has to know any of our business. I came over here because I thought we could talk. And because you look so damn pretty. I didn't come over to listen to her shit."

Neither of us said anything for a few moments, and it nearly suffocated me. I had to get away, for a few minutes at least. I drained my drink and then pointed to Angie's glass. "You want another?" I asked. She shook her head.

At the bar Travis asked, "Are you and Angie getting back together?"

"We're not apart," I said.

"But I thought — "

"How's your mother doing?" I interrupted.

"Pretty good."

"You sure?"

"The insurance companies keep screwing us around, and that drives her nuts. Otherwise, she's okay. We don't talk about it much anymore."

One of the bartenders said, "Travis, go get me a couple of cases of Bud," and Travis left while the bartender changed one of the soft drink canisters before mixing my drink.

Waiting at the bar, I felt all the old grudges between Angie and me resurface. The last time I saw her, I had just returned from a three-day run to Tucumcari, and I hadn't slept in thirty-six hours. I stopped at Mr. Wonderful's and talked to a bartender friend of mine who used to work for Santa Fe but had been laid off after three suspensions. We exchanged some railroad stories, then I said I had to go home, but I didn't go to my efficiency. I felt a little loose and guilty, so I drove out to the trailer park. The light was on, but the door was locked, and when I tried my key, the door wouldn't open. I jammed the key in the lock and shook so hard that the whole porch on the trailer house started rocking.

"Gene, is that you?" Angie asked from the other side of the door.

"What's the matter with the goddamn lock?"

"I changed it," she said.

"Why'd you do a thing like that? Open up the door."

"You can't come in, Gene."

"My key's stuck."

"You're not coming in."

"I paid for this tin box," I said. I tried to yank the key out, but it wouldn't budge.

"Stop it. You're going to break the whole door down."

"Let me in," I said.

"If I let you in, how can I be sure what happened before won't happen again?"

I didn't say anything. She had a right to be wary. The night before our last separation, I'd been working a long shift, whipped and edgy. Almost as soon as I got home, we started arguing about the truck and the plumbing, piddly stuff that seemed to be tunneling dangerously toward the more tender grievances of our marriage — money, drink, my hesitancy about having kids. I could feel the heat expanding like a balloon in my chest and head. Sleep, I knew, would take the heat away. But she had me trapped in the kitchen. So I shoved her, just to get by, but she banged into the corner of the counter and crumpled to the floor. I'm not trying to make excuses for myself, but I honestly didn't mean for that to happen. It wasn't the first time, though, and she was not ready to forgive me. The next day I was gone.

"What am I supposed to do with my key?" I asked.

"Leave it. It's no good anyway."

Our neighbors, Mr. and Mrs. Jameson, were looking out their trailer window. Mrs. J's hair was done up in pink curlers and she had on the pink smock she wore all day, every day. Her cat was on the windowsill with its back arched. Toward the sewage ditch that ran in back of the trailer park, Staubach, an oversized black lab with a cataract in his left eye, stood eyeballing me. Once, about six months before this latest breakup with Angie, I had followed Staubach down to the far bank of the ditch and found a man, face down in the brown water, drowned. I was so shook up over seeing that man's face when I lifted it, all bloated and blue with grizzled little hairs on his chin and his eyes rolled back in his head, that I didn't go to work for three days, and stayed drunk most of the time.

Staubach waggled over to see what the commotion was all about. "I've been in Tucumcari this past week," I said. "I just want to talk."

"Get some sleep, Gene. Call me in the morning if you want, and maybe we'll talk then."

I sat on the steps and scratched Staubach's tick-ridden ears and looked into his smeary eye and at the way the moon made the aluminum siding of our trailer look this shimmery shade of blue.

About ten minutes passed before Mr. Jameson opened his front door and shined a flashlight in my eyes.

"You better go," he said coolly, like he owned the damn trailer park.

"I guess I better," I said and did, leaving my useless key in the lock and Staubach on the porch.

I didn't call Angie the next morning. How could I? I felt embarrassed, stupid. I couldn't make myself see her, not for a while at least. I sent her checks every two weeks, sometimes with little notes, sometimes not. The last one unfortunately had bounced.

I got my drink and headed back to the table, ready to make amends. Gloria was sitting with Angie, their heads bent toward each other.

"I hear you got rubber in your checkbook," Gloria said.

"That was an accident," I said to Angie. "I wrote it expecting payroll to come last Friday. There was a mix-up in Dallas, and we didn't get our checks until yesterday. I should have called you."

Gloria leaned over and kissed Angie on the cheek and said, "Don't be a stranger." Then, as she left, she called back, "The two of you get on that dance floor. Now."

"Sorry about that check," I said.

"I'm sure it was a mistake," Angie said.

"I've got a little money in my wallet if you need some," I said.

"Send me a check tomorrow. That would be better for both of us. For records and all."

"I suppose you're right." I didn't keep records, and it hurt to discover she did. Why in the hell did she need records?

"Hey! Angie, Gene!" Over by the pool table Rich was standing on a chair. He hollered, "Arriba!" trilling the r. The band had begun a Marty Robbins's tune, the one about falling in love with a Mexican girl in El Paso. Rich liked Marty Robbins. He did a Mexican hat dance on his chair, then yelled, "Dance! Now! Or else you'll have to answer to Señor Stomp-on-Your-Toes."

Angie and I laughed.

"We better follow orders," I said.

We two-stepped, but it was not an easy song to dance to, and we never found our rhythm. I didn't want to hold her too close, though I knew her ribs couldn't still be bruised. I lost my step several times. After the song we went back to the table and sipped our drinks.

"We're out of practice," I said.

"It's been over a year," she said.

"Has it been that long?"

"Last summer. You and me and Rich and that girl. What was her name? She was pretty and had dark hair, looked like a little kid. Barbara, Babs. We all went dancing at the Western Club. Remember?"

"I didn't think it'd been that long," I said.

Another silence. We didn't dance to "Your Cheatin' Heart," but when the band started "The Orange Blossom Special," I said, "Give it another try?"

"I guess," she said.

"The Orange Blossom Special" had always been one of our favorites because the tempo's so fast and the fiddle playing so screechy and wild. We liked to show off, covering the whole dance floor with under-the-arm twirls and twists, and an impromptu jitterbug. This time, though, we had more trouble. I stepped on her toes again. But we laughed, and then I pulled her hips close to mine and took a few long two-stepping strides, and suddenly I felt we had never been separated. We knew just how our feet fit together, when to unhook our arms and swirl. At the end I twirled her out, and when she flipped into the crook of my shoulder on the last note, I kissed her hard on the lips. Several older couples sitting at tables nearby smiled and clapped, evidently ready to adopt us. The band started playing another old standard, a slower-paced Tammy Wynette hit, "Stand by Your Man."

"I better go check on Shelly," Angie said.

"She's a grown woman." Angie started to leave, but I still had hold of her arm. "Please."

"Okay. One more and that's it."

We danced that song, then a polka, then a fast waltz, and a slow Willie Nelson number. I held her close as we swayed in a circle, shuffling in the sawdust. I had one hand on her sweaty neck, the other in the small of her back, my nose nuzzled in her

French braid. I swam in her smell, a sweet mixture of sweat, fresh bread from the bakery, a little whiff of bourbon, and spearmint gum.

The smell made the future roll out before me like a plush carpet. Tonight, maybe tomorrow. Soon. I would return. Already, as we danced, I felt her softening toward me, the barriers dropping. Later, in the dark of the trailer, with the familiar hums and rumblings from the highway outside our window, we'd lie on the bed, whispering. I'd gently stroke the long curve of her back, kiss her ribs. This time I wouldn't disappoint her. I'd work double-length shifts so we'd have enough money. I saw two little boys tussling with me, laughing, Angie big-bellied beside us in a house, not the trailer. I'd never wanted children before, but at this moment I wanted it so badly it hurt. I didn't want to open my eyes, the picture was so strong.

"The song's over, Gene," she said.

I turned her face to mine and kissed her again.

She looked away for a few seconds, then back at me. There was a wrinkle in her forehead.

"This isn't right," she said. "You and me. Here. Like this. It just isn't right."

"If this isn't right, tell me what is?" I tried to kiss her again, but she pulled away.

"Don't," she said.

"Angie, I'm sorry."

She slipped from me and walked quickly away. I stumbled after her, knocking into a table, tipping a couple of drink glasses onto the floor.

"One more dance?" I called.

She turned around and, with a pinched expression that reminded me of Shelly, she said, "You've had your dance."

She rushed to the restroom. I followed, but she was inside before I could catch her.

Rich came over. "You two were cutting one hell of a rug out there."

"Yeah," I said. "We were."

"Everything all right?"

Angie opened the door to the restroom. I could see Shelly sitting on the floor, her back against the wall, a wet paper towel draped over her face like a brown veil.

"What's wrong?" Rich asked.

"Shelly's sick," Angie said. "Can you give us a lift to Skagg's, Rich?"

Shelly sat in the passenger seat of Rich's Nova so she could hang her head out the window. Angie and I sat in back. It was an awkward situation, her asking Rich for the ride instead of me. But Rich was eager for Angie and me to reunite, so he insisted that I come along. We'd said good-bye to Gloria and Travis and then helped Shelly to the car.

The wind from Rich's open window made wisps of hair that had come loose from Angie's French braid blow around wildly like spiders dancing on her face. I reached for her hand, but she jerked it away. All the way down Eastern to I-40, Rich gave us a passionate inventory of the additions he had made to his Nova. He had overhauled the transmission, put in a 450 Chevy engine, cut the chrome tailpipe, and painted two purple stripes on the hood like his old one.

Shelly finally pulled her head back in the car. "Why do men always sound like they're masturbating when they talk about their cars?"

"It's better than screwing a woman like you," Rich said.

"If you believe sticking your thing in your gas tank is love, you got some serious problems," Shelly said.

"I've seen this all too often," I said, anxious to get a little revenge on Shelly and to divert attention away from mine and Angie's awkwardness. "A woman pukes all over herself in a bar, you're nice enough to give her a ride home, and she insults you, your car, and your sexual practices."

"You two are modern-day Gallahads, all right," Shelly said, smirking again.

"Do you want me to give her one right in the kisser, Rich, or would you like the honors?"

"There's a tire iron under the seat," Rich said. "Use that."

I picked it up and tapped Shelly lightly on the head with it. "Don't pull that shit on me," she said, batting away the iron. "I'm not your wife."

I could feel Angie's eyes on me.

The car fell silent. We passed Bonham and Washington streets, Angie staring out her window, Shelly with her head still on the car door so that her hair whipped back in my face. Rich caught my eye in the rearview, smiled, and mouthed, "Oops."

Shelly lifted her head and swiveled around so that she could see Angie and me. "I swear you struck gold when you married into this dead-end family," she said to Angie.

I laughed. "I don't see how we're any more dead-end than you. You think a grocery store bakery is a career?"

Shelly turned toward me, her chin on the headrest. "Well, tell me this, slick. How's it gonna feel when Angie starts bringing home more money than you?"

"Shelly!" Angie said. "Don't."

"From Skagg's?" I said and laughed again.

"Ha! You don't even know, do you?"

"What are you talking about?" I asked.

"Do you have any idea how much a radiologist makes?" Shelly continued.

"Damn it, Shelly!" Angie said. "Please!"

"What's going on?" I said.

Angie took a deep breath. "Nothing."

"Nothing, baloney. She's gone back to school. In two years she'll be a radiologist," Shelly said. "She'll make a hell of a lot more than you do at Santa Fe."

"I won't be a radiologist," Angie said. "A radiology technician. Or maybe a radiology therapist."

Rich said, "I thought they did all the nuclear work out at Pantex."

"It's not like that," Angie explained, halfheartedly. "x-rays. After two years I'd be a radiology technician, which basically means that if you had to have your x-ray taken, I'd do it. It's not that big a deal."

"What about that other thing?" Rich said, trying to be helpful. "What's that?"

"Radiology therapist. They work with cancer patients, do probes to see how much cancer they have and where it's at. I just found out about it yesterday in class."

"When did you decide all this?" I asked. I hadn't heard anything about any of this business, which made me both suspicious and guilty. I didn't like that the checks I had been sending her were going to books and classes. On the other hand, where the hell had I been?

"Last spring."

"When last spring?"

Shelly said, "In the spring semester, stupid."

"Shut up!" I said.

"Middle of January," which meant one month after we separated.

Rich asked, "What made you want to do this?"

"Better now than never. I don't want to frost cakes the rest of my life."

"That's great," Rich said. "I think that's really great."

Shelly said, "It is great. Isn't it, Gene?"

"Yeah," I said. Angie stared uneasily at me, and I could see her green and brown-flecked eyes even in the dark of the car. "It's fucking stupendous."

As we drove, Rich asked Angie more questions and wouldn't stop. "How much money will you make? Does Skagg's let you off for classes? I thought about taking some courses in auto repair. Do you know how much mechanics make? Where do you take your courses? Do you actually get to look at lungs and broken bones and stuff?"

"Pull over at that Toot 'n' Totum," Shelly barked. "I need some milk and laundry detergent before I go home."

"Get it in the morning," Rich said.

"I can't get it in the morning. I have to be at work at six. I need to wash my uniform tonight."

"Can't you say 'please'?" he said.

"Please your ass. Pull over."

Shelly obviously felt better. When she got out of the Nova, she actually jogged into the store like she was warming up for the New York Marathon, as if shoving Angie's new life in my face had lifted her spirits. For a moment I thought I understood why her son was on drugs.

"I better get some more chaw," Rich said, uncomfortable.

After Rich closed the door, Angie said, "I was going to tell you."

"Hey, don't worry about it. You could have just sent me a graduation announcement."

"You're a free agent too, Gene. I don't answer to you, and you don't answer to me. Besides, it isn't like you've shown an interest."

"I'm sorry. I've been a little busy. Didn't I tell you?" I said. "I certainly meant to. I've been practicing law on the side. All this time you thought I went on railroad runs. Actually, I was trying cases, winning landmark decisions, storing away the bucks. The president just called today. He wants me to be attorney general. I told him I couldn't 'cause I've decided to become a nuclear scientist next month."

"This is just like you. You make it sound like I'm committing a federal offense. It's just a couple of classes at Amarillo College, for Christ's sake."

"That I'm paying for."

"That's bullshit," she said. "And you know it."

I suppose it was bullshit, but it pissed me off to hear Shelly's attitude coming out of Angie's mouth.

"What I don't understand is why you feel compelled to change everything about your goddamned life," I said.

"Maybe that's the problem," she said, turning her head slightly to the side, one eyebrow raised, a smirk creeping into the corner of her mouth. "You don't understand."

I could have done a lot of things, and it may sound crazy, but what I wanted more than anything else at that moment was to hear the sound of my palm hitting the seat beside Angie. It smacked, almost like a gunshot, about six inches from her shoulder. Angie gasped, then stared at the indentation and then at me. Neither of us moved.

"I think I need something inside too," she said calmly and got out. The way she moved as she walked in front of the car, the way she swung her arms, made me see her for the first time away from me, really apart from me. I could see her in a lab coat in a hospital, clipping up an x-ray of somebody's chest and pointing to parts of it with a lacquered wooden stick. A young doctor with black hair would be standing behind her, looking over her shoulder at the x-ray, nodding his head as he slipped his hand inside her lab coat.

I picked up the tire iron from the floor and hit the back of the seat a couple of times hard, making long white nicks in the nubby red vinyl. Then I inspected the seat, wet my fingers, and tried to smudge away the white.

In the store Angie cornered Shelly and Rich, and all three stared at me through the window. Rich's keys dangled at the wheel. I climbed over the seat and quickly started the engine. Not much was said once everybody got back to the car. Everybody knew. Angie got into the backseat through the passenger side and then slid behind me so I couldn't see her very well in the rearview. Rich slid in back beside Angie since Shelly would be the first one out and since she'd been sick.

"You okay?" Rich asked, once we were all in.

"You bet," I said and gunned the engine.

"Let's go," Shelly said.

I suddenly was ready for this night to end. I would drop Angie and Shelly off at Skagg's on Bell Street, the next exit, let it all be finished. I saw the sign for Bell Street. I put my blinker on, but at the last moment I had a crazy idea and passed right by it.

"Skagg's is back there, you dummy," Shelly said.

"I know."

I put on the blinker and got off at the next exit, Coulter Road. But instead of turning left, under the underpass and back towards Bell, I turned right, which led to the medical district, the Baptist Hospital, and Medi-Park.

"Where are you going?" Rich asked, uneasy.

"Let's go see where Dr. Kildare here takes her x-rays," I said.

Shelly said, "For Christ's sakes, I've got milk here that'll spoil."

I tilted the rearview at a weird angle so I could see Angie. She stared out the side window, her black hair teased around her forehead and jaw line, but her face was a blank, expressionless. She must have known I was staring at her, but she refused to look at me.

"We'll just drive by the hospital, and Angie can point to it, show us where she's going to make her fortune, buy her ticket out of here. Isn't that right, babe?"

"Take us to Skagg's, Gene," she said. Her expression didn't change a bit. Blank. Calm. She wasn't going to let me get to her.

"Now, honey. Don't get testy. I'll take the Medi-Park road back up towards Bell. It's just as fast that way."

I felt myself on dangerous territory, not sure how far I would take my comments, but I couldn't stand Angie back there ignoring me. It was like being spit on.

"Besides, show a little pride in your new life," I said, my face itching with a sarcastic grin. "You'll be leaving us peons soon enough. You should gloat."

None of them said a word.

In the middle of Medi-Park is a small lake. There's a sidewalk around it that runners and joggers use. On one bank are private offices, a lot of high-priced doctors, heart surgeons, eye specialists. At the north end there is a planetarium, and on the other side sit the three wings of Baptist Hospital, the tall wing rising above everything else on this side of town. Along the same bank there's a cancer lab and other research offices. I'd heard it was one of the biggest medical centers in the state, but I didn't know if that was true.

When Rich and I were younger we used to sometimes come to Amarillo and tube down the hills and onto the lake when it was frozen in winter, and for many years in summer we raced the long, down-sloping strip of road wedged between the lake and the Baptist Hospital. It was a good drag strip.

Down the hill some sprinklers were doing a pretty good job watering both the grass and the road. I drove slowly.

"Okay, we've seen it," Shelly said.

I revved the engine.

"Careful," Rich said.

In the mirror, Angie shook her head, as if she expected this from me.

"So this is the place that's going to make a successful woman of my wife? Get her the job that will change her life? Who knows, maybe get her a new husband?"

"This is stupid," she said. "Just let us out here, Gene. We can walk."

"It's not a very big place, now is it?" I went on, unable to stop myself. "Hard to believe it will do all that for you, Angie. But I guess that just goes to show you, it's not the size that counts."

It *was* stupid, I know, but I didn't care. I wanted to make a goddamned fool of myself. I wanted her to pay.

I revved the engine again, and Shelly said to Angie, "He just wants to show off this metal penis."

That was all I needed. I'd had it with Shelly and Angie both. The sooner I was away from them, the better. I gunned the engine. We bucked forward once, twice, then plunged down the swervy Medi-Park drive, as if we had just hit the top of the climb in a roller coaster and were hurtling down.

"You jackass!" Shelly screamed.

Angie braced herself in the seat. "Gene, what are you doing?"

"Trying to keep this woman's milk from curdling," I answered as I wheeled tightly within the white dotted lines and picked up speed.

"Watch out for the sprinklers!" Shelly said.

She grabbed the steering wheel, and I tried to tap the brake but hit gas pedal instead. We barreled into and over the curb. All of us lifted out of our seats, and though what happened next only took a few seconds at most, I had the strangest sensation of time slowing down, all of us floating in the air. We were sailing out into the night, only the stars visible, for the longest time, over Medi-Park Lake. I actually felt that we might fly right over it onto Bell Street and skid right into Skagg's parking lot since we were going in that direction anyway, or maybe sail right out into space and never touch down.

When we finally hit the lake, the Nova made a sound like a fat man doing a belly flop. Water sprayed out in instant waves beside us. We floated for a second or two, and I thought, *We won't sink.* But the water rose quickly to the door, then to the window, and I thought, *We're going to drown, right here, right now, and no one will find us until tomorrow.*

"Get out, get out, get out!" Rich yelled.

"How?" Shelly asked.

"Through the windows, crawl through the windows," I said, trying to stay calm. "Hurry up!"

Shelly pulled herself through her window, and I pushed her the rest of the way into the water as the car started to rock. Rich crawled through the same window.

"What do I do?" Angie said.

"I'll pull the seat forward, then go out this window. You push the seat and crawl through behind me."

Water started to gush over the door on my side, forming a small waterfall into the seat. I leaned over, found the lever, and pulled the seat forward as much as I could. But when I sat up, the car rocked to the side suddenly. Dark water hit the windshield, and I fell through the side window, but my legs and feet didn't leave the car, so it seemed as if I was lying on top of the lake, half in the car, half out. The seat had pitched forward and my feet were caught inside, and I thought for a second they were broken or cut off altogether, but then the car tilted, and I fell into the water face forward.

It was murky, but not as dark as I thought it would be. I paddled under water, tried to slip my boots off, but they wouldn't budge. My clothes were heavy, and it took me some time to find my way to the surface. The moon and the street lamps lit the lake. I spit out water, looked past the sinking car, and saw Rich already on the bank with Shelly swimming toward him. I tread for a couple of seconds, caught my breath, and scanned the bank and the lake for Angie, but I couldn't see her. I thought, *Oh my God, when I rocked the car forward, she got trapped. She's sinking with the car.*

I yelled for help, but Rich couldn't hear me. I gulped air and dove underwater, an awkward half-flip because of my clothes. The car was going down slowly. Even in the dark I could see it rocking, sinking. The seats were forward, and it was too black to see very clearly. My lungs caught fire. I swam to the surface. I saw Shelly and Rich on the bank.

I called, "Where's Angie?" and they called back something I couldn't hear.

I swam to them. We would have to strip and come back for her. I swam as quickly as I could, over the Nova, which I could miraculously see right below me, not far down. The purple stripes on the hood shone and the silver ball on the radio antenna peeked above the water. I swam on, trying to get rid of my shirt, sputtering every few feet, "Angie's trapped in the car! Angie's trapped in the car!" They kept calling something back to me, but the only thing I could hear was my heart pumping in my ears and the water splashing around me. About twenty feet from the bank, I called again.

Rich yelled, "Are you all right?"

"Angie!" I sputtered, flailing ahead.

"It's shallow, Gene," he said. "Stand up."

"What?"

"Stand up!"

I put my feet down on the muddy bottom and was surprised to find the water only came up to my waist.

"Angie's trapped in the car!" I rasped, choking with water and confusion.

Shelly said, "She's right there, you fool."

Fifty yards away, Angie was on her hands and knees in the grass.

After we all caught our breath, Rich said, "I'll tell you one thing. I'm not getting another Nova. Those things are bad luck."

He'd taken his white undershirt off and was pressing it against his face. There was a gash across his forehead and cuts on his chin and cheeks, bloodying his beard. His nose looked crooked and swollen.

Shelly sat on the grassy slope of the bank leading up to the curb. Angie, behind her, stood facing the hospital.

"I'm sorry, Rich," I said.

"Well, if nobody else is hurt, I'm going up to the hospital and call a tow truck, see if they can pull this damn thing out without the police and fire department getting involved," Rich said. "Anybody got change?"

I reached into my wet jeans and found a couple of quarters.

Shelly looked up from where she was sitting on the grass. Tears ran down her cheeks.

"I'd like to call my son," she said. She stood and flapped her wet blouse sleeves, and I suddenly felt sorry for her. While Angie wiped grass from Shelly's soaked jeans, Shelly grabbed hold of her, hugging her there in her dripping arms for a long time. "Come with me," she said.

"I'll stay here with Gene."

Shelly met Rich at the top of the bank and continued on without him toward the hospital. Even though it was dark, I could tell his face was cut up bad, and I knew this time he wouldn't get his good looks back. This time his scars would show.

He called out to me, "Aren't we the luckiest sons-of-bitches you ever knew!" before trailing Shelly to the hospital.

Angie sat on the grass, facing the lake. It was quiet out, only a few bullfrogs croaking. The water was still except for a few ripples circling out from where we had landed, about twenty-five feet from the bank. The surface of the water was made bright by the moon. The silver nipple of the Nova's radio antenna glittered on the surface of the water. I felt again the sensation I had in the car, when I thought we might sail right out into space and never land. At that moment a dragonfly landed on the antenna.

"You're not hurt, are you?" I asked.

"No. Just wet," she said. "We could have all been killed."

She wanted to say something else to me and was working herself up to it, and I felt the way you do when you think a tornado is about to hit, and you are scrunched down in the bathtub, beneath a mattress, hearing the swirling cloud that could wreck everything in your life. I almost demanded she speak her piece, get it over with. But then I thought, *This is the most important moment of my life. Don't let it end like this.*

The lake was calm now, the sky clear, the moon three-quarters full and bright, everything around us silent, only the faint hum of cars in the distance. No one had seen us fly into the water. No one. The place was desolate.

"Take off your clothes," I said.

"What?"

"Let's swim."

"You're crazy! I'm not going back in that water."

I undid the button on my wet jeans and started wriggling out of them.

"I need to talk to you about something," she said.

"We'll talk later," I said, hopping, pulling at my pants.

"I'm serious, Gene."

I left my pants in a wet crinkle in the grass and pulled off my shirt.

"You can't do this. Your brother will be back soon. A tow truck and the police will come. You'll be arrested."

"I don't care. Come on." I pulled off my socks.

"You're out of your mind," she said.

"Maybe." I stripped off my underwear and waded into the

lake until the water reached my knees, then I did a shallow dive, skimmed the bottom, sifted my fingers through the loose mud before rising to the surface. I swam toward the antenna of the Nova and stood on the hood. The purple stripes shone very faintly below me. I waved at Angie, still sitting on the bank fully clothed, but she didn't wave back.

"Come in," I called.

She stood up, but she didn't answer me, and I feared she might never answer me again. She was just a thin sliver on the bank in the dark. I thought about swimming back to her, but at that moment I wanted to swim through the Nova, felt I had to get back inside. I took a deep breath and went under, drawing myself down the antenna to the car. I grabbed both sides of the passenger window and pulled myself into the cabin. It was completely dark, except for Shelly's white milk jug bobbing up and down in the back dash like a jellyfish.

My eyes burned, so I closed them. I could hear only a faint buzzing in my ear and the quickened thump of my heartbeat. Being inside set my mind afire. I thought of the time Rich was trapped in his first Nova, how I had resigned myself to him being dead. Then I remembered the first time I had hit Angie, an accident, long ago, over what I couldn't even remember. I thought about the bloated, grizzled face of the old man in the ditch near my trailer, of the man who'd broken his neck on the mechanical bull, then of Gloria's husband and son, trapped dead in a snow-covered car last winter. Right now, I thought, I could be in the basement of the Baptist Hospital, some coroner pumping water out of my lungs.

My chest felt like it might explode. I pulled myself through the driver's side window and up to the surface in one motion. On the hood of Rich's car, I shook my head free and gasped for air. My heart beat wildly, as if it would tear itself right out of my chest and rocket into space.

I tried to open my eyes, but they stung too badly.

If I had opened them, then I would have seen Angie walking up the grassy slope and down the road towards the hospital, and from there, eventually, to Colorado Springs, where she and a man who fixes x-ray machines would move soon after we divorced. I might have glimpsed the days ahead for me when I would sit in my underwear on my green couch and catalog in my mind the mistakes I made and try to figure out how I should have done things differently, then think, *What's the use?* and throw ashtrays and bourbon bottles against the wall until my landlord evicted me.

But the water lapped against my stomach and my back and my sides as it lifted me up every few seconds. And what I imagined I saw instead was Angie's wet captain's shirt and jeans in a heap beside her, her body glowing like a whitish-blue shimmer in the dark as she waded in and dove underwater. With my eyes tightly shut against the stinging, I pictured the Baptist Hospital, the lights making a tic-tac-toe pattern in the sky, Rich in the lobby calling a tow truck and Shelly calling her son in the detox center, water from her hair dripping as she waited for the phone to ring.

When I finally opened my eyes, I hoped to find the thin ripple and bubbles that would be Angie. Standing there on my brother's Nova in the middle of Medi-Park Lake, with the moon on my back, I waited for my wife to resurface.

Last Call

1978

Last call had been made over the intercom, and I began to scrub the stockpile of cocktail and beer glasses on the three-pronged bristles, rinsing them quickly in standing water, a glass in each hand. Enrico and Boozer stood at the far end of the counter, splitting what we'd made for the night, even though not all the customers had left. I was only the bar-back, their gopher, but they were good about dividing the money equally, giving me a full third. I doubt they would have been so generous if we worked at some little dive, but the Texas Moon was a big place — it used to be a roller skating rink — and when I worked there, it was full most every night. We made well over a hundred dollars regularly, so the split was usually good. Plus Boozer and Enrico knew I worked for my money, sweating like a frothy dog, changing the liquor and soda guns, hauling fifty, sixty cases of beer a night from the walk-in, and washing so many glasses that my back hurt from bending over, and my hands were permanently pink and wrinkly with flaky white circles all over my palms.

Arlene set her empty glasses on the counter and smiled at me. She'd been working at the Texas Moon for about a week, tall and slender and blonde, almost twenty. She wore loose-fitting shirts because her breasts were large, and I admired her modesty. We'd been winking at each other since her first day, accidentally bumping together near the walk-in. Earlier that night she let me chew a lime slice off the plastic sword she was holding.

I was examining her walk-away when somebody leaned over the counter and poked his finger in my chest. It was an older man in a cheap straw cowboy hat, creased at the top and banded with a little brown feather stuck in the side.

"How old are you?" he asked me. His voice was gravelly, like he had ice chunks caught in his throat. It reminded me, oddly, of my father's voice.

"Old enough," I said, guarding. For all I knew, he could have been with the Texas Liquor Commission. I tried to judge whether or not I should say anything else. If I made a mistake, the Texas Moon might have shut down since I was not, at seventeen, legally old enough to work there. My mother got me the job. She liked to know where I was (not in any trouble that she wasn't supervising), and if men started hitting on her, which they sometimes did, she could point to me and that usually got rid of them.

"That waitress over there," he said, looking at the pool tables, "claims you're her son. Is that true?"

Boozer leaned over the counter beside me. "Which waitress you talking about?"

The man sized Boozer up, not a hard task. Boozer was short, brawny, about ten years older than me. He had to stand on his tiptoes to lean over the counter. The man pointed at my mother, bent over a table, waiting for the two men there to pay their tabs.

"That good-looking blonde over there," the man said.

"That's my mother," Boozer said.

"I just want to know if she's his mother," the man said, trying again to poke me in the chest. I jumped back, and a little soapy water splashed on the counter. A couple of drops landed on the man's arm above a red tattoo of a fish.

"Sorry," I said. He scowled at me and wiped his arm.

"What's the problem, Travis?" Enrico called to me from the other end of the bar. I laughed, as I did whenever I looked at him suddenly. He was about fifty, at least six-foot-eight, bone thin, big marbly eyes, with a long neck and shaved head, only a few gray prickles around his ears and along the back of his skull. An ostrich's head.

"Well, are you or aren't you?" the man demanded.

"That's not his mother," Enrico said, deadpan. "That's my mother."

"Fuckin' bartenders!" the man said and waddled off toward the bathroom.

"Hey, Mother!" Boozer bellowed so loudly everybody still at the tables on our side of the Texas Moon stared at us. When she turned, we all waved. Then Enrico counted one, two, three, and we yelled, "Who loves you, baby?"

"My boys," my mother called back, laughing, her teeth flashing like neon in the half-dark. She turned back to her table, but that laugh stayed with me. My father used to say she had a laugh that "could melt butter and make invalids dance." And drunkards tip, I could easily add. At thirty-eight, she was good looking with silvery-blonde hair that kinked sometimes on the ends. She had high cheekbones and girlish dimples etched around the corners of her mouth and, to me, the saddest blue-green eyes, flecked with white, like a choppy wave in the sunlight. She had, too, what she called a "bump" on her nose, her only unattractive feature. I knew she got it from my father, though exactly how and when and why, I never discovered; they never told us kids, and we understood that we weren't to bring the subject up, that it was somehow a private symbol of an earlier, more desperate time in their marriage.

Our landing the jobs at the Texas Moon several months prior was the luckiest thing to happen to us since the accident. My father hadn't had any life insurance. My mother hired a lawyer, Raymond, to sue the trucking company and the driver who hit the car my father and my brother Carroll were in, but the whole process had seemed so long and drawn out, with them making an offer, then us, then the string of nasty letters, the threats and counterthreats, the delays. My mother finally just told Raymond not to tell her any news that wasn't good, and she more or less resigned herself to getting nothing. The Texas Moon was the first real money we'd pocketed. She seemed calmer now, more relaxed than I'd seen her in the past year.

Yet, it wasn't just the money that made the Texas Moon important to us. Part of it was being around Boozer and Enrico. They were a strange pair. Boozer had an ex-wife and a three-year-old boy named Cody in Brownsville. Enrico, I'd heard, served a couple of years in prison in El Paso, for what I didn't know. One waitress told me assault and battery (which I didn't believe) and another said he'd been a spy (which I wanted to believe). Enrico was old enough to be Boozer's father, but they weren't related. They had bartended together for several years, at the big clubs all around the state, some country and western, some rock, even some punk and gay bars. I didn't know if they were fired from all those places or if they were on a bartending circuit. I figured a circuit, if there was one, since I couldn't see why any manager would want to lose them. They were masters on the liquor and soda guns, lifting them high in the air, like six-shooters, creating carbonated waterfalls that threatened to, but never did, splash all over the counter and rubber drink strips.

Every evening, around six o'clock, before the band showed up and after I prepped, I flipped through *Hoyle's Bartender's Guide* and called out a drink — starting with something easy like a Hurricane, say, or a Long Island Tea, then moving on to the trickier drinks like Mau-Maus and Siberian Russians — and they alternated back and forth explaining how to make it. They played the game strictly, too, at twenty bucks a miss. "Verbatim," they'd shout at each other, angry sometimes, laughing mostly, hitting the counter with their fists. Since I'd become their bar-back for the summer, I was the official referee and score keeper, which was easy until they got bored with *Hoyle* and started in on the regional drinks only they'd heard of: Gooseberry Fizzles, Papa John Goolagongs, Laredo Spritzers. I didn't plan to make a career out of bartending, but it didn't seem like a bad life if you could manage it like Enrico and Boozer, working the big-money bars with a sense of humor and style. It was easy for my mother and me to forget ourselves in their routines and in the drum-thumping nights at the Texas Moon.

"Fix us up, Booz," Enrico said.

Boozer poured tequila shots. After Enrico finished splitting the money, he called us over. I rinsed two more glasses, so as not to seem too eager or greedy, and wiped my hands on the towel tucked in the front of my blue jeans. Enrico shoved my stack of bills and change over to me. It looked like a lot, maybe fifty bucks.

"Big night," he said. I never counted the money in front of them, just stuck it in my pocket.

"We busted our butts," I said.

Enrico elbowed me. "You want a chance to lose some of that?"

"Huh?"

"You play poker, don't you?"

Carroll and I used to play in family games. I was pretty good too. Better than Carroll, at least, who could never bluff. In that respect he was like my mother. He'd get a good hand, three of a kind, for example, and he'd start chewing on his upper lip, or his knee would bob up and down like a jack hammer, or he'd rub his cards so hard my father would have to replace the deck. I could have a full house, though, aces over kings, and wouldn't show it. Or sometimes I'd purposely start imitating Carroll when I had nothing, and then I'd bid like I held a royal flush. Three-quarters of the time my uncles would fold, and I'd rake in the kitty. My Uncle Gene refused to play with me; he hated losing to a kid.

"Yeah," I said to Enrico. "I play."

"Come over after we finish," he said. "We're having a party. You and your mammy can take our money from us."

"I don't know," I said.

"Stakes aren't that high."

I wanted to say yes, but I couldn't. My older sister, Julie, was in labor down in Beaumont, had been all day. She'd had complications, toxemia, and been bedridden for three months. The doctors said not to worry, but my mother had the same thing when she was pregnant with me, and my father's mother had died when she was pregnant with her third baby. My mother and I had bought an answering machine on sale at Radio Shack so we wouldn't miss any updates from Julie's husband, Bub, while we were at work.

"I really don't think we can," I said. "We're going to Beaumont tomorrow. Maybe some other night."

"Suit yourself, but I warn you. You don't have your fun early, you wind up cruel and cynical with premature wrinkles and gray stubbles." He patted his head and smiled, then went back to work.

I would have liked to play. But I'd learned from my father that you shouldn't press your luck. If you felt it coming on — and I could always feel it like a cool space around me, a clear-eyed alertness — you should channel it into one thing and one thing only. I wanted to give the luck to Julie, if that was possible. When I was younger, she let Carroll and me smoke in her car, and every weekend she'd take us to the caves in Palo Duro Canyon. She and Bub had been trying to get pregnant for four years. My mother was excited. Ever since we heard the news, she had been sending gifts: baby clothes, bottles, packages of disposable diapers, a playpen, a Johnny Jump-Up. And we had more things at home that we were going to take down that weekend.

"You boys thirsty?" Boozer asked, stuffing his bills in his shirt pocket and his change in his slacks. He had a stack of lemons and the salt shaker and a small Coke chaser (for me) lined up by three shot glasses of Cuervo.

My mother whizzed over, dropped off a tray full of empties, and handed a check and some cash to Boozer, who put it all in the till. She noticed the shot glasses.

"You two wouldn't corrupt my son, would you now?"

"Don't worry, Mom," Boozer said. "I'm already corrupted."

She laughed, then said to him, "You fix me up."

"Yes, ma'am."

Enrico leaned over the bar and put his head down. My mother took her towel and buffed his knob of a skull. Then she wrapped the towel around her own head, turban style, and ran her palms over his gray prickles like it was a crystal ball. They did this every night, their closing-time ritual.

"Have you called yet?" I asked her.

"Not yet, Travis," she said. "I'll check the machine in a little bit. Quit worrying. That's my job. Everything's going to be fine." She picked up her tray and said to Boozer, "Don't start without me."

I put away most of the glasses, mopped, and eyeballed Arlene as she bent over to wipe off a chair.

A few days earlier we had climbed onto the roof of the Texas Moon during our break. It was cool up there, the air curling in from the east. I drank a Coke while she smoked a cigarette. She asked how my mother and I got the job at the Texas Moon, and I told her, though I didn't get into the details about Carroll or my father since I figured she had already heard from Boozer or Enrico.

I was suddenly nervous talking about myself with her, afraid she would peg me for who I was: a kid. But either she didn't notice or it didn't matter, and that fact tickled something inside my chest, made me bold and giddy. "How about you?" I asked. "What's your story?"

She told me about North Carolina, where she grew up, and where there were tall pines and oaks and an ocean. A man from Kansas brought her to Texas. He knew how to operate a culti-packer, and when he'd come to the Texas plains for the haying season, she tagged along. He began working in Midland-Odessa in March and had planned to work his way up to Canada. Arlene stayed behind in Amarillo, and she figured he was somewhere near Minnesota by now. She hadn't heard from him since he left, didn't expect to. I didn't say much in response, but I felt privileged that she had confided in me.

From her table Arlene suddenly turned and caught me staring, raised her eyebrows, and smiled before coming over to the bar.

"What do you need, honey?" I asked.

She lifted her hair off the back of her neck. Perspiration lined the top of her forehead and beaded above her lip.

"A big glass of soda water with lime and another rag."

"Is that all?"

"For now," she said and seemed to blush. I squirted up a soda water from the gun and gave her a towel, my last one.

"God, it's hot in here," she said.

"It's just me," I said. I took a napkin off the counter. "Lean over."

"Why?"

"Just lean over and close your eyes," I said.

I dabbed the little sweat mustache off her lip. She opened her eyes and smiled, then leaned back and drank all of her soda water in one long gulp. She took the lime slice out of her glass, bit the pulp, and plopped the thin rind back in the ice. She wiped her lips with a napkin, tossed it over my head, basketball style, into the trashcan behind me, then headed to her waitress station.

My mother alcoholed her tables and napkined the ashtrays, then came over to the bar. I asked her if she had called home to check the tape machine yet, and she said she would in a little bit. She wanted to rest her feet. When Boozer and Enrico returned, Enrico pulled out a deck of cards, shuffled them a couple of times, then slapped down two cards in front of my mother: a three and a ten. There was a gap between them.

"You ever played Between?" Boozer asked my mother.

"Plenty of times." She waited a perfect beat. "How do you think Travis was conceived?" Enrico laughed; his Adam's apple, as big as a cue ball, bobbed on his skinny neck. I didn't laugh, but I was proud and a little shocked by her timing. She used to hate off-color jokes. She'd leave the room when my father and brother started in on them.

Boozer said, "We're not talking Between the Sheets."

"I'm so happy," she said. "Because you're much too young for me."

"It's a poker game," Enrico interrupted. "Everybody take out ten dollars."

My mother said, "We can't play in front of the customers."

"It's a quick game. We'll play on this side of the register. Come on."

The dealer put down two cards and the person betting wagered if he thought the third card would fall between the other two. Boozer and I got bad splits to start with, a nine and a six, and a ten and a jack, so we passed. Enrico slapped down an ace for my mother and said, "Call it. High or low."

My mother looked puzzled.

"Low," I advised.

Her next card was a queen. "What should I do?" she asked.

"Bet the pot," I told her.

"No coaching," Enrico said.

"Bet the pot, Mom."

She did. Enrico slapped down a king. He cackled. "You should get yourself a new coach."

My mother pushed her money toward the center and patted my head. "I'll keep this one, thank you."

I told her to play my hand while I went back to the office to get more towels. When I returned she was telling Enrico and Boozer and Arlene, who'd joined them, about the time she saved my life when I was six years old. The money was gone and the deck of cards was by Enrico's elbow.

"It was just a regular hamburger," she said. "The kind you get at old drive-in restaurants. Anyway, it looked fine to me, so I gave it to him."

I knew this story, heard it a million times. I was accident prone as a child, and my mother enjoyed recalling her moments of motherly heroism. She used to tell this story to friends and relatives at Christmas and Thanksgiving, birthdays and summer campouts at Lake Meredith, but this was the first time I'd heard her tell it since my father and Carroll's accident.

"Who won the game?" I interrupted.

"Your mother won it on your go round," Enrico said.

She winked at me. "You'll get your split later."

Boozer said, "She's ratting on you now."

"Go on," Arlene said. She had put her hair up in a ponytail. She looked more girlish, and for a second I wondered just how old she was.

"I went into the kitchen for a second," my mother continued, "just a second, mind you, and when I came back, there he was, poor baby, on his back, scooting across the floor, gasping for air, his eyes rolled back in his head like he was having a seizure. I thought I would die myself. I rushed over and straddled him to hold him down. He thrashed and squirmed and, my God, I was so certain that he'd swallowed poison."

"Were you poisoned?" Arlene asked me.

"Just listen," I told her. She rested her elbow against the counter and brushed against me. I leaned forward a couple of inches from her ponytail and examined the back of her neck where there was a little V-shaped pattern of black hairs leading down to her top vertebra.

"I pried his mouth open," my mother said, demonstrating the maneuver with her fingers. "When I looked inside, what did I see?" She held a moment for suspense. This was my favorite part of the story. "A toothpick sticking in the back of his throat."

"Oh, gross!" Arlene shivered.

Boozer mimicked, "Oh, gross," and clutched his throat.

"What did you do?" Enrico asked, grimacing.

"I reached back there as delicately as I could and tried to pull it out. But I couldn't get all of it since it was splintered. Part of it had lodged in the back of his throat. I thought for sure it had pierced that little thing that hangs down. What's it called, Travis?"

This was my part of the story. "The uvula," I said.

"Did you call an ambulance?" Enrico asked.

"I didn't think I had time. I was in such a state. My adrenaline must have been high because I carried him all the way to the car and rushed him to the hospital, bleating the horn the whole way. A policeman clocked me going a hundred and nine. And I had to stand in the emergency room, trying to hold Travis still, as the doctors tweezed the rest of that toothpick out."

"Yuck," Arlene said.

"It had broken in two and punctured the side of his throat."

"You poor baby," Enrico said.

"I have a little hole in the back of my throat," I said proudly. Enrico got a flashlight, and they all took turns looking. My jaw hurt from opening my mouth for so long, and when Arlene scrunched her eyes to search for the hole, I was suddenly convinced that the inside of a person's mouth was his least attractive anatomical feature.

"So what's the moral?" Enrico asked my mother, putting away the flashlight and deck of cards.

My mother said, "I don't know. I haven't considered the moral. Watch your kids all the time, I guess."

"Check your hamburgers for toothpicks," I said.

Arlene laughed.

My mother followed me back to the walk-in freezer, where I stacked the dolly with another load of beer, my last for the night. She took out a wad of bills from her apron and pockets. I took out my money, and we counted it.

This was a good place to count money. The cool air made our breaths steam and chilled the sweat on our bodies. It smelled good in there with the cardboard cases of lemons and limes and oranges and the malty smell of the beer kegs. I felt closer to her there than I often did at home, where the absence of my father and brother — practical jokers and talkative punsters both of them — made easy banter somehow wrong.

I counted fifty-six dollars and some leftover change for myself, the most money I'd made since I'd been working at the Texas Moon. My mother wound up with over a hundred, which was pretty good for her. Plus sixteen more from the Between game. She handed her money to me, and I uncrinkled the corners and stacked each bill face up in the same direction. I folded it in half and slid the wad in my back pocket.

"Nothing new from Bub?" I asked.

"Oh, I forgot. I'll call in a minute." She started for the door.

"Bet you ten it's twins," I said.

"There aren't any twins in our family." Her breath misted in front of her. "Or Bub's."

"I've got a hunch."

"That's a sucker bet," she said.

"There's got to be two or three kids in there," I said. In the bleached Polaroid they sent us, Julie's belly pooched out like a medicine ball. "I think it's twins."

"No, that's just the way we carry children, honey. When I was pregnant with Carroll, your father thought the same thing, was sure I was gonna have quadruplets. He'd never seen anything so big. He'd thump my stomach, say I was as ripe as a watermelon."

She paused, smiled, and fingered the bump on her nose. "And I was. I was ready to bust, I tell you, couldn't wait to get the pregnancy part past me. All that waiting and worrying and feeling like you're not yourself."

She reached into the ice chest by the lemons, pulled out a couple of ice cubes, and threw one to me. While we ran them over our necks, the water dripping through our fingers, I thought about how little she'd mentioned my father or my brother since we started working at the Texas Moon.

For the first few months after the accident, she couldn't do much of anything. It had been snowing heavily when the policeman knocked on our door. My mother answered and I heard some muffled noises, and when I rounded the corner to the den I saw my mother leaning against the door frame, her face in her hands, her slender little-girl's back moving in spasms. The policeman had his head down, and when I saw him he looked, strangely, like a polar bear, draped in a white fur of snow. He started to speak to me, but my mother turned at that moment, her face creased. "Oh, Travis," she said and then, "Oh, God." She turned back to the wall, and I went to her. She tried to stop herself from crying, from making a scene, but she couldn't. The policeman stood there, dumbly, and said, "I'm sorry." The only thing I could think of then was how terrible his job was, how I'd never want one like that. He looked so pathetic, his eyes down, embarrassed, the snow spitting at his back.

The doctor gave my mother Valium. She would sleep all day and when she woke, she would sit in front of the fire in the living room, draped in one of my father's old air force sweatshirts, looking through family albums. Or sometimes she would write long letters to Carroll or my father, as if they were on a trip and she expected them back soon. My uncles helped and Julie came to stay with us for a couple of weeks, but after that I took care of us. I made most of the meals. I did the laundry and grocery shopping. I had to coax her out of bed in the mornings, force her to go to movies and play Scrabble with me. She liked to tell the toothpick story, how she had rescued me, but I knew, firsthand, how fragile she was.

She took another ice cube and put it in her mouth, crunched, swallowed. "Anyway," she went on, "it's not going to be twins. I promise you that."

"Bet me," I said.

"I can't just take your money like that."

"I'd take yours."

"True," she said. "But I'm not as selfish or as greedy as you." We both laughed.

"Okay, then, I bet you it's a boy."

She thought about it for a second before saying, "Okay. That's fair." Air misted from her lips again as if we were outside after a January snow. I noticed her eyes were a little red, probably from the tequila.

"Well, go call," I said, nudging her shoulder.

"I'm going, I'm going. You're worse than a nervous father."

She opened the door, and it was like walking into a furnace after the chill of the walk-in.

Enrico handed me a few more dollars, my share from the last customers. I reloaded the cooler and then washed the rest of the glasses while Boozer wiped his cash register and Enrico refilled the margarita and daiquiri mixes. A couple of pot-bellied bouncers gabbed at the front door, and I saw one of them usher out the man who had poked his finger in my chest earlier. He staggered, and I wondered if the Texas Moon was the only place he had to go at night.

Arlene was cleaning the sawdust from the carpet with the big clumsy vacuum cleaner, the crap job given to new waitresses. I watched her right hand bear down on the long hose as she moved it back and forth, her left hand at her hip holding the cord up and back so that it didn't get tangled. Already she was an expert. She maneuvered that thing all over, fast and thorough.

Most of the musicians had left, but the manager talked to one of the roadies by the stage, haggling over something. My mother'd been in the office on the phone for nearly ten minutes before she finally emerged, slowly, her face pale. A couple of the other waitresses went up to her, but she just waved them off.

Boozer tapped my shoulder. "What's wrong with your mother?"

She sat down on a stool at the bar. I recall very clearly lifting my shriveled hands out of the water and wiping them on my towel. Enrico didn't set the mixers down, but he watched her. She didn't say anything, just stared at the wall behind us. Her eyes were swimming, and I saw her throat tighten, the muscle thickening right under her chin.

"What's the matter, Gloria?" Boozer asked.

"Did we get the call?" I asked.

She turned to me. "Yes," she said. She looked away and blew out a long breath of air.

I started to say something more, but then Enrico cut me off.

"Gloria? Who called?"

His voice sounded different, rich and soothing, like a preacher's voice almost. My mother looked at me for a few moments, searching for something, but for what I didn't know. She said, "Raymond called."

"Who?" Enrico asked.

"My lawyer," my mother said.

"Didn't Bub call? Has she delivered yet?"

"No. No, not yet." She paused again. "I don't want you to get your hopes up too much, Travis, but Raymond said they've agreed to settle. Or at least have made a decent offer. He's going to talk to them again on Monday."

She looked at me funny, then nodded, and I wondered for a half-second if she was telling the truth. She seemed disappointed, half-frazzled.

"You're kidding, aren't you?"

"No, honey, I promise. Monday." She took a napkin from her apron and pushed it over to me. Right below the picture of the lassoed moon were the numbers. Enough so my mother would probably never have to work again.

"Congratulations!" Boozer said. "It's about time." He immediately pulled up a clean rock glass, poured a shot of Cuervo, and pushed it in front of her. She drank it. He quickly refilled it.

"I've had enough," she said.

"I understand. I'd want to be sober too if I received a call like that."

"That's great news," Enrico said.

He took her hand and held it for a second. Just the corners of her lips turned up. She leaned over the counter and kissed me on the cheek.

"I think we should do something tonight. Celebrate. I don't want to go home right now."

Enrico insisted again that we come to his party, and my mother told him she thought it would be a good idea.

She talked to the manager to make sure we had tomorrow and Monday off so we could drive to Julie and Bub's. I started washing the glasses again, ready to be done with them, knowing I might not ever have to wash another glass in my life if I didn't want to. My mind was already off on the million things I might do with the money.

I told Enrico that I had to go to the bathroom, but instead I slipped out the back, propped the door open with a brick, and climbed the ladder to the roof. The Texas Moon was a good five miles outside of Amarillo. It was a hot, clear night, and I could see the downtown lights in the distance and a few neon signs on this side of Amarillo Boulevard, but nothing much else except a few trailer houses butting against the back parking lot. I thought, *What the hell?* I pulled about ten ones from my back pocket, threw them up in the air, watched them flutter over the parking lot like birds. I took change from my pocket and whisked quarters and nickels towards the trailer houses, listened to them clank on the sidewalk and tin roofs. I ran a couple of laps around the gravel roof, staying close, but not too close, to the edge. Then I took a five dollar bill out of my pocket, climbed up the back of the Texas Moon sign — a big, smiley-faced blue moon with a yellow lasso squeezed tight around its middle — and pinned it on the nail of the lasso knot.

"I caught you," a woman's voice shouted, and I nearly fell off the sign. "Over here, Travis." Arlene stood on the ladder, just her head visible.

"Come on up."

"I gotta get home."

"Wait." I climbed down from the sign, went to the ladder, and offered my hand.

I helped her up, and she looked around for a few minutes, commenting on how flat it was. "No water. No trees."

"Do you miss him?" I asked suddenly, then tried to take it back. "Sorry. I don't know why I asked that. It's none of my business."

"It's okay. He got me out of North Carolina. I've got a good job now. And here I am on the roof with a guy who throws money away. What more can a girl ask for?"

I asked her if she'd ever been to Palo Duro Canyon, and when she said no, I told her I'd take her out there one afternoon next week when I got back from Beaumont. "I can show you the caves," I said.

"Sounds scary."

"I'll hold your hand."

She smiled and then walked toward the Texas Moon sign. The moon and lasso blinked, casting blue and yellow rainbows on her face and the sides of her slender body. I followed her, and she turned and kissed me. My lips were dry and a little cracked from the summer wind, but they moistened quickly. For a moment I smelled smoke and thought wildly that the neon lasso had touched us and would burn holes through our shirts and jeans, brand us both, which sounded romantic, but before I pulled away I figured out the smoke was on Arlene's clothes. She wasn't burning. She just smelled the way my mother did each night when we got home.

"Good to see you two working hard." Boozer's head peeked over the ladder at the edge of the roof. "We're about to wind up down there."

"We'll be down in a minute," Arlene said.

"Why don't I get these fringe benefits?" he said, then laughed. "I'll have to renegotiate my contract." Then to Arlene: "You coming to the party?"

She quickly glanced at me. "Don't worry," Boozer said. "He's coming too."

"Yeah," she said. "I just want to run home and shower." Boozer cackled at that and then slipped back down the stairs.

We followed, and I walked Arlene to her car and promised to meet her at Enrico's. I kissed her again, but it wasn't the same, and I hoped the spell hadn't been completely broken. As she drove away, I took another quarter out of my pocket and flung it as far as I could. The silver whirled in the air, but then I lost it, never even heard it hit.

I decided to call the answering machine to hear for myself. I went to the pay phone at the back of the Texas Moon. The voice I heard was Bub's: "The doctor says the baby is not in a very good position, so he may have to do a cesarean. But we'll wait and see. It could be a while."

Then Raymond's call: "I've got good news." He provided the details quickly about the settlement meetings on Monday, and he said what he thought the new offer would be. When he gave the figures, even though my mother had already written them down, my heart flip-flopped.

I was about to hang up and redial to listen to those figures one more time, when I heard another beep. It was Bub again.

"I've got bad news, I'm afraid," he said and paused. I thought wildly for a moment that something had happened to Julie, but then he said, "Julie's okay." Another short pause. "But the baby didn't make it."

I felt as if someone had dumped a block of cement into my stomach.

"Julie's okay, though. She lost a lot of blood, but she's resting now. She'll probably be here for a week recuperating." He paused again. "It was a girl," he said, and his voice shook so badly that I thought of glass shattering. Then he hung up.

I sat down on a stool by the back door. A couple of the waitresses walked by me on their way out, but I didn't want to be seen, so I stepped into the walk-in. I didn't turn on the light, so it was both cold and dark in there, just the smell of the fruit and beer. I held my breath and pushed on my stomach as hard as I could. I bit down on my finger. I felt that I should go break the news to my mother, but I couldn't move. I didn't know how she would take it. We'd known there were complications. We knew that she might lose the baby.

But still.

In the dark chill of that freezer, I made impossible comparisons. I wondered if losing a baby was as hard as losing a father or a brother. They'd sent us lists of prospective names. And what were we going to do about the boxes of stuff we planned to take tomorrow? I had even found in our attic the mobile that went over my crib, little blue and red wooden ducks.

I thought, *Here I am. Sweating, joking, flirting, doing tequila shots. Throwing away dollar bills. Pitching quarters off the roof. Kissing Arlene underneath the neon sign on top of the Texas Moon. I've made plans.*

Wouldn't it have been better not to know? Wouldn't it be better never to hear that phone call or, for that matter, to see that policeman at the door, snow flecked and cold and ashamed and somehow still proud to be carrying the news, to be the one to knock on the door and stare at his boots and, later, to tell his children, "I was the one. I had to tell them. That was my job. You should have seen their faces. You don't know what it was like. Particularly on such a miserable day. So cold that frost built up on the inside of the windshield. So cold."

Like the inside of the cooler. Locked away with the beer and the fruit and the ice, I was convinced it would have been better not to know, better never to know such things. I opened my eyes, but it was just as dark. My nose ran, and gooseflesh covered my arms. I pried open the door, and the heat blurred my vision.

When I went back into the bar, most of the bouncers and other waitresses had already left. My mother sat at the counter, her head in close to Enrico's and Boozer's. There was only a thin glow from the neon beer clocks. My mother whispered something to Enrico and Boozer. I couldn't hear what it was.

"I thought you'd flushed yourself down the commode, boy," Enrico said.

They all smiled. I searched my mother's face. She smiled too, her smile — the corners of her lips barely turned up. "Are you ready?"

I planned to tell her right then, right there, but she fingered the bump on her nose, leaving me speechless.

"Let's go, kiddos," Enrico said. He threw the bar rag on the counter and grabbed my mother's hand. Boozer edged around the corner of the bar and threw his arm around my shoulders, the way Carroll used to do when he was drunk or feeling brotherly.

My mother asked me to drive. The Texas Moon sign clicked off as Boozer and Enrico wheeled out in front of us. We followed.

"My back's killing me," my mother said.

"Why don't you crawl in the backseat?" I said.

"Good idea," she said. "I can look at the stars and you can chauffeur me around."

At the next red light, she climbed over the seat and stretched out with her head behind me so that I couldn't see her face in the rearview.

"That feels so much better," she said and sighed. "To the cocktail party, James."

We drove down Amarillo Boulevard. I saw a few hookers in matching blue dresses sitting on the curb outside a Motel 6 and, a little farther up, a cop putting a wino in the back of his car and, not far from that, an ambulance with its lights flashing.

"It's a pretty night, isn't it?" my mother said. "Tell me what we should spend the money on. A car? A speedboat? A vacation to Acapulco? You could invite Arlene." She laughed, that rich laugh my father appreciated so much.

"I don't care," I said.

"Got you with that one, didn't I, Mr. Smooch-lips? Come on. Name something. Make a wish."

Ahead, Boozer, in the passenger seat, turned around and waved. I didn't wave back. I had to tell her, but there was something beautiful about her not knowing, all stretched out in the backseat, depending on me not to say a word. She was so vulnerable. But how could I stay quiet? How can anyone?

"I wish . . ." I choked up and had to clear my throat. "I wish I didn't have to tell you what I have to tell you."

"What is it, honey?"

"I called the answering machine."

"You did?" she said and lifted up in the seat. I could only see the outline of her face silhouetted in the rearview, no details, her profile only a silver-edged blade.

To catch the interstate, Enrico turned left down a dark and narrow two-lane road unfamiliar to me. I put my blinker on and stayed with him.

"There was a message after Raymond's," I said. I could no longer see even my mother's silhouette.

"I know," her voice said. "I know."

For a year my mother and I had been fumbling to protect each other. It struck me at that moment as a futile thing to be doing. How strange it was to think that you could ever protect someone else. Or to think somehow your life could stay the same — frozen, still and unharmed. What faith. What ridiculous faith.

Our lives were never the same after that night. The money came through eventually, and we quit the Texas Moon soon after. But the money came between us, made us feel both guilty and resentful, and separated us in that house in a way that the deaths of my father, brother, and Julie's baby could not do. I left home the following winter, not returning for my final semester of high school. I took my new car and drove across the country with Arlene, as far away from Texas as I could go.

Later, when Arlene was pregnant with our first child, we returned to Amarillo and visited my mother in the hospital. I had not seen her in several years, and only came then because the operation had been a serious one, and she had made it clear to Julie that she wanted to patch things up with me while she still had time. I felt sure my mother was exaggerating, as had become her custom.

We sat in her hospital room, playing cards. She looked tired, her hair messed up, an IV sprouting from her hand like a plastic flower stem, her gown draped loosely around her body. Doped up at first, she talked about Carroll and my father in the syrupy nostalgic way that had begun to sicken me over the years.

Then she fell asleep. We watched television for a while, and then, as I was massaging Arlene's shoulders, my mother woke and was remarkably lucid.

She asked Arlene if she could touch her stomach, so Arlene sat on the edge of the bed, and they talked about babies and doctors and hospitals and, jokingly, about the trouble women go through putting up with men. Then my mother grabbed Arlene's hand, and her tone changed. She talked again about my father and brother's accident, but this time her voice had no self-pity. She spoke lightly and honestly, in a way that made me grateful to be there.

"I didn't think I would make it," she said. The moonlight from the blinds made slatted images on the bed and on both their faces. "And part of me didn't want to. Travis's father had practically raised me. When I first met him, he was twenty-four and cocky, in the air force, decorated with medals. I was sixteen and amazed that such a man could be in love with me."

Arlene nodded.

"I never thought there would be a time without all of us together," she said, and I could sense in the shift of her voice, a slight lowering of her pitch, that she wanted me to pay attention. "And then afterwards I never thought there would be a day of my life when I wouldn't feel him and Carroll gone."

"I know," Arlene said.

"No, you don't," she said. "Not really." She closed her eyes for a few quiet moments. "For a long time, what I couldn't admit was that it was okay that they were gone. I didn't want to forgive myself for feeling good again."

Then she smiled, turned to me, and seemed to change the subject. "Remember what fun we all had at the Texas Moon, working together that year? You remember, don't you, Travis?"

"Of course," I said.

The smile left the corners of her mouth, and she seemed to stare past Arlene, past me, out the window. She tugged on her cover, pulling it up to her neck, jostling the IV so it looked like it would tear out. Her lips barely moved as she spoke. "You want to hear something ironic?"

"What?" I said.

"That was the happiest time of my life."

In the dark of the car, after my mother told me she had heard the call from Bub, I said, "Maybe we shouldn't go to Enrico's." I waited for her answer. I wanted to see her face but still couldn't.

"I think we should go. For a little bit at least." She stretched out in the seat again. "I'm going to shut my eyes," she said. "Can you get us there?"

"Yeah," I said.

"Good," she said. "I'm trusting you."

My eyes felt blurry. I blinked a couple of times to clear them, then opened them wide. I could hear her breathing in the backseat, soft and steady, and I heard my own breathing too. In rhythm. I thought of the little v-line of black hair on the back of Arlene's neck, how sexy it made her. I could picture Julie in the hospital resting, Bub in a chair beside her, waiting to comfort her if she should wake. I wondered where they put the little girl, if there was a special place for her.

Ahead, Enrico drifted in and out of his lane.

I gripped the steering wheel tighter. I could see clearly now the green and silver interstate signs for Paramount and Washington streets. Enrico and Boozer slowed down, but the car still moved back and forth like a slow-swinging pendulum. I eased up on the pedal, fell behind a few car lengths, but not far enough to lose them.

"Travis," my mother said quietly.

I didn't answer. There was no need to, really. There was a calm spot in our silence.

"Thank you," she said.

I didn't really understand then what she was thanking me for, but I said, "You're welcome." I concentrated on the road, and I tried hard to stay within the white dotted lines. I just wanted to get us there safely.

Knock Down,
Drag Out

1980

The pickup was a rusted-out Ford with a black canvas tarp sealed over the bed and a jagged hole the size of a fist in the back window. Rich rumbled up to the apartment complex and parked on the chalky gravel in back, the area reserved for visitors. He unbuckled his seatbelt, edged out, and after shaking loose his legs and arms, twisted his neck until it popped. He still wore the thick blue jeans, steel-toed boots, and light flannel shirt he'd worn his last day out on the rig, twenty miles off the Galveston coast.

It was a little after eight in the morning, and having just driven fifteen hours to his old apartment in the Texas Panhandle, Rich felt relieved to finally be here, excited and a little scared at the prospect of seeing the wife he hadn't heard from in over two months.

For the past few weeks he'd been moping around the rig, dumb and distracted, like a lovesick cow. He'd gone stir crazy, nothing but water everywhere he turned, reflecting up in his eyes, the thought of coming back for Babs the only thing on his mind. The third week he was on the rig, he took off his shirt, and by the end of the day, the direct sunlight, along with the reflection off the water, had scorched his back and shoulders enough to put him in the rig clinic. The doctor applied zinc oxide to the blisters with a large Q-tip and gave him green pills that numbed his itchy pain a little but didn't help him sleep. For a week he lay in a constant sweat, listening to the hydraulic roar outside, and tried to watch television and read old magazines.

But sprawled, belly down, on the hard-coiled infirmary bed, his back and shoulders like a feeding ground for fire ants, he had visions. Babs would appear, each time urging him to return. At first she came only in his sleep, but before long he was seeing or hearing her in the mornings and afternoons too. He knew these appearances were probably a product of his exhaustion from the long work shifts, the heat blisters, and the medication, but as the days went by and his wife's appearances increased in number and regularity, he also thought they could be a sign. As a gambler, and thus a believer in such mysteries, Rich knew better than to ignore or — worse — simply laugh off the signs. Babs was telling him something. He'd better pay attention.

So, even before he was out of the infirmary and back to work, slagging the pump and running the cord line, he knew he'd head north first chance he got, convince Babs to move to Houston with him and forget their separation. There would be lovemaking to refresh them, then they'd pack her stuff in the bed of his uncle's truck and drive back that very day.

He gave the front door three quick raps and covered the peephole so the only thing she would see would be dark, maybe the ridged callus of his finger. He waited, heard shuffling as she made her way from the bathroom or kitchen to the hall. The floors were hardwood, and he knew the sound she made when she walked on them, a sort of *swoosh-swoosh* because she didn't pick up the balls of her feet. He waited as she looked through the peephole. She would go to the window next, so he squeezed himself into the door frame, his finger still over the hole. No response. Smiling, he knocked again.

"Who is it?" she said from inside.

He disguised his voice, tried to sound gruff, put out. "Flowers."

"For who?"

"Barbara Tate."

"Just leave them on the doorstep," she said.

"No can do. Somebody's gotta sign."

"I don't like to open up for strangers," she said.

"I'm in a hurry, lady. Do you want the flowers or not?"

She unlatched the chain on the door and clicked the deadbolt. He stepped to the side of the frame and pressed his body between it and the windowsill so she wouldn't see anybody when she first opened the door. He waited for a few seconds to heighten the drama.

"What's going on here?"

As she stepped beyond the doorjamb, he jumped in front of her, his arms thrashing wildly, comically over his head, his imitation of an enraged baboon.

"BOOGEDY-BOO!"

He saw her eyes roll back in her head, and just as he put out his hand to grab her arm, her head whacked the door. The knocker clanked loudly, and then she fell like a cut tree onto the hardwood floor, landing with a dull *thunk*.

He held his index finger up to her nostrils and felt warm air, then tried to rouse her, but she didn't respond. Moving her didn't seem smart in case she had, God forbid, broken her neck or back. Her eyes were closed, and she looked awkward, which scared him even more, her legs spread apart, one knee bent out. She wore the raspberry, midthigh kimono he'd given her a couple of years ago for their first wedding anniversary, and it had fallen open, revealing panties that also seemed familiar, purple hearts and a lacy waistband. Covering her with the open flap, he checked for blood on her hair, still wet from the shower, found none, and then rushed for the phone in the kitchen and dialed 911.

The dispatcher put him on hold, of all things. He felt foolish and wondered if he should have at least dragged her into the apartment. He imagined Bob Kendable, his old preening landlord, peering out his window at the half-naked Babs.

They had not been ideal tenants, and though Kendable liked Babs, he didn't care much for Rich. There had been all-night poker parties, often loud and raucous, sometimes ending with Rich's drunken friends screaming at one another in the courtyard. There were other episodes with Rich and Babs arguing late into the night. Once, banished from his apartment because he'd lost his paycheck in a round of blackjack, Rich slept the night on Kendable's prized azalea bed, crushing the poor flowers before they had a chance to bud.

The night Babs sent Rich packing, Kendable stood at the edge of the courtyard, leaning against the cement fountain, water sputtering wildly over his head like fire-stand sparklers. He didn't say a word, just stood there with his arms folded and watched Rich load his clothes and what belongings would fit into his truck. It was creepy, Kendable monitoring his every action like he was her father. Like he had a right.

Just as the dispatcher came back on the line and asked Rich where to send the ambulance, Babs sat up and rubbed her head.

Her hair hung across her face in long wet ribbons, like burnt-orange licorice. She cleared her throat. "What happened?"

"Are you all right?" She looked woozy, lifting up onto one arm. "Seeing double or anything unusual like that?"

"I'm seeing one of you, and that's one too many."

"I wanted to surprise you, a joke, and you slipped and hit your head on the door."

The lady on the phone asked him again if he needed assistance. He muffled the receiver with his palm, turned to Babs. "Do you need an ambulance?"

"No."

"Don't worry," he said. "I'll pay."

"Aren't you sweet," she said. She rose slowly, motioning for Rich to put the phone down. He told the dispatcher to forget the call, then hung up. When he turned back, Babs wobbled, her knees buckling like a staggered boxer's.

He barely caught her this time. "Whoa!" he said as he steered her to the couch, cushioned a pillow behind her head, and propped her legs on the armrest. The flap of her kimono had come open again, this time revealing, in addition to her panties, her stomach and one of her breasts. It had been a long time since he'd seen her like this, and her body seemed new. It took a few moments before he could bring himself to close the kimono, and when he did, he let his fingers brush over her breast. He sat down beside her and pulled the hair from her face, caressing her cheek and forehead with the back of his hand. Her skin, so smooth compared to his own still-blistered back and shoulders, seemed one of the reasons he'd come, why he'd longed for her so badly out on the oil rig, the sun reflecting everywhere off the water until his own skin was all bubbly and tender.

She squinted. "God, my head feels like it's been cracked open with an axe."

"Let me check." He held her neck gingerly and probed the back of her head. It seemed like years since he'd touched her.

"Ouch!"

"There's a little knot right here."

"Thanks for informing me," she said.

He examined her pupils, not really sure what he should be looking for, but he thought he'd recognize it if he saw it. "I should take you to the hospital. You may have a concussion."

"I'm okay," she said, pushing him away.

"Let me at least get you some ice."

"I can get it," she said, rising halfway off the couch, but her knees gave again, and she fell back.

"God, this hurts." She gently touched the back of her head again and winced.

As she closed her eyes, he impulsively leaned down to kiss her but thought better of it, saw the disadvantage of taking too many liberties so soon.

"What are you doing here?" Babs asked.

"I came back for you." He hadn't meant to blurt it out like that. A wave of panic washed over him. He decided to make the most of his temporary position as nursemaid. "Let me get you that ice," he said.

He got the ice trays from the freezer, put cubes in a Ziploc bag, wrapped it in a dishtowel, and twisted it on top. This activity bolstered his confidence. He still knew where everything was. This was still his home. Nothing had changed. He felt justified in coming to get her, even if things were not going according to plan. But, he reminded himself, he hadn't really expected her to be overjoyed to see him at first. *Stay calm*, he told himself. *Be patient.*

He found her in the bathroom, where she held a hand mirror, trying to get a look at the knot on her head. "I don't think it's that bad. Just a little bump with a nick on it."

He reached up to put the ice pack on her head, but she quickly swatted away his hand.

"I'll do it," she said. "And don't look all hurt. You are not going to worm your way back," she said. "Don't even consider it."

"What do you mean?"

"I don't want you here. Get out of the doorway and get out of the apartment."

She brushed past him, obviously feeling better now, which upset him a little.

Okay, yes, they'd separated. A trial separation, though, was what they'd agreed to. Not for good. She knew that. He wanted to move the situation back a few steps. He liked helping her to the couch, propping up her head, brushing her hair from her eyes, feeling the lotion on her stomach and legs. He liked getting her ice packs. He could do that.

"I've got good news," he said as he followed her into the next room.

"I don't even want to hear it."

"You're gonna love it, Babs. I promise. Just listen."

He had come a long way, and she couldn't expect him to just turn around and leave. He had a plan to win her back, a plan he'd rehearsed the whole seven hundred and fifty miles in that bitch of an old truck, from Houston to Dallas, from Dallas to Childress, from Childress to Amarillo with the tires whining on the hot asphalt and the night air whistling in the cabin.

She pointed to the door. "Just go away."

He felt the urge to sentimentalize his own ordeal, let her know just how far he'd come, stopping every seventy miles to check the transmission fluid. He wanted her to know he'd gotten a steady job on an oil rig, offshore, with Texaco, twenty-eight days on, twenty-eight off; let her know just how much money he (they!) stood to make; let her know she didn't have to work again if she didn't want to, at least not for another mall hair cuttery.

Things would be different now. He had even put a down payment on a house in Spring Branch, and it was clean with three bedrooms. Zoned so she could run her own hair-styling business out of the house if she wanted. There'd be no more gambling. No more arguments. He'd throw their furniture in the truck bed, sling the tarp over it, tie it all down with rope, and haul everything to Houston this very second. Start fresh. It'd be that easy.

"I want you to come to Houston with me," he said.

She stood in the doorway to the living room, her shoulder leaning against the wall, one foot on top of the other. She seemed almost relaxed, amused by what he'd said. "You're certifiable. You know that, don't you?" she said, chewing a hangnail.

"I'm serious," he said, eager to get to the good part.

"Of course you're serious. Crazy people are always serious."

He could feel his anxiety swelling. He knew that she wouldn't consider him crazy once he explained to her about the job and the Spring Branch house, all the evidence that would convince her of his good intentions.

He was about to start again when there was a knock at the door.

It was Kendable. He hadn't changed a bit. Still looked like a California version of Santa Claus: hard blue eyes as big as marbles, a closely cropped white beard that extended up the sides of his face and formed a fuzzy band around the back of his head, the darkly tanned knob of his skull a sharp contrast to the white hair. He was not particularly tall, but he was thick. The way his chest bulged, you would hardly believe him to be a man in his fifties. But the backs of his hands were wrinkled and liver-spotted, his breath stank of coffee, and there was a nicotine stain in the shape of a crescent moon on his top front teeth. Kendable sized up the situation, examining first Babs, still in her kimono, then Rich behind her.

"Are you all right?" he asked her.

"Don't worry," she assured him, drawing the kimono band tighter around her waist. "Everything's fine."

"What's he doing here?" Kendable asked.

"Leaving. Right now. Aren't you, Rich?"

"He'd better be," Kendable said forcefully.

Here this man was again, Rich thought, poking his nose into his and Babs's affairs, ordering him to leave as if Rich was some frightened teenage boyfriend who could easily be chased away. It made him sick.

"Listen here," Kendable said, lowering his voice menacingly. "You get your candy ass out of here in half an hour or you'll find yourself in the county jail."

"I can see my wife whenever I want to," Rich said.

Kendable smacked his lips, revealing the nicotine moon. "Not on my property, you can't."

"I have things under control," Babs said, sighing as if the whole matter was being blown too far out of proportion.

"You can do what you want," Kendable said to her. "You know that. But he's not allowed on the premises. He's trespassing. I want him out of here, or I'm calling the police."

He reminded Rich of those bonehead, Vaselined wrestlers on late-night television, threatening opponents and fans alike with clenched teeth, flexed biceps, and fierce, melodramatic talk.

Rich was normally not the sort of man who was easily provoked. He'd been in some wild poker games, and he'd worked as a bartender in cheap little dives in the North Heights of Houston, where the Mexicans and blacks and white trash all sported switchblades and routinely brawled, but he had usually managed to keep his distance. Even as a roughneck, offshore or out in the hot Panhandle fields with the other mean-tempered, grumbling riggers, he tried to avoid scraps, a remarkable feat when he thought about it. But Kendable really ticked Rich off. Who did he think he was, coming between a man and his wife?

"You got that?" Kendable said. "Thirty minutes."

Babs rolled her eyes, exasperated. "Wait here," she said to Rich and then asked Kendable if he would step outside with her for a moment.

Rich watched them through the window. He wanted to listen, but they moved away so that he could only hear muffled conversation. They stood about two feet from each other. Babs waved her hands, motioned to the apartment, shrugged her shoulders, expressed her regret that all this had happened. Kendable nodded appreciatively.

The air conditioner clicked on, startling Rich. Cool air blew down the back of his neck. He noticed, for the first time, that the living room was different. Hanging over the recliner was a picture of a woman sitting in a wheat pasture, staring at a house on top of a hill. On the television set was a wooden statue of a smiling Buddha. He was sure that they would've never chosen these things together.

Even more disturbing were the plants. Babs had never done well with them. Any plant in their house had died in a matter of days. He used to kid her about her brown thumb. But now there was greenery all over the place, and the remarkable thing was that it was flourishing. A large cactus with white flower buds hung in a rope basket. What seemed to be a small tree towered imposingly in the corner, and the windowsills were filled with violets and other flowers he couldn't even name.

Suddenly Babs laughed, her arms crossed and her head thrown back. Kendable smiled, happy with himself, looking slyly through the window at Rich.

They used to joke about Kendable. "Dependable Kendable," they called him because he could always be depended on to fix the toilet, to mow the lawn, to demand the rent the first of each month, to meddle in his tenants' affairs. Rich would lather his face with shaving cream and thrust out his chest, do his Kendable routine until both he and Babs lay on the floor in stitches.

But now she and the landlord were acting like old friends, and Rich figured he was the butt of the joke this time. He had been gone for over two months, but he had no reason to distrust Babs. As far as he knew, she had never been unfaithful to him.

She was a woman separated from her husband, though, needing someone to confide in, an ear to pour her troubles into. Vulnerable. Wouldn't that be the way Kendable would have perceived it, spying on them from his window during their arguments, watching her after their separation as she moped around the house, alone, heartbroken? In her kimono! The purple-hearted panties underneath! And wouldn't it be just like Kendable to make himself suddenly available, to repaint the walls, install new faucets, stain the hardwood floors, change the locks, enlist her help with his garden, the two of them sifting their hands through the dark, thick mulch?

At that moment, outside, Kendable reached up and touched

Babs's cheek. It wasn't really a caress; he seemed simply to be shooing a bug away from her face. But the mere sight of his wrinkled, liver-spotted fingers on her face made Rich's stomach churn. He could picture it all. Kendable weaseling his way into her heart, his mouth opening up to her like a pot of stale coffee, his teeth like a grimy tattoo. "Oh, Babs, I don't know why you put up with him as long as you did! You deserve much better. Yeah, go ahead and cry. Cry it all out now. Yeah, that a girl. No need to thank me, honey. A woman like you deserves some pampering."

Dependable Kendable.

Stay calm. Be persistent. Stick with the plan.

But get her out of this place. And fast.

As soon as Babs was back in the apartment, the door safely closed behind her, Rich exclaimed, "You'll never believe the job I got." He waited for her to follow his lead, ask about the job, but she didn't, so he forged on. "Texaco. Offshore from Galveston. Twenty-eight days on, twenty-eight off. But I can get switched to a two-week schedule soon. The money is great, Babs. You won't believe it. Three times what I was making in the fields. No kidding. And that's only for starters."

"I'm happy for you," Babs said.

"That's not the half of it." He felt the need to overwhelm her with the details, thoroughly persuade her. This was his chance. He couldn't blow it. "I bought a house, Babs. A house. Not a trailer. Not an apartment, either. The real McCoy. Can you believe it? My sister scouted around while I was offshore, and as soon as our boat came in, I had the real estate agent show me the place. It needs a little electrical work and a new shingle job, but I got it for a steal. Wait'll you see. You will absolutely love it, I swear to God you will. It's only ten years old. Brick. Twelve hundred square feet plus a garage. Three bedrooms, plush blue carpet. There's even a fenced-in backyard. And my buddy Willie promised to give us one of his puppies. He had a new litter of blue collies."

"Hold on now," Babs said, raising her hands as if warding off a blow.

She sat down on the couch. Rich had been talking as fast as an auctioneer, reeling off the speech he had rehearsed during the drive up here.

"What makes you think I want to leave here with you?" she asked.

"But you'll love Houston." He sat on the edge of the coffee table, facing her. "You can even use the front part of the house to open your own hair-styling place. I called about that too. There's no zoning problems. Perfectly legal. It won't cost us a dime. The house is in the good section of town, up in the northwest, called Spring Branch, not far from Laura and her kids. It's close to grocery stores, two malls, all sorts of restaurants. And still only an hour from Galveston. Ten minutes from the Galleria. Thirty minutes from the Astrodome."

She seemed puzzled. She started to speak, but he cut her off. "Babs," he said, reaching out for her hands. "You have to see it to believe it. It's paradise."

"Poor Rich." She placed her hands on top of his. "You're a sweet man sometimes. You really are."

He felt a rush of sympathy from her; he would prevail after all. She rose from the couch and went to the window, pulled the separate sides of the kimono closer, and ran her fingers through her still-wet hair.

"But I don't want to be married to you anymore," she said. "I've talked to a lawyer and filed for divorce." Turning back to him, she said, "And don't bother to act shocked."

He was shocked, though. He'd thought she might refuse to

come with him, but he had not prepared for this. Maybe he hadn't explained it well enough. If only she could see their new life together as clearly as he could. If only he could make her understand how it would be. Show her.

"I've changed," he said. "Really, I have."

"I'm late for work," she said.

"Please, Babs. You don't know what it was like on the rig. I swear, I thought you were following me around. I'd see you in the shop, clipping hair. Or pulling groceries from the trunk of the car. Or whispering to me. Not like a dream, either. It was in the daytime. You were like a ghost or something. I couldn't get rid of your face. And you'd talk to me. You said, 'Come back.' I know it sounds weird. But that's what you said. 'Come back!' And I have."

"Well, Rich, I'm not responsible for what I say in your imagination."

After an awkward silence, she said she had to go to the bathroom. Heading down the hall, she shook her head, as if she still couldn't believe what he'd said.

He could see himself returning alone to Houston and in another twenty-four days, out to the rig, where the sun and the water and the other riggers would make his isolation that much worse. Nothing to look forward to, nothing to come back to. But as awful as it seemed, he thought he might be able to tolerate that.

What was absolutely intolerable was to consign her to a life here, with Kendable, where she stood no chance of happiness. She'd already changed. The painting, the plants, her expression, her condescending attitude, even the pity she seemed to feel for him, scared him. This wasn't like Babs at all. In his short time away from her, she had been overthrown by this imposter. He was sure that the old Babs would have listened, would have eventually seen it his way. He had to get her out of here so that he could break whatever spell had gotten hold of her. It was, he realized in a moment of absolute clarity, his responsibility as her husband to do what was best for her. To protect her.

As she turned the corner into the living room, he made up his mind. What did he have to lose? He bent low and rushed, grabbed her at waist level, lifted her up and over his blistered shoulder. He felt a hot tingling there. She kicked and tried to stiffen so that he would drop her, but he gave a little jump and boosted her back so the edge of her waist rested on his collarbone.

"Goddamn it!" she yelped after a startled moment.

"Watch your head," he warned.

She started pounding on his kidneys and his ribs. He swiveled around on the balls of his feet until he found the door. She rocked on his shoulder, and he could feel her arms sway free, whirlybirding as she tried to regain her balance. They tipped over the tree, and on its way down it hit the rope basket, sending the cactus flying over the coffee table.

"Rich, stop it!"

He had to get to the truck, and he knew it wouldn't be easy with Babs punching and screaming and Kendable at his window ready to pounce. He made it through the door, but then jerked backward, almost lost her, and nearly toppled. Over his other shoulder, he saw that she had somehow managed to grab the knocker on the door and was holding on with both hands.

"Let go," he said, "or we're taking the door with us."

"We can talk about this, Rich. Okay? I'll call in sick. Come back inside. I'll fix us some breakfast."

Nobody had stirred in the courtyard, not even Kendable. Not yet. He expected him to come running out of his apartment any second, charging, chest forward, like a white-grizzled buffalo. Somehow Rich had to make it to the truck, open the door, put Babs inside, and keep her there while he started the engine.

Then what? He wasn't sure, but it felt good to be committed to a course of action.

"Let go of the door, honey," he said. "Please."

By way of response, she started kicking her legs, but he clenched them tight against his chest, jerked forward, and pulled her away from the knocker. He walked as fast as he could, Babs screaming wildly, "Help! Somebody! Help!" as she continued her assault on his back while thrashing her legs.

He squeezed tighter and quickened his pace, then found he could cover more ground without losing his balance if he skipped sideways. Ahead was the white gravel of the visitor's lot, the truck bed facing him with the black tarp on top.

She pummeled and screamed. "You're gonna regret this. I mean it!"

Still no sign of Kendable. Rich skipped to the truck bed. On the other side of the parking lot, a gust of wind blew a red and black For Rent sign end over end across the empty field. A large tumbleweed followed, and behind it, plastic lids skittered across like mice chasing a thorny doughnut.

With his free hand, he peeled back the front driver-side corner of the tarp, located the coil of rope on the inside edge.

"Rich, let me down," she said, more calmly now. She stopped thrashing. "This is ridiculous. You're not proving a thing."

Winded, he set her down. She breathed hard too, her eyes wide, and he could tell that she was as perplexed as he was. He expected her to run, but she didn't.

"What are you going to do with that?" she asked, pointing to the rope in his hand.

"Come on," he pleaded as he opened the driver's door. "Get in. That's all I'm asking. Things will be different. I promise you."

She nodded and stepped in the direction of the truck door, touched the handle. "Okay," she said. She was going to give him a chance. Finally.

"You'll love Houston," he said.

But then she turned suddenly and bolted back toward the apartment. He took four long strides, caught her arm, and pulled her to him.

"Let go of me!"

She left him no choice. He'd have to take drastic measures now and then convince her later. He pulled her thin wrists back and gripped them tightly in his left hand. He hooked the rope over his left thumb and with his right hand he whirled it around her waist, her belly, below her chest as many times as he could, and holding her close to his body, he wrapped the rest of the rope around her wrists, careful not to hurt her.

"Jesus," Babs pleaded. "You can't do this!"

Maybe she was right. But to set her down now and pretend none of this had happened was the unthinkable thing. He picked her up again, this time from behind. She kicked his shins with her heels. He started to put her in the cab but feared she might fall out once they got on the road or tip over and land on the gearshift.

"Please stop. This is insane."

He peeled back the tarp, lifted her up and over, and placed her in the truck bed as gently as he'd placed her on the couch just moments earlier.

"You're absolutely crazy," she said, her voice raspy now, her forehead twisted into wrinkles.

His hands shook. He felt as if a jagged rock was working its way down his throat. The exhilaration of seizing the initiative was beginning to drain from him. This *was* crazy. He felt pulled, though, forced to carry on, despite himself, as if caught in an undertow.

He got in the truck. In his rearview he saw Kendable coming out of his apartment. Rich fumbled with his key before putting it in the ignition. He turned it, but the engine didn't kick over. Through the fist-sized hole in the back window, he heard Babs call for help. Kendable shouted her name. Rich's heart thumped wildly, and his ribs and back ached. He thought for a second that maybe he should stop this right now before it was too late, but Kendable was barreling toward him.

He turned the key again. Nothing.

"Babs!" Kendable shouted again.

Rich tried the key again, fed some gas. The engine sputtered, coughed, then finally turned over.

He gunned the engine to keep it from dying, then slipped into first gear and carefully let out the clutch, so as not to jostle her too much. He sucked in a breath, and it felt hot and raw on his throat. The truck moved forward. The tires wheeled up a cloud of dust into Kendable's face. Pieces of gravel crunched and shot like pellets. He pressed down harder on the gas pedal.

He could feel Babs in the bed, squirming, rocking slightly from side to side, crying, calling to him in what now seemed like a song he'd heard long ago, a lament or a hymn. As he pulled onto the main road, the black tarp whipping like an angry flag in the wind, he felt the way he sometimes did in poker games, early in the morning, when he'd lost everything he had or could borrow before he realized that his luck had run out.

Pool Boy

Costa Rica

1970 − 71

In 1970 my father quits selling carpet and goes into business for himself. He and my mother and his parents get in on the ground level of a cosmetics firm. They sell lipstick, aloe vera, eyeliner, face powder, blush, fingernail polish, fingernail polish remover, the works. My mother is pretty, blonde, a model, so that helps selling. They travel around Texas and Oklahoma in a car and give speeches in bank lobbies and restaurant banquet rooms and sell cosmetics out of briefcases. Though only six, I preach the powers of positive thinking. People love me. I'm a star on the cosmetics circuit. My father gets some distributors underneath him, in a pyramid structure, and then he is in business.

In six months we are rich.

Success breeds success. My grandmother and mother discover a wonderful bra, something special about lifting and supporting. My father thinks it's funny. "Push those titties up and create some cleavage," he says and demonstrates on my mother, pinching her nipples through the fabric of her blouse, then squeezing her breasts together so that a dark line appears where her flesh meets. He laughs.

"I'm serious," she says and slaps his hand away.

They prove it to him by selling, door to door, over four hundred bras in a week and plop down five thousand dollars on the coffee table. So my father buys a warehouse in downtown Dallas and starts a bra and lingerie business. He puts my grandmother and my mother in charge, president and vice president. They make more money.

I stop giving speeches about positive thinking and instead start playing with Max, the son of the manager of the huge condominium complex where we live. I go over to Max's place one day, and he shows me the master key to all the mailboxes in the complex.

"Come with me," he says.

By now my father is driving a Cadillac Eldorado and is making deals, big deals, with men named Donald Duck and Carlos Esposito and Bob McKay. Carlos is married to the daughter of a Costa Rican diplomat, who owns twelve thousand acres. My father and his friends put their heads together and decide to buy Costa Rica. All of it. Start a timber and cattle operation. Clear-cut and then have the cattle graze the land.

With Carlos, Bob, my grandfather, and my uncle, my father flies down to Costa Rica to scope out the situation. Once in the country, they rent a pilot and a Cessna. The plane is small, though, so only my father, Carlos, Bob, and the pilot can go.

They take off. There are miles of hundred-foot trees in Costa Rica. The plane dips down low in a valley so they can survey the jungle. Then the pilot tries to nose the plane over a mountain range. My father and Bob and Carlos are looking out the windows, taking lots of pictures — both snapshots and sixteen millimeter. It starts to rain, suddenly, hard, and one of the engines sputters. The pilot doesn't want to hit the mountain, so he tells them, in a mixture of English and Spanish, to fasten their seatbelts because he is going to try a crash landing. Everybody goes nuts.

"Are you crazy?" my father shouts. "We'll die if we hit those trees."

"We have no choice," the pilot says. "Better the jungle than the mountain."

Meanwhile, I am at home, sitting on the bed beside my mother. She is holding a belt in one hand, and she is crying because she does not like to whip me but knows that I must be whipped, and whipped hard, because Max and I threw one hundred and thirty-four mailboxes full of letters, bills, and magazines in the gutter before Max's father caught us.

My mother says, "You know this hurts me to do this, don't you?"

I remain still, look at the belt, a thin red one with a thick gold square buckle I've seen her wear many times. Whatever I say will be wrong. Then she is holding on to my arm with one hand and hitting my butt and legs with the belt. She is the hub of the wheel, our connected arms the spoke, and I am rolling in painful circles on the carpet, shrieking for her to stop. The phone rings, but my mother does not answer it. I put my hand out to stop the belt and receive a whop. I scream.

"Don't put it back there if you don't want it hit," my mother says calmly.

We are in the middle of this when my grandmother opens the door. Her face is sad, her eyes bloodshot, and it is clear she has been crying.

For me, I believe.

My mother stops with the belt, and I feel overwhelming love and gratitude for my grandmother, this woman with white cotton candy for hair.

She says, "Laura, Neil's plane has crashed."

When my father regains consciousness, he discovers three things more or less simultaneously: one, he is alive; two, his ribs are probably broken and his back and arms lacerated; and three, it is incredibly humid and dark. He calls out for Carlos, Bob, and the pilot and hears, about ten feet away, the voice of the pilot, gibbering in Spanish. In the dark he tries to dislodge himself from his seat, but when he stands the pain in his ribs stabs him and he only feels a white-hot flash in his head before he topples over.

My uncle stays to help the search party while my grandfather immediately flies back from Costa Rica to comfort us and to tell us the brutal truth of the situation. There are rescue crews searching, but quite frankly, there is very little chance — one in a thousand — of even finding the plane in such impenetrable forests, and even less chance of survival. My grandfather tells us that a DC-10 crashed in the jungles a year ago and no one even found the plane. My mother begins to sob uncontrollably, keening, but my grandmother, a Sun Belt Baptist and sometime reader of fortunes, looks my grandfather in the face and calmly tells him, "Neil will not die young. I know it." We turn to her, expectantly.

We believe her, though she will be wrong.

When my father awakens again, it is daylight. He rises slowly this time, and though he feels pain, he does not pass out. He discovers two things then. The cockpit was torn completely off in the crash; he can see it several feet away. And Carlos is slumped on the floor, two rows up, still unconscious. My father does not see the pilot or Bob. He bends down and nudges Carlos, who is groggy. His back hurts, but he's alive and able to sit up.

Minutes later they discover the pilot lying outside the cockpit, about ten feet away. He is awake and talking rapidly in Spanish to his wife and sons and to the trees. He is shaking his head back and forth, as if he has a nervous tick. His eyes are glazed over. Only after they prop him against a stone do they notice that a large shard of his thighbone, startlingly white, is protruding from his bloody pants. My father stuffs a part of his shirt between the pilot's teeth as Carlos tries to set the leg and bandage it with the pilot's shirt. The pilot shrieks, and my father tells him to bite down on the rag, which he does, before he passes out, his jaw clenched tight.

It takes them a while before they find Bob, fifty feet from the front of the plane, facedown on a flat thorny bush. They turn him over and find huge slashes across his face and chest, and thorns and glass lodged all over his nose, cheeks, arms, chest.

"He looks like a goddamned bloody porcupine," Carlos says.

My father nods and says, "He must have flown right through the windshield."

They shake their heads in disbelief. Bob is alive, however — miracle enough. As gently as possible, they move him closer to the pilot, remove most of the thorns and glass from his face and arms, and try as best they can to swab away the blood.

My father and Carlos decide that it is unlikely that anyone will be able to find them, so they better try to find somebody. From the plane they bring the bottles of water and the snacks they brought with them — two apples, a papaya, and one Milky Way. They make the pilot drink and eat, and when he is somewhat lucid, they ask him what they should do.

He speaks more gibberish, but then he says, "Agua, agua, agua," and they eventually understand that he is telling them to find a stream and follow it. Not having the least clue where water might be, they set out east, move away from the blaring sun, and hope for the best.

At home my family waits impatiently for news from my uncle in Costa Rica. My mother feeds my baby sister. My grandfather chain-smokes his unfiltered Camels. My grandmother reads aloud from the Bible. Everyone has forgotten about my whipping or what I have done except me, but now I wish I could have the whipping back, ten times harsher and longer, and not have this happen to us. I have begun to think that my throwing away mail with Max is somehow linked with my father's plane crash, and though I want to believe my grandmother when she says that she is sure my father is alive, and I try to comfort myself with my old stories of the powers of positive thinking, I have started seriously to believe that he is dead and that it is my fault, and this is the way that God, in His divine wisdom, has seen fit to punish our family for my sin.

A miracle happens forty-five minutes later, as my father and Carlos come upon a healthy stream that runs south. They hear the water before they reach it, hear the lap and gurgle and splash, and when they finally do reach it, after twisting through jungle vines and briars, they are so happy that they start jumping up and down in the stream, hugging each other tightly, spinning in circles, despite their pain. Exhausted from their joy, they sit in the water together and my father and then Carlos begin to cry. It is the first time this has happened to either of them since the crash. There has been so much to do that they have not had much time to think about their situation or their chances. Now they realize their chances are much better, but looking down the stream, the way it twists and turns out of sight, disappears into the thicket of trees on either side, they also understand that they may never get out, may never see their families again, and that if they do, it is doubtful that either the pilot or Bob will make it.

In fact, though they do not know it, Bob is already dead.

They wipe their eyes and my father says, as lightheartedly as he can, "Let's get this show on the road."

So they start downstream, walking in the water, the leather on my father's shoes starting to shrink and squeeze him. There are fish swimming around their feet, small ones, and Carlos tries to catch one, then my father tries, but they both fail. The slick fish flop out of their hands before they have them, and soon they realize it is futile to waste their time, and besides, the bending over hurts my father's ribs and Carlos's back. The sooner they find somebody, if they find somebody, then the sooner they can eat. They plod along in the shallow water. My father tries to ignore the pain in his ribs, the hunger in his belly, tries to stay focused on the water between his ankles, flitting away the bugs that are attaching themselves to him — the gnats and mosquitoes — and successfully stays focused until twilight descends on them, suddenly, two hours later. They lie down on the bank with some light still filtering through the thick foliage of the overhanging trees, and they close their eyes.

Though raised on a farm in Oklahoma and accustomed to country nights, my father, when he opens his eyes a few minutes later, cannot believe this darkness, so thick and black that he is not sure if he does, in fact, have his eyes open. He checks. They are. He expects his eyes will adjust, but they do not. The trees block out the stars and moon completely, and he wonders if perhaps he has gone blind until Carlos says, "I can't see a goddamned thing."

"Me either. Get some sleep."

"I'm scared," says Carlos.

"You're not the only one," my father says. "Get some sleep."

With the blackness come the sounds of the jungle: the high-pitched cicadas, night birds squalling, the far-off roar of a leopard or something more exotic and unnamable, the breaths and scurries of smaller animals nearby, the rush of the water, the gnats and bugs whirring, constantly whirring. My father feels mosquitoes landing and sucking, and he fights them off for a while before he gives up, exhausted, lets them feast as he tries to think about sleep, and soon he is asleep and discovers his wife there, my mother, on their bed in Dallas. There is a yellow glow from the lamp beside her, and he gets into bed and fingertips her soft flesh, slips away the blue cotton nightgown she wears and examines her body, so white and unscarred, like before the babies. She pulls him to her, and then she shifts nimbly on top of him, and as they make love, she starts to cry and her tears as they drop on his face and chest do not disintegrate, but puddle there and are warm and then suddenly so cold they burn him.

"We'll miss you," she whispers, and then he is suddenly very cold, and he is awake and shivering. He gropes to his right and finds Carlos and huddles against him, clutches tightly to his friend.

"What the hell are you doing?" Carlos says, groggy.

"Cold," my father chatters. "Hold me. It'll keep the bugs from eating us alive."

Shivering, they huddle together like lovers and soon fall into a dreamless sleep.

That same night my grandmother also has a dream. In it she sees a clearing, a large village, the forest at the edge. And from the density of the trees, she sees my father sitting on top of a white horse, being slowly led by a naked, dark-haired, brown-skinned boy.

When my father and Carlos wake the next morning, they are sore and exhausted, and there are red welts all over their arms and faces and necks from the mosquitoes.

"I hope we don't catch malaria," my father says.

"I thought that was only in Africa," Carlos says, and then they move on, knowing they have more important things to worry about.

They travel down the stream again, this time more slowly. They are hungry, but they do not know what they can eat. They are afraid of the berries and foliage along the banks. The villagers in Limón warned of the many poisonous shrubs and trees and fruit, and my father wishes he had paid closer attention. Later, in midday, when the sun beats down so hard and hot and humid that they have to rest in the shade on the bank, Carlos catches a frog, a big slick one with a huge gullet. He twists the frog's head off, tosses it away, and then pulls off a leg and eats it. Carlos gives my father a leg. My father is surprised at how delicious it tastes. They consume what they can of the rest of the frog, rinse their mouths with the stream water, sleep while it is hot, again bundled together to keep the bugs off them. A couple of hours later, they are moving again.

Carlos's back has spasmed several times by late afternoon, and though my father feels as if he has daggers lodged in his sides because of his broken ribs, he helps Carlos walk, draping his friend's arm over his shoulder as he wraps an arm around his back. They trudge on, slower and slower, and as they walk, my father begins to sense that he will die, that their chances are so slim that it seems futile to even go on. They stop and sit in the shallow portion of the stream. Carlos lies on his back in the water so that only his face is above the surface. His face looks like a mask, and my father thinks it is a death mask, like the ones he had seen at the festival in Limón. This is the way Carlos will look in his coffin if they find them at all. This is the way Carlos's children and wife will remember him, just this face, swollen and scabbed with bites.

The longer my father stares at Carlos, the sun beating down on their exhausted, half-starved bodies, the more transfixed he becomes. He wonders if this is what a life is, if this is all we ever learn about ourselves and the world, just a portion of ourselves above the surface, while the rest stays submerged and then is lost forever. My father thinks that maybe it would be okay to die. He tries to think about my mother and about me and about my sister, who is so new to the world that she does not really count as a significant part of his history. But we all seem too far away. He can't even picture clearly what we look like. He knows he loves us, but he is not sure, in his state of mind, if love matters, and if it does matter, he wonders, how does it help? My father just wants to go to sleep, so he lies down like Carlos and the world is muffled by the stream, and as he closes his eyes, he drifts back to a time when he was very young, and he lay down in a tub full of water in his grandmother's bedroom on a farm in Reed, Oklahoma, and fell asleep.

Two planes, a helicopter, and over two hundred men, divided into five crews, search for the missing Cessna, but after three days they find nothing. The officer in charge of the rescue tells my uncle that memorial services should be considered. With each day the chances of survival diminish a hundredfold.

"Don't expect bodies," the officer says.

My father wakes to the dark and the feel of something slimy and thick slithering over his stomach. He thinks that he is dead, and so goes back to sleep, goes back to the watery blackness. Then, later, Carlos is tugging at his arm.

"Neil, get up. We'll freeze in the water. Come with me."

Holding Carlos's hand, my father crawls through the darkness to the bank. Carlos clutches tightly to him, and in the strange silence and pitch of the night, they are asleep again and do not believe they will wake.

I go with my mother to the funeral home so that she can talk to the director about memorial services. She listens attentively to the possibilities he offers, but halfway through she breaks down, hysterical, and says she cannot do this. My grandfather, smoking his Camels, his forehead wrinkled and liver spotted, drives us home. He helps my mother to her bed, and I go into my grandmother's room, where she is sleeping with the open Bible across her chest. I crawl up beside her and put my arm over her stomach, press myself against her old warmth and sleep.

When daybreak hits, my father and Carlos are surprised to be alive. They do not feel they can go much farther. But what choice do they have? They see another frog beside them, but neither has the energy nor strength to catch it, kill it, eat it. They rise and slosh dumbly through the water. They are not even sure they are going in the right direction. It takes them three hours to travel a hundred yards to the bend in the stream. Their bellies gnaw. Black birds circle above them, but they do not know if the birds are vultures, crows, or the exotic Montezuma Oropendola that the natives told them about.

When they make a turn in the stream, my father is shocked to find a boy standing there, splashing naked in the water. The boy does not notice them at first, just keeps on playing. My father believes he is dreaming — this boy is a mirage or perhaps a ghost child, his son there to comfort him as he dies.

He calls out my name — "Lee!" — and Carlos jerks his head up suddenly, and the Indian turns and is shocked by the sight of these two ragged men, three-day beards on their faces, their eyes bloodshot and half-crazy. He starts to run, whipping through the greenish-brown water, to the bank and away from these creatures. My father calls my name again, but the boy does not turn back. Carlos kneels down in the shallow water and my father watches as I run from him, disappear into the trees, frightened of my own father.

He kneels down beside Carlos, and the two men wait to die.

The next morning my father is inside a hut on a handwoven rug. Above him there are two dark-skinned women, naked except for a thatch of grass over their pubic hair. One is applying some jelly to his wounds and bites. The other holds a gourd out to him. It is coffee, or something that tastes like coffee, wonderfully rich, and he gulps it down though it scalds his throat. She gives him another gourd that has cooked bananas and papaya in it. He spoons the goo into his mouth with his fingers, asks for more, eats it, then sleeps.

The next morning he and Carlos are taken to a village nearby where there is a Catholic hospital. Carlos rides a brown donkey, my father a white one.

The next day, against the wishes of the doctors, my father flies out in a reconnaissance helicopter to help locate the pilot and Bob. They discover the pilot sitting in the stream, in shock, but alive. They find the plane and search for Bob's body but find nothing.

We see the news stories about my father before we see him.

He is the lead story in the *Dallas Morning News*, and *Time* does a small story about him that next week. In both he is bearded and smiling and pointing to a map of Costa Rica. When he returns to us, we cannot believe our good fortune even though he does not look like the same man who left us. He has lost sixteen pounds. There are black circles under his eyes. His face, neck, arms, and hands are scabbed with bites, so that he looks like he is in the later stages of the measles. He wears soft leather moccasins, his feet bandaged, swollen three sizes larger from walking in the water.

We feel blessed, though, touched by the impossible.

That night, the night my father returns home, I stay up late and listen to him tell the story for us, saddened by the death of Bob but also transformed by the event, changed by what has happened to him. My grandmother says a prayer for us all, and we hold hands together in a circle and thank the Lord for delivering us this miracle. My mother clings to my father as tightly as I imagine he and Carlos held on to each other to stay warm.

We are at this moment, in 1971, the beneficiaries of ignorance.

We cannot, for example, know that my mother and father will soon divorce, remarry, then divorce again, heartbreakingly, because my mother fears my father will go to jail and take her with him. We cannot foresee that little more than a decade from now, my father, not yet forty, still a young man, will die mysteriously in Las Vegas, and though I am the last of my family to see him before he dies, I cannot prevent it. And I cannot know that I will still dream of him more than a quarter of a century from now, see him sloshing along in the waters of Costa Rica, rounding the bend and calling my name, calling for me to rescue him.

All that we know now is how happy and lucky we are.

Later that night, in bed, beneath the soft sheets, in the dark, I relive my father's story again and again. I close my eyes and imagine the kind of darkness he must have experienced, the tall trees looming, the whir of insects, the gurgle of the stream, the breath of exotic animals dangerously close. I listen intently to the night, re-creating it all, as my parents make love in the room next to mine. And the sounds of their lovemaking become the sighs and moans and gentle sobbing of the jungle.

Breaking Glass

1973 — 74

Houston. I was nine years old and awake in my room with a flashlight under the covers reading *Boy's Life* and listening to Chubby Checker, The Four Tops, and the cocktail chatter in the living room. My parents were throwing a party, and when I heard the last guest leave, I slipped out of my room and into the hallway. My father sat in his orange recliner, his eyes focused intently on the ceiling, while my mother stormed about the apartment, picking up empty chip bowls, crinkled napkins, beer and wine glasses. After a few minutes she stopped and stared at my father for several seconds until he became aware of her. She had a half-full beer glass in her hand.

"Doesn't it bother you that Dub made a pass at me again? Doesn't it bother you in the least?"

"He didn't mean anything by it, Laura."

"He's your best friend," she said.

"He was drunk. He won't even remember it in the morning."

"He was not drunk, Neil, and you know it."

163

Dub and my father worked together as salesmen at Salem Carpets, and Dub usually spent most weekends with us, at the beach in Galveston, or fishing on his speedboat, or playing Gin Rummy or Spades or poker, or going up to College Station to watch the stock car races. He was a small, gentle man, much shorter than my father, with straight black hair, a thick mustache that curled handsomely around both corners of his lips, and a little pot belly that hung over his heart-shaped turquoise belt buckle. My father had been working at Salem for only six months — his first job since he and my mother lost their cosmetics and bra companies to bankruptcy — but it seemed that he and Dub had known each other for years. I liked Dub because he didn't treat me like a kid. Every weekend he would play Rummy 500 with me for a penny a point, and he didn't hesitate to take my money when I lost or to fork over his own when I won.

"Big deal. It was a joke," my father said. "Don't take it so seriously." My father absently twisted the hair on the back of his head into knots, a habit that drove my mother berserk.

"What bothers me, Neil," my mother said, "is that *you* don't take it seriously. You know I hate it, and you still won't do anything about it."

"What do you want me to do?" he asked.

"Just tell him to quit it. Let him know it bothers you."

My father looked at my mother for almost a full minute, trying to interpret what lay hidden beneath her request, though it seemed obvious to me. Then, as if what he discovered profoundly disturbed him, he suddenly lurched from the recliner, turned on my mother, who knelt startled by the chair, and said, "You expect me to make a big fucking deal over something that's not worth mentioning. Just forget it. Jesus Christ, I work with the man every day!"

"Okay," my mother said, grabbing his arm. "Don't tell him anything. I don't care. Just tell me it bothers you. At least let *me* know you care."

He paused, then opened his eyes wide and pitched his voice high, as if telling a story to a child. "I *care*, darling. I *really* care."

Her eyebrows looked as if someone had run a drawstring through her forehead and pulled.

"Satisfied?" he said.

They stared at each other for a few moments, then he turned and walked to the bedroom. She stood there a long time, not moving, the beer glass still in her hand.

Then something weird happened.

She flung the glass to the floor, and it did not shatter. Its thick bottom hit the hardwood in the dining room with a thud, and the beer splashed up and over the chair like a wave. I made a noise then, a sudden intake of breath, but my mother did not seem to hear me. I remained still, crouched in the dark hallway, watching her as she examined the glass. Like me, she was stunned that it didn't break. She picked it up and again flung it to the floor. The bottom hit with a *thunk*, wobbled for a second or two, then stood upright, still unbroken. My mother just stared. Then her arms tensed and the veins in her neck began to knot beneath her skin. She snatched the glass from the floor and reared back her arm, prepared this time to hurl it against the door that separated her from my father.

My mother had taught me to throw a baseball the previous year, and when she threw her fastball, my palm stung. I knew if she wanted to, she could explode that beer glass against the door. I held my breath. But her arm fell slack to her side, and she slumped to the floor, dropped her head, and started to cry.

I should have slipped back to my room, hidden beneath the

covers, and forgotten what I should not have seen. But I was fascinated by my mother's pain. It reminded me of the time I saw my best friend Gordy Thompson fall off the monkey bars and break his leg. I had stared, mesmerized, at the bone protruding from his torn thigh. Gordy wailed only when he saw it, and I knew I should have gone to get some help for him, but I couldn't move. That bone looked so absolutely white and clean. It paralyzed me.

In the hallway I felt the same as I watched my mother sitting on the floor. I inched closer until I was standing right behind her. She didn't move. How could she not know I was right there? I could see the white crease of her part running like a river down the center of her head, and I reached out to touch her thin yellow hair. My hand shook as I held it not six inches from her. But then, for some reason I still don't understand today, I pulled my hand back and retreated to my room, where I lay awake watching like a criminal the thin strip of hallway light seeping beneath my door.

Much later that night, my mother woke Cindy and me and huddled us close to her.

"Your father loves us," she explained. "It's there underneath. He just doesn't know how to get at it sometimes."

Usually when my mother said something like this, I rolled my eyes at my sister. But not this time. Cindy and I just nodded.

"I just want you to know that," she said.

Two weeks later my father packed his things and moved into an efficiency apartment on the southwest side of Houston.

The night he left, I crept down the stairs around midnight and found my mother sitting cross-legged on the living room floor, drinking beer out of an iced tea glass. In front of her, precariously stacked in a misshapen pyramid, were her other used glasses — tumblers, beer mugs, crystal. She stared at the pyramid, and I thought for a moment that it would all come crashing down if I took another step or even breathed too hard.

"I want you to know," she said without moving, without even looking at me, "you never get over your first love. You remember that. Okay, buddy?" Her words were slurry.

"You think you'll get married again?" I asked quietly.

She shook her head. "It's gonna be just you and me and Cindy holding down the fort from here on out."

She drained the last of the beer and flashed me a bittersweet smile. Then I held my breath as she reached out to complete the pyramid.

A week after the divorce was final, my mother started dating Dub.

He took us to his parents' ranch, outside of Houston, where we ate brisket, romped with the Irish setters, and rode horses. He showed me how to lasso (though I was never very good at it), how to shoot rabbits without ruining the meat, how to plant corn, and how to butcher a hog. We even saw two headless chickens run around, bumping into each other, blood spurting from their necks, a sight so disturbing to Cindy that she had nightmares for weeks and would do anything I asked so long as I didn't torment her with stories of timber wolves stalking her window at night, searching for chicken heads.

I was under orders from my mother not to tell my father about Dub.

One Sunday night, about two months later, when my father brought Cindy and me home after a weekend with him, Dub's white station wagon with carpet samples in the back was parked in the lot. I saw it before my father did, so I immediately told him I was not ready to go home yet. I begged him for a chocolate shake. He took us to Dairy Queen, but when we drove back to the apartment, Dub's car was still there.

"What's going on, Lee?" my father asked when he recognized the station wagon.

"I'm not supposed to tell you," I said, but then promptly told him.

He didn't seem all that surprised, nor was my mother when she answered the door.

"You're early," she said.

"It's seven-thirty."

"Hello, Neil," Dub said, smiling uncomfortably. He stuck out his hand, and my father shook it and smiled as if he was glad to see him. "Hi, Lee. Hi, Cindy."

We said hello but did not hug him, as we usually did, both of us sensing the betrayal in that act. My father and Dub talked for a few minutes about work as the rest of us stood by, watching carefully. Suddenly, my sister started to cry.

"What's the matter, honey?" my mother said.

"She didn't take a nap today," I said.

"Then some little girl needs to get ready for bed."

"I want Daddy to put me to bed," Cindy whined.

"You're home now, honey," my mother said.

"I want Daddy to do it."

My mother looked at my father. "All right. Daddy'll be up in a minute." She turned to me. "Lee, you too."

"It's not even eight," I said. My bedtime had recently been moved to nine o'clock, and I was ready to argue, on principle alone, any regression. But I also had a feeling—like someone twisting the inside of my stomach with pliers—that something bad was going to happen. I figured as long as I stayed downstairs, the adults would have to behave.

"Do what your mother tells you," Dub said, sharply. He had never spoken to me that way, never given me orders. We all looked at him as if he had uttered an obscenity.

"You're not my father."

"Go on," my father said. "I'll be up in a minute."

"Dub, why don't you make Neil a drink," my mother said as she escorted us upstairs.

In my room I told her I made Dad take us to get some ice cream when I saw the car. But then we came back, and the car was still there.

"It's okay," she said.

"I'm sorry."

"Honey, it's okay. Really."

When my father came up, my mother kissed us, then started back down.

"I'll be down in a minute," he said.

"Take your time," she said lightly.

He read us two books and sang lullabies until Cindy was asleep.

"I'm sorry," I said as he tucked me in.

"What do you have to be sorry about?"

"I don't know."

"If you don't know, then don't apologize."

"What's going to happen?" I asked him.

"What do you mean?"

"Are you gonna kill Dub?"

He laughed. "No."

"Are you gonna still be friends?"

"Your mother and I are divorced. She can see whoever she wants."

He kissed me on the forehead and went back down. I listened

for a long time but couldn't hear what they were saying. They seemed to be having a good time, though. There was loud laughter at one point. I nodded off, not waking until I heard the front door slam shut. I jumped out of bed and raced to the window but couldn't see anything.

A few minutes later I heard footsteps on the stairs, and then my mother's door shut. I waited for a while, then slipped out of bed and went to her door. I pressed my ear against it and heard whispering, then went back to bed rather than listen to anything else.

My mother woke us early the next morning and fed us doughnuts. She was cheerful. No one else was in the house.

"Is everything okay?" I asked.

"Couldn't be better," she said.

We spent the late morning and afternoon at the apartment complex pool. Cindy played in the kiddie pool. My mother lounged on a plastic chair, rubbing her homemade suntan lotion — baby oil and iodine — onto her arms and legs, as I jack-knifed, cannonballed, and back-flipped from the diving board.

About one o'clock that afternoon, Dub opened the pool gate, dressed in blue bathing trunks and chest hair, drinks in hand, swizzle straws and cherry stems peeking above the rims of the frosted glasses. He waved at me, kissed Cindy on the cheek and then my mother on the mouth, sat in the chair next to hers as I double-jumped, soared high into the air, curling tight before can-opening the surface of the water.

Underwater, I flipped my head into my stomach like a fetus, crawled through my own bubbles, and discovered the quarter glinting on the black drain. I reached for it, but it slipped through the grate, and my chest tightened in an omen as I failed to finger it loose. Empty-handed, I pushed from the bottom and scissor-kicked upward, turning my face toward the sun refracting through the chlorinated blue. Breathless, I emerged no more than thirty seconds later to the double *thwack* of the swinging iron pool gate.

I swiped the water from my eyes and saw Dub receding, as if pedaled away. Around the pool, the mouths of the other sunbathers were o'd, their feet off the ground. My mother sat statued in her lounger, a strange half-smile on her lips. Her stomach glistened, puddled with liquid. She brushed a maraschino cherry off her bikini bottom. Around her, on the hot cement, lay cubes of ice, one swizzle straw, and a thousand shiny slivers of frosted glass, that cherry like a dollop of blood in the middle.

I see this moment even more clearly now than I did then, as if the instant itself—that sensation of rising from the watery depths into the aftermath of the violent, critical moment in a relationship—is a slow-developing photograph that becomes more vivid and distinct, yet still mysterious, still elusive, as the years slip by.

"What happened?" I asked, treading water, careful not to touch the side of the pool, which shimmered with watery shards of light and glass.

She lifted her sunglasses so that I could see the whites of her eyes circling her green irises. I could see far into the green, and it was as complicated as a fractal. The half-smile escaped, but she was not frightened or unhappy. She seemed to me assured, triumphant really, calm, as if she'd won something she knew was hers all along.

"Your father and I are getting married again," she said.

Marty

1975 – 80

For a while my parents were happy to be married to each other again. He bought her roses, and she would fix us huge break-fasts — pancakes with fresh strawberries, Mexican omelets, T-bone steaks and fried potatoes — which we would eat in bed on white wicker trays. On Friday or Saturday nights, they would drive to Rotten Red's, a nightclub in Galveston, and would not return until four or five in the morning, drunk and in high spirits, stumbling in the door and to their bedroom, where I could hear them making love through the air conditioner vents.

But in the fall of 1975, without any warning, my father quit his job as a salesman at Salem Carpets and started spending all his energies again on what my mother called "his deals." By the following summer two of my father's colleagues, Carlos Esposito and Lenny Shumacker, were indicted for tax evasion and international mail fraud. Lenny was convicted and Carlos, whose wife was from Costa Rica, disappeared. My mother begged my father to go back to selling carpet.

"I'm not doing that grunt work again," he said.

"You were so good at it. We were doing all right."

"I worked my butt off for a measly two-and-a-half percent commission. That's chump change."

"I don't want you to go to prison."

"Don't be paranoid."

"I can't help it."

"Just trust me."

"Is that what Lenny said to his wife and kids when he was carted off? 'Trust me'? Is that what Carlos would say to his family if he hadn't already left the country? 'Trust me'!"

"Do you love me, Laura?"

"Love doesn't have a damn thing to do with this."

Right before my thirteenth birthday, they divorced again. This time it seemed for good.

Soon after the divorce, and against my father's wishes, my mother moved us to Amarillo. She had grown up in the Texas Panhandle and wanted to be closer to her family. She had an older sister, Gloria, an older brother, Manny, and two younger brothers, Gene and Rich — all of whom lived there. My mother was particularly close to Aunt Gloria, and we lived with her family. My sister and mother slept together in the oldest daughter Julie's room.

I slept on a cot in Carroll and Travis's room, and every day we read aloud the Edgar Rice Burroughs's Tarzan books, and then we'd all horse around, wrestling like apes, lifting weights so we'd look like the illustrated version of Lord Greystoke, muscled and loin clothed and bearing down angrily on a saliva-dripping gorilla who was trying to do unspeakable acts to the frightened, blonde-haired Jane.

My mother worked as a waitress at my Uncle Manny's barbecue restaurant and did some temp secretarial work. Every couple of weeks the whole family would come together for big poker games that would last until three or four in the morning. Carroll and Travis taught me to play, and we'd get to join in if there was room at the table, which was usually late at night after one of the aunts or uncles ran out of money, or Uncle Gene and his wife, Angie, got really drunk, cranked up the music, and started two-stepping around the house like mad until they passed out on Aunt Gloria's floor or went home, sweaty and kissing. Cautious, I usually broke even, but Travis always seemed to win, partly because everyone else was drunk and foolish by the time he sat down to play, and partly because he was lucky, almost as lucky as Uncle Rich, who was the baby of my mother's family and, by general proclamation, the luckiest son of a bitch in the world. He'd been in half a dozen car accidents and had always come out fine. He worked as an oil rigger in the Panhandle and sometimes offshore, and he'd had so many close calls with fast-swinging two-ton pipes, jet hoses, steel cables, and swimming sharks and poisonous jellyfish that you'd think the law of averages would have had him dead long ago. But he was charmed, and he always seemed to win big at the poker table — at least at the family poker table.

I loved this time, and though my sister and I missed my father, I could see myself living here forever and thought that's just what we'd do. At first my mother seemed to truly relish being back with her family, but then as the summer wore on, and after several tearful phone calls with my father, she grew depressed and lonely. She quit working for Uncle Manny and stayed home all day, sometimes lounging, asleep, in Aunt Gloria's backyard in her bathing suit, sometimes not even getting out of bed.

Finally, near the end of August, she declared that we were

moving back to Houston. It was where she had made her home, and she felt guilty about taking us away from my father. My uncles had always liked my father and seemed to understand, but Aunt Gloria and her husband felt it was "dangerous" for my mother to be back in town with my father. They knew about my father's shady deals, and Gloria's husband had been in the air force and felt that it was stupid to "fuck around with the government," as he said. She was "susceptible to his charms," they said, and they begged my mother to stay in Amarillo. But her mind was made up.

Within a week we had packed up and made the seventeen-hour drive with the trailer back to Houston.

For a while my father started hanging around more often. He'd always been a handsome man, but over the summer he'd grown heavy again, as he had been when he and my mother were happiest together. Sometimes he'd spend the night, and though my mother said that it was "unlikely" they would marry again, Cindy and I didn't believe her. Though it was sad to leave Amarillo, we didn't mind being back in Houston with our friends. The summer had been like a vacation, and we were ready to return to our normal lives. The expectation of our parents reuniting once again made us hopeful.

But then my father started traveling a lot — often to South America and Las Vegas and California — and we began to see less and less of him. When he was around he seemed preoccupied and worried, always on the phone, chain-smoking.

Then we hardly saw him at all. His child support checks came irregularly.

My mother started working as a waitress again, and on nights off she would go out with friends and return home, sometimes drunk, sometimes with men, who would come in for a drink or other things. They would always be gone by morning.

This period lasted for about six months. Then our lives changed for good.

My mother's second husband, Marty, sold hydraulic tools, was six years her junior, drank vodka, and weighed only as much as I did at fourteen. I liked him at first. He bought me Tarzan novels, a blue-green fiberglass skateboard with a fancy fishtail curve on the back, a hockey stick autographed by Gordie Howe. He would take Cindy and me to Astroworld and to Oiler and Rocket games and, if we pleaded, to a restaurant called T.G.I.F.'s, where we ordered virgin strawberry daiquiris dolloped with whipped cream and watched a man in a gorilla suit play banjo and graze ladies' hairdos as he swung through the dining room. Marty gave us fifteen-dollar-a-week allowances. He taught me how to drive and didn't even get angry, as my father surely would have, when I once ran his van off the road and hit a cow.

In the first few months of their marriage, I milked his generosity for all it was worth, even though I felt jealous and uncomfortable as he and my mother suffered through (to my mind at least) the awkward stages of intimacy. At twenty-seven, he didn't have much experience with children, so he was alternately hesitant and then aggressive about showing his affection for my mother in front of us. Sometimes he would not even kiss her while we were in the same room, but then later he would slip up behind her while she was at the stove and nibble her ears, cup his palms around her breasts, or slide his fingers inside the front of her jeans. At such times I felt wronged and strangely embarrassed for all of us, yet almost scientifically interested in the inner workings of their physical intimacy.

In the winter of their first year of marriage, Marty and my mother began to drink and argue. They'd return home from nightclubs or parties screaming at each other, Marty's face clotted red, the veins bulging in both his and my mother's necks, his hair ratted like a woman's. Then in the middle of the night, I would sometimes hear through the air conditioner vents muffled *thunks* and sobs from their room. The next day I would watch for telltale signs — a black eye, fingernail scratches, hostile glances, sunglasses, or too much makeup.

One time, on a hot afternoon in late April, when my mother came inside after sunbathing in the backyard, I saw a bruise on her back.

"What's that?" I asked her, touching the purple center.

"Ouch! What are you doing?"

"There's a bruise on your back."

She quickly put her shirt on and began buttoning it. "No, there isn't."

"Yes, there is. Right between your shoulder blades."

"That's my business, Lee."

In my most confidential voice, I said, "You can tell me."

"Look, mister," she declared, "you worry about your body, and I'll worry about mine."

I was grateful that she did not involve me then. I saw my mother's dilemma through the refracted waters of adolescence. I was more concerned with hormonal shifts, body hair, and the alternating ridicule and elation of junior high and early high school. I was trying to work up enough courage to ask Susan Gloyna, the envy of my ninth-grade class, to go steady, a difficult hurdle since my voice could not be trusted to stay in the lower registers. I had no time, really, to concentrate on my mother's problems. Besides, those sobs and *thunks* I heard coming through the vents late at night would often wake me from not so very chaste dreams of Susan. So when my mother covered up her bruise and told me to worry about my own body and let her worry about hers, I thought she was onto me, that she had a direct pipeline to my more carnal fantasies. It was best to leave well enough alone.

The following summer when I returned home from a three-week track and field camp, Marty and my mother had separated. Marty's ten-speed bicycle, gas barbecue grill, favorite vodka jigger, and maroon sofa were gone. My mother divulged no details about their breakup.

"We've decided to split up for a while. That's all," she told me when she and Cindy picked me up at the bus station. Cindy was nine by then, and she looked at me, her brown eyes wide, her jaw clenched tight. She shook her head covertly, warning me not to press. I didn't.

In fact, nothing was said about the separation for two days.

On the third night I sat in my bedroom lost in *Tarzan and the Jewels of Opar*. It was raining and cool for summer. The rain beat against the window, and the water from the drainpipe gushed over the bushes just outside my room. My mother was in her bedroom watching *Happy Days* on television and circling job prospects in the classifieds. Cindy opened my door a crack and whispered, "Let me in."

"What do you want?"

She carefully closed the door and tiptoed to the end of my bed. She wore one of my mother's old nightgowns, white flannel speckled with pink roses. It was too big for her; the frayed hem dragged the ground.

"What's the matter?" I asked.

"Shh!" she snapped. "I'll get in big trouble if Mom catches me."

In low whispers, she then told me that while I was gone, my mother had left the house several times for the whole night and not come home until after Marty had gone to work the next morning. Then one night Cindy and my mother were playing Canasta on my mother's bed while Marty was out. He came home drunk and laughing and popped the telephone cords from the walls and stood in the doorway of the bedroom, flipping the light on and off. He asked my mother who she'd been sleeping with, and when she said no one, he said that the Little Bluebird of Truth Tellers told him that she'd been sleeping with mine and Cindy's father. She said that wasn't true. Marty asked her where she went all night then, and my mother said it was none of his business. He went to his chest of drawers, pulled out a pistol and waved it at them, then forced the barrel into my mother's mouth. A few minutes later, my sister crying, he shuffled into the living room and passed out on the sofa with the gun on his chest. The next day when my sister came home from Connie Taylor's house, all of his things were on the sidewalk, and a policeman smoked a cigarette while Marty loaded them onto the bed of a white truck.

Cindy swore it was all true, but said that I couldn't say a word about it.

"Why not?" I asked suspiciously.

"Mom told me not to tell you. She said you would be real mad at her. I told her you wouldn't, but she didn't believe me. You're not mad at her, are you, Lee?"

"No."

"Promise you won't tell."

"I promise."

"What're you going to do?" She was close to tears, as if the burden of silence had almost been worse than what had happened.

"I promise. Now go back to your room."

"I'm not a tattletale?"

"No, you're not."

Cindy tiptoed out. Then, though I didn't hear her, I sensed my mother was right outside my door.

"Come in," I said as calmly as I could.

"I just wanted to tell you good night."

She opened the door, and I could tell she wondered if Cindy had said anything. I got the feeling that she almost wished I knew. I wanted to evade the issue, and not simply out of loyalty to my sister. I said, "Did you find anything good in the want ads?"

"If I didn't mind black fishnet, I could make a fortune."

"Huh?"

"I'm not too thrilled about being a cocktail waitress."

"You'd be good at it," I said.

"You don't think I'm cut out for better things?"

I wasn't sure how to answer that. Actually, I'd never thought seriously about what my mother was cut out for. I said, "You'd be good at anything."

"Smart answer."

"Maybe you'll have better luck tomorrow."

"I hope so. Somebody's gotta feed you."

"We could always go back to Amarillo," I said.

She smiled wistfully and shook her head. "No, not now. It wouldn't be right. They wouldn't understand."

"Sure they would."

She shook her head. We didn't say anything more for a minute, then she laughed and asked me to stand up. "I think you've grown since you've been gone. I bet you're as tall as your father now, aren't you?"

"Only five-ten," I said.

"Almost grown up."

It was an awkward moment. She had not seen my father, as far as I knew, for several months. Last I heard, he had been out on the West Coast, visiting friends, scouting out jobs. But this sudden mention of him made me wonder if Marty's accusations were justified, if my father perhaps had been back for a tryst with my mother. I felt the hair on my forearms tingle.

My mother stared at me, and I thought again she might confirm what Cindy had told me, and I didn't want her to. She must have sensed my anxiety because she just shook her head and sort of bit her lip, then gave me a quick kiss on the cheek.

"Don't stay up all night reading," she said.

In the next few months I ran the scenario that my sister had detailed through my mind again and again. In the daytime, watching a football game or daydreaming during boring lectures at school, I saw myself disarming the drunken Marty, delivering a quick, efficient uppercut before the police arrived to cart him away. Yet, at night, as I lay half-awake in the dark, listening to the wind howling past my window and the insistent gush of rainwater from the drainpipe, I envisioned more gothic scenarios. I saw myself not moving toward him quickly enough, and the gun exploding through my mother's skull. At other times I saw him murdering my mother, then turning the gun on Cindy and me, and finally himself, in the kind of kamikaze wholesale slaughter that I read about in the papers and had actually seen in one of the gruesome R-rated movies I sneaked into. In one dream of black comedy, I saw him pull the trigger, and a bouquet of flowers — red, white, and blue — blossomed from my mother's nose, mouth, and ears.

Despite these dreams, I was so preoccupied with my own life that fall that I had little time to think about my mother's or sister's problems. My voice was under control, and my face cleared up because of the summer heat. I landed a job at a non-union movie theater as an usher and projectionist for two dollars and twenty cents an hour and learned how to load the giant reels onto the projector and thread the film and splice on previews. My birthday was not far away, and a friend's father who owned a junkyard agreed to let me have an old, beat-up (but running) Delta 66 if I worked for him five hours each Saturday and Sunday morning for the rest of the year.

And as if these breakthroughs weren't enough, I began to make headway with Susan Gloyna, who was at home recovering from mononucleosis. I didn't know if she'd contracted the illness by kissing, as rumor had it, but I felt her misfortune was my chance to make my presence known to her. First I sent humorous get-well cards that I made myself. And then I started visiting her. She lived in a powder blue and white three-story Colonial house in a wealthy subdivision called Memorial Drive. Though not contagious, she was too weak to get out of bed, so I was allowed to talk with her in her bedroom (with the door open, of course). She had a thick white comforter on her queen-sized bed and posters of animals all over the walls — zebras, tigers, giraffes, lots of bears, elephants — a jungle, really.

It was thrilling to be there, alone, in the bedroom with her, even though nothing would or could happen between us. She wore a bulky terry-cloth robe, enforcing modesty, but the very top of her nightgown was visible, a thin, almost transparent silky material through which I could see the pale skin at the base of her neck, making me aware that under the robe she must look like one of the heroines depicted on the covers of my Tarzan novels, buxom beauties wrapped in gauze. I couldn't help but imagine myself in Burroughs's world, inside the sanctum sanctorum of the high priestess, parrots shrieking, drums thumping, the incense filling up the room, Susan, scantily clad, a finger crooked in feline temptation, her breasts threatening to topple out, and me on the verge of passionate confession.

I tried to take all this in, memorize it as I relayed the latest school gossip and helped her with her theorems and proofs since I'd had Mr. Gibler's geometry class the previous spring. I could tell she wasn't in love with me, but she did find me funny and, as she said, "more attractive than you used to be." Plus she was grateful for what I had done for her. Gratitude wasn't love, but it was a start. Although she declined my invitation to go steady, she did agree to go to the Snow Dance with me in December if she was well enough.

Life at home was not so good. In late September Cindy broke her arm while learning to vault in her gymnastics class. My mother had let our insurance lapse, so she had to dip into savings to pay the doctor's bills. My father had recently moved to Las Vegas to start a financing company and didn't return our calls. The child support checks stopped coming.

To make matters worse, my mother could not find and keep a job that made her happy or that produced enough income to support us. She went back to secretarial work. She'd always been an excellent typist, boasting a speed of 102 words a minute with only six errors. The bosses loved her because she was fast, efficient, and good looking. But the work hurt her back and strained her eyes and never paid enough.

Despite her aversion to black fishnet, she tried cocktail waitressing, and though she could make seventy to a hundred dollars a night at a small club up the street called the Contico Lounge, she found the work "abhorrent." She had never established her own line of credit, so we couldn't get a bank loan, and she didn't think it was right to borrow from her family, not even from Uncle Manny, who had the money. One month I gave her my paycheck to help pay the electricity bill and buy groceries, but she refused my help after that.

On Halloween Marty moved back in. For a few weeks both my mother and Marty remained on good behavior, obviously conscious of Cindy's and my scrutiny. They took us out — to nice restaurants, to football and hockey games, for a boat tour through Galveston Harbor — in an effort to reestablish a firm footing in the household. They even took us to T.G.I.F.'s, but the man in the gorilla suit now seemed like a fraud.

By Thanksgiving they were drinking again. I tried to maintain a neutrality, but it wasn't easy. We were better off financially, but more than ever, I was sensitive to the undercurrents of violence. The story my sister told me the previous summer clung to me day and night. They bar-hopped nightly and returned home arguing. My mother grew despondent, moping about the house during the days, distant in her conversations with Cindy and me. At night I heard again the muffled cries through the vents and tried to distinguish their lovemaking from their arguments, sensing that sooner or later I would be drawn in.

A couple of times, when my sister slept over at a friend's, my mother left the house without Marty and didn't return until morning. After he left for work and before I left for school, she would sneak in, as if she'd been watching to make sure he was gone. She would fix herself breakfast or go in the bathroom, where she would unpin her wig and drape it over a white Styrofoam head, unpeel her eyelashes from her lids, and Vaseline the mascara and makeup from her face, the sink filling up with gray water. When she'd catch me looking at her, I'd leave.

These all-night absences were, I suppose, gestures of resentment or vindictiveness. Perhaps she just needed to be away from Marty and us for a while. I never questioned her. He did, though, interrogating her when he returned from work like a man possessed; I could almost see his mustache twitching, his face knotted in anger in the other room.

In early December I woke one morning around two-thirty and heard Marty yelling in the kitchen. I lay in bed for several minutes, cursing them both. Then I put on my sweatpants and a T-shirt and went into the kitchen. Marty was obviously drunk. I didn't know about my mother. He had her cornered against the stove, and he tottered back and forth in front of her, chanting, "Where've you been? Where've you been?"

"Hey!" he shouted when he caught sight of me in the doorway. "Look who's here, Laura. Lee-roy's here. Lee-roy, film man, junkyard dog, what do you know? Lee-roy's here, Laura. Tarzan, come to save you."

He howled like Johnny Weissmuller, then staggered over and put his arm around me, his eyes bloodshot, his breath reeking of cigarettes and drink and some other smell that made me think of formaldehyde.

"Go back to bed, Lee," my mother said.

Marty grinned at me. "Ain't it just a pisser when they don't want to be rescued? After you come all this way to save them. After you make sacrifices, put food in their mouths, put a roof over their heads, save them from the wild beasts. And all they can say is 'Go back and live in your tree, Tarzan, like all the other dumb monkeys.'"

"Go on, honey," my mother said. "Everything's okay."

"That's the thanks you get for rescues these days. But she's right, Lee-roy, old buddy. You need some beauty sleep, a growing boy and all."

"Maybe you should get some sleep, Marty," I said.

Suddenly, he whipped his forearm around my neck and jerked me close to his ribs in a tight headlock. "Don't you tell me what to do. You hear me?"

"Yes," I wheezed.

"I could smash your pimply-ass face in, you know that, don't you? I could do any damn thing I want."

"I just thought we could use some sleep, that's all. I have a trig test tomorrow."

"You owe me, you little son of a bitch. All of you owe me. I bailed your asses out of debt, and I'd like to see a little goddamned gratitude around here for a change."

"Shut up, Marty!" my mother said.

"You know that, don't you, Lee-roy?"

My heart was pounding; I could feel it like a knot in my throat. He clutched my face, drawing it closer to his own so that his breath enveloped me. But, just as I thought he might carry through on his threat to smash my face in, he smiled, slapped me playfully but hard on the cheek, and let me go.

"But I wouldn't hurt a big old pup like you. You know why? Because I pity you, Tarzan. You know why I pity you? Because I think it's a goddamned shame to have a mother here who will let a man pay her bills while she boffs all the other apes in the tribe."

"You bastard!" my mother said and pushed him away from me.

"Oops." He covered his mouth and raised his eyebrows like a naughty child. "I forgot. Tarzan hasn't learned about boffing yet. Have you, Tarzan? Better go to bed now, ape-man. Need rest. Tarzan got big test tomorrow."

That next week I tried on several occasions to call my father. I had the notion, despite all that had soured between him and my mother, that he could somehow patch up our lives. One part of my mind actually believed that he would and could rescue us, that we could start over again. But I only got a message that said his line had been disconnected, and there were no new listings for him in Las Vegas.

Friday night was the Snow Dance. It was Susan's first time back, and she spent the majority of the date talking with her friends and dancing with other boys. I got only two dances. I wanted desperately to take her to the Artesian Well, a favorite make-out spot, and spend a couple of hours kissing her and smelling her perfume, but when several people asked us to go to the Pizza Planet, she said we'd love to go. The place was full of other couples from the dance.

Susan spent the entire time hopping from table to table, "catching up on the news." All of which I'd told her during my long afternoon visits. To my amazement, she acted as if she'd never heard any of it, pretending surprise, laughing, expressing regret, all of it done as if I wasn't there, as if she was counting on me not to reveal that I'd told her all of it before. Or as if the news hadn't counted before, since I was the one who'd told her.

I sat with a couple of guys who didn't have dates, but I didn't have anything to say. I drank too much tea and had to go to the bathroom four times and felt compelled each time to examine my face in the sallow, fluorescent-lit mirror. When it got late Susan went to the restroom, and everybody gave me money for the pizza and left. There wasn't enough, so I had to pay extra. We drove to her house in silence, and at her front door I only got a quick peck and an obligatory thank-you-for-the-wonderful-time before she was inside her house and away from me. I felt stupid and full of a frustrated anger that made me sick.

I drove to the Artesian Well and threw rocks hard against the stone wall. There were cars parked above the rim on the south, the sound of muffled music from the radio drifting over to me. Some of the cars moved slightly side to side. I wanted to throw some rocks at those cars, shatter some windshields, make them stop what they were doing.

As I drove home around midnight, I noticed my mother's car was gone again. Marty was in the living room, reading a magazine, a drink in his hand. My sister had gone to bed.

"Do you know where your mother is?" Marty asked me.

"No."

"How did your date go?"

"Lousy."

He nodded and took a drink. We hadn't spoken to each other the past week, so this was a form of apology. In my bedroom I put on my sweatpants and a T-shirt, then rummaged through my closet, found my baseball bat, and leaned it carefully against the wall by my bed. I lay down and tried to finish *Tarzan and the Forbidden City* since I lacked only twenty-five pages, but I seemed to keep reading the same page over and over again.

Then Susan suddenly appeared. She had changed clothes, out of her dance dress and into a green and white-striped terry-cloth robe held up by her breasts. Her black hair was long, twice as long, down to her waist, and loose around her face. She came to me, slowly, as if walking through water, and pulled my head close to her chest and held me there. I could see the freckles on the exposed top of her breasts and light hair all down her left arm, smooth and soft and warm like down. When she smiled at me, I could see a small, beautiful sliver of pink gums and teeth, white and glinting in the moonlight that streamed through my shutters.

She said she was sorry about the dance and that she was here to make it up to me. She led me to the window, and we just slipped out with no trouble whatsoever. It was snowing and the roads were iced over completely, two inches thick, but the air was warm, not cold. We had on skates, and we skated across the ice over the Thatchers' and the Wilsons' lawns past Morell Avenue, where cars, glassed over in clear ice, reflected light from the street lamps. We skated to the Artesian Well and edged onto the frozen water there, which was so clear and smooth you could see fish, orange and yellow and red ones, swimming beneath, as if you were looking through a window pane. Susan skated backward as I held her in my arms. I kissed her on her neck and then on the lips and then open in her mouth. We kept skating like that, in circles, without any muscles aching, not our thighs or arms or backs, without any disruptions, no one on the outskirts threatening us, just a drummer beating a drum slowly to the rhythm of my pulse.

When I woke I heard the slamming of a door, followed by a loud banging, and finally my mother's scream, shrill as a referee's whistle, cutting through the silence.

I bolted from my bed and ran to the hallway. Cindy stood there in her white flannel nightgown, chewing her fingernails. There was another crash, the sound of glass shattering, two quick thumps, and a scream from my mother. I threw open the bedroom door. A lamp lay cracked on the floor, the bald light spilling over the room like a white gash. One end of the curtain rod dangled loose and swung back and forth across the window. The headboard banged against the wall as Marty, straddling my mother in the middle of the bed, flailed his drunken fists against the desperate forearms she raised to protect her face.

For a second I felt a sick nausea rise in my throat, and then my head seemed to fill with fluid. I jumped to the bed, rolled him, and began punching him in the face, windmill style. He raised his hands, and as I hit him on the side of his head and in his mouth and over his arms so quickly he didn't know what was happening, I could see through his laced fingers his eyes squint shut, surprised and scared. Over his left eye was a jagged cut, not deep, just a trickle of blood, probably from my mother's fingernails, running up over his forehead into his scalp. His lips were moving but he wasn't saying anything. My mother crouched beside me on her hands and knees, delirious, frantic, her mascara cutting two black streaks down her cheeks, screaming wildly, "Hurt him, Lee! Kill him!" His hands fell away; his eyes closed. But his face was there, and my mother was screaming, and I could see the whites of her eyes making a full circle around her green irises like a moat, and I could see far into the green like it was rich and thick and textured. It seemed so easy just to raise my arms and clasp my fists and come down with them on his face, which wasn't really a face at all, just something white and red with hair on it. My mother screamed again, "Kill him, Lee!" My fists came down on the bridge of his nose, and it gave easily.

His head bounced twice on the mattress.

Afterwards I began to shake. Cindy screamed and ran from the house in tears, and my mother ran after her. Leaping off the bed, she seemed capable and young.

For a few moments all I could hear was the sound of my own breathing, fast and whistling, and the blood pumping into my head. I knelt beside Marty and placed my hand on his chest to feel his heartbeat. His chest rose and fell. I touched his nose. It was bent to the right and was already starting to swell. His mouth was open, his blood-rimmed teeth and his tongue barely visible. I touched his beard, and it felt almost like water. It was that soft.

I got a washcloth from the bathroom and wiped the blood from his forehead and cheeks and nose, but he didn't wake up. I guessed that he wouldn't come back after this, that I'd probably never see him again.

From the phone in the bedroom, I called the police and peered out the window into the yard, but it was so bright in the room that I could not see very well through the pane, only the faint outlines of my mother and sister huddled beneath our oak tree. Much more clear was the bedroom itself, and it seemed in the reflection transformed into something oddly beautiful. The lightbulb, orange in the window, shone on the room like a stage light. The closet door was open, my mother's blue and green dresses drooping from their hangers like shy, flimsy dancers. On the rumpled sheets, Marty lay, his face propped toward me, disfigured, his eyes closed, his lips curved up in an unconscious smile. In the foreground was my own face — pale and puffy cheeked, blood speckled, stunned in a slack-jawed way that made it seem in that brief moment as if I could really be related to Marty, as if he was really my father and not just my mother's second husband.

Pool Boy

1981

The plane slipped over the mountains and began its descent into Las Vegas, the heat shimmering on the runway like in dreams or movies. Everything far away looked smeary, wavy, even McCarran Airport, which wasn't as big as I'd imagined. When we filed into the connecting metal sleeve, the weather seeped in through the seams, not just hot, but desert hot, about twenty degrees worse than I'd ever felt in my life. I suppose it was the heat that made me feel suddenly uneasy, a warm nausea, as if I was a fugitive, escaping to a place I didn't belong.

A few months earlier I called my father. I hadn't heard from him in almost a year, not since he moved to Las Vegas to start a financing company. I had tried to call him several other times, but his line had been disconnected, so I was startled when he answered.

"Lee? Oh, how are you, boy?"

I told him I was doing well in school and that I'd won a few medals in track meets, and that my little sister had broken her arm a few months ago in gymnastics but was fine now, and that my mother was divorcing Marty, which he, surprisingly, already knew. After a few moments I finally blurted out why I called: "Can I come out there?"

I immediately regretted asking him. I wasn't sure how he would respond and was embarrassed by the desperate sound in my voice. When he and my mother divorced, three and a half years earlier, I asked if I could live with him, but after consulting her, he didn't think it would be such a good idea; he thought she needed me. I never knew for sure if my mother manipulated the situation, or if my father just didn't want me in the way while he tried to make his fortune.

"I don't know," he said on the phone, which seemed the worst answer, so noncommittal. He would say no, but he needed some time to figure out how to let me down gently. "I'll tell you what, hoss," he continued. "I think that's a great idea. I really do. But business is sorta hectic right now. I'll consider it and get back to you. Let me talk to your mother."

My mother was surprised when I told her my father was on the phone. She talked to him on the extension in her bedroom while I waited nervously in the kitchen. After a few minutes she yelled at me to pick up the phone again.

"How would you like to be a pool boy at Caesar's Palace?" my father asked.

"A what?"

"Pool boy!" He explained that a pool boy was someone who brought towels, drinks, and messages to guests at poolside, and that Caesar's Palace, in case I didn't know, was only the most famous casino in the whole goddamned galaxy. He said he had connections and thought he could get me a job. In the meantime

I should get my lifeguard's certificate, and once school was over, he'd fly me out for the summer.

My mother came into the kitchen after I hung up, her face blotchy. I dreaded talking to her. We had not been on good terms since the police carted Marty away after that fight with my mother and him and me all on the bed flailing away at each other, my sister crying nearby. Though Marty was gone and none of us were hurt, I didn't really trust her anymore. I knew she felt I was abandoning her when she needed me most, but I wasn't about to be pulled into anything like that again. I wanted to escape.

"Are you going?" my mother asked.

"It's just for the summer."

She sat on the couch and started to cry, which she usually tried not to do in front of me. "Lee, I told you I was sorry."

"It's not that," I said and put my arm around her shoulders to comfort her, but my heart wasn't in it. I was ready to go, giddy at the prospect of being a pool boy, ecstatic that my father had come through for me when I didn't expect him to.

She dried her eyes on the sleeve of my T-shirt, ran her hands through her blonde hair, then stood up, her back to me. "Just don't tell your father about what happened," she said quietly.

When I didn't answer, she turned around, her eyes at once threatening and pleading.

"I won't," I promised.

It only took me ten Saturdays to get my lifeguarding certificate at the YMCA, and when my junior year finally ended, I watched as my mother waved to me from the huge airport windows, a long sorrowful wave. But as the plane nosed up, the wheels retracting, I suddenly felt like a colorful hot-air balloon rising into the clouds, drifting toward the West, weightless, full of possibility.

When I broke into the windowed light of the Las Vegas terminal, I didn't recognize my father at first. When he was married to my mother, he was overweight from drinking screwdrivers and falling asleep on our orange recliner. He had puffy cheeks then and white bags under his eyes. But the man who suddenly stood in front of me looked like Ichabod Crane, gaunt with pockets in his cheeks and shadows around his eyes. His shoulder blades and the ridges of his ribs poked through his sweaty shirt as we hugged.

"You lost weight," I said as I pulled away. He wore black slacks, black dress shoes, a black silky dress shirt, even black sunglasses. Stupid, I thought, given the heat.

"Forty-five pounds. Been running every morning for the past two years. Running builds your stamina, boy, it builds your stamina." He forced a laugh.

"So does swimming," I said, examining his face for clues. He didn't seem that excited about me being there, or at least not as excited as I wanted him to be.

He shifted uneasily. "Well, things haven't cleared completely, son." He put his fingers together, only a pinch space between. "I'm this close, though. We should have you poolside in no time." He slapped me on the back, a hard slap that stung afterward, then pulled a roll of quarters out of his pocket and handed it to me. "Here you go." He pointed to the slot machines lining the tall glass windows of the airport. "You go win us some money from the one-armed bandits, and I'll wait here for your luggage."

As I stood before the first slot machine I'd ever seen in my life, mindlessly shoving quarters into the thin holes and pulling the heavy chrome handle, I wondered if I'd made a mistake. This seemed like an ominous beginning. My father was nervous and distracted, fidgeting by the silver luggage bins, smoking a cigarette. (I wondered, oddly, if he smoked while he ran.) I was still shocked by the weight he'd lost. He seemed taller now, without the girth, more like a fat piece of taffy that had been stretched lengthwise. He was a stranger to me, not one, under normal circumstances, I would necessarily trust. For a crazy moment I thought I might just get back on the plane and head home. No explanations. Just fly away.

But my luggage — a couple of red and blue duffel bags and my mother's old gray hanging bag — came around, and he picked them up immediately. He flicked his cigarette on the linoleum, stamped it, and we headed out in the brilliant daylight and away in his van.

I assumed that Las Vegas was not like other American cities. While swimming my laps and practicing my lifesaving procedures in Houston, I'd begun to imagine, then expect, glitz, expect that even normal men such as my father lived in plush hotel suites overlooking golf courses, majestic pools, and the neon of the famed Strip. Just like Howard Hughes. (After all, my father did have "connections" at Caesar's Palace.)

So I was surprised and, though I tried to disguise it, disappointed when my father ushered me into a one-bedroom apartment with gold shag carpet, cheap paneling, a red velvet sofa, and a black vinyl chair. Some wicker fans and postcards from West Germany, France, Switzerland, Colombia, Costa Rica, and Brazil were tacked up on the walls. He did have a balcony, but the view was less than spectacular — a carported parking lot, a small pool, and other balconies.

"I'm just biding my time," he said. "I'll be outta here before you can say 'Nigger pickin' cotton.' Lucky I've got you here to help me move and choose new furniture. Ha ha."

He threw my bags in a closet on top of some shoes, then he made a phone call. A few minutes later Abbey, a blackjack dealer who lived downstairs, walked in. She was short and heavy lidded with blonde-gone-gray hair.

She said, "So, you're Neil's kid."

"As far as I know," I said.

She laughed and said to my father, "The kid's got a sense of humor. I like that." She turned back to me. "But I hope you're not a smart-ass."

I tried to figure out whether she was pretty or not. It was hard to tell. What struck me as significant was how much she looked like my mother: same slim build, same color hair, dimples in almost the same places when she smiled. It dawned on me then that the two other girlfriends I'd met also resembled my mother in some distinct way. I wondered if my father was aware of this pattern. Was this just his taste in women, or did he carry the same sad torch for my mother that I believed she still carried for him?

Abbey sniffed and rubbed her nose with the back of her hand. "So what are you going to do with yourself while you're here?" When I told her about Caesar's Palace, she glanced covertly at my father and shook her head. I figured then that the pool boy job had fallen through completely. "I've got to go to the store," she said. "You need anything, Neil?"

"Cigarettes and Sweet 'n' Low."

She turned to me. "Your father's on a diet of nicotine, caffeine, and saccharine. He'll starve you, if you're not careful."

"I'll feed him soon enough, Mommy."

She winked at me. "Good luck." She kissed my father and left.

After he lit up a cigarette, I asked him, point-blank, "Is there a job or isn't there?"

The smoke wisped out of his nostrils. "Well, let me put it to you this way," he said. "There's no opening just this minute. Pool boy is a great job, mind you. Every kid in Vegas — every kid who has a wop uncle or aunt connected to the casinos — wants the job. You understand? These jobs don't grow on trees."

"It doesn't really matter," I said.

"Now wait," he said. He took the cigarette out of his mouth and pointed it at me as if it were an extension of his finger. "I didn't say that the job was out the window completely, did I?" He squinted against the smoke. "It will take some wrangling, that's all. I don't want you to lose confidence in your old pop now. Don't you lose faith, you hear? I'll send you back to Texas lickety-split if you lose faith."

We drove to a McDonald's, where my father stared out the window while I ate. He smoked half a pack of cigarettes and drank four cups of coffee. He looked like a ghoul, his face lost in swirls of smoke. I found myself thinking that he could easily be mistaken for a lost cause, one of those men you try to ignore in elevators and gas stations, but as I polished off my second Big Mac, I decided, for the time being, not to lose faith.

I did spend most of my days poolside. Not Caesar's Palace, of course. The closest I'd been to the Strip since I arrived in Las Vegas was the airport. My father told me that locals didn't spend much time at the casinos, though Abbey worked at Circus Circus, and my father sometimes dressed up in his Johnny Cash getup and went to the Dunes or the Sands hotels for what he called "Adventures in Brokering."

No, I spent the 110-, 115-degree afternoons at the dinky apartment complex pool. My father loaned me his raft, which was good since there wasn't a diving board. I don't think anyone even looked after the place. Burnt weeds sprouted through the cracked cement. A thin line of clear jelly rimmed the tile above the water, and the wire fence surrounding the pool had jagged, violent holes in it, as if somebody had gone berserk with a pair of shears.

At night my father and I would watch television or play Liar's Poker or Canasta or some other game he invented and wanted to teach me. Occasionally Abbey would join us after work. The first few nights, he slept with me, the two of us sharing his double bed, but when I told him I didn't mind if he slept with Abbey, he began spending the nights at her apartment. I'd stay up and watch old Humphrey Bogart and horror movies on cable or listen to the late-night talk shows. The nights were sometimes cool, desert breezes slipping in from the west, and sometimes I'd watch the sun creep up over the mountains — all orange, purple, blue, and silver.

My mother called twice a week to make sure I was doing okay and to let me know she missed me.

Although Abbey and my father took me to a few delis and once to Henderson for a car show and then across the border into Arizona to see the Hoover Dam, those first few weeks were mostly uneventful, the days slipping into each other, my father sitting in a pair of running shorts, his feet propped up on the kitchen table, talking long distance to Costa Rica, Mexico City, and southern California.

According to my mother, my father's enterprises were always dubious. He hadn't paid his taxes in years, companies he'd started went bankrupt, partners had been indicted. My cousin Travis once told me that my father and my Uncle Manny had trucked bootleg oil from the Brownsville-Mexico border to my uncle's gas station in Amarillo. And once, when I was only six, he and some partners had cooked up a crazy scheme to clear-cut most of Costa Rica and start a timber and cattle operation. My parents' second divorce, my mother claimed, was because she feared that my father would go to prison and that she would somehow be connected to his deals and either have to go to prison herself or be held liable for his debts.

From my father's phone calls, however, I could deduce little. He'd smoke cigarette after cigarette. None of his notes looked very important to me, but he sketched cartoon characters — Mickey Mouse, Daffy Duck — and an elaborately detailed drawing of the Taj Mahal while he talked and cackled on the phone.

"You could be an artist," I told him the morning he finished the Taj Mahal, and he said, "But I am. I am. We're all artists in our own way. You just have to find your particular talent and exploit it, son." He took a deep drag off his cigarette and slowly exhaled so that white swirls shrouded his face. "Cultivate it, hone it, prune it, sell it, exploit it."

The fourth week I was there, on a Tuesday morning, my father received a huge package from Bogotá, Colombia. He signed for it and then, without opening it, he ashed three cigarettes in five and a half minutes. I timed him. Then he went downstairs, carrying the bulky package with him, to make a call from Abbey's phone, though there was nothing wrong with his own. When he came back upstairs, he told me he had to go out for a little bit.

A little bit became a lot. I waited all day for him to return, torturing myself by imagining the contents of the package and the gruesome tragedies that might result when my father opened it. The package could be filled with snakes (maybe just the venom) or killer bees (I'd just made my sister watch a movie about them with me). After toying with these wild scenarios, I realized it could actually be something more dangerous, something illegal—poached animal skins, elephant tusks, drugs. Maybe my father wouldn't even be opening the package himself. I considered going down to ask Abbey what she thought, but I didn't want her to know I was worried.

Eight hours later my father burst into the apartment, without the package, toting two bottles of champagne in a brown sack, dancing around, singing "Hound Dog" and "Amazing Grace" in a gaudy voice.

"What's going on?" I asked, laughing because he was and because I was relieved he'd come back.

"You just leave everything to Pops, you hear me. Isn't that what I said? Huh?" He rushed over and wrestled me to the carpet. "Do you wanna be rich? Do you, boy, do you wanna be the son of a king?" he chanted, tickling me so fast and so hard that I couldn't answer. I thought I might wet my pants any second. "Answer me, boy. You wanna be the son of an emperor? Las Vegas Prince? Bring towels to those chickeroos at the hotel? Hell, I'll buy you a casino. You can be pit boss and whorehouse manager, for all I care!"

I didn't think I would ever stop laughing. Tears streamed down my face. My sides ached. The last time I'd seen him this happy was when I was ten years old. He and my mother had been divorced for a year, and then they decided to get back together, to give their marriage another try. At the wedding my sister, though only six, was the maid of honor, and I had the rare privilege of giving my mother away to my father. Afterwards he was manic, swinging my mother around wildly, kissing her passionately and unapologetically, dousing all of us with champagne. At that moment I glimpsed that part of him that was still boyish—pure and hopeful.

On the eve of their second divorce, three years later, my mother went out with some girlfriends, leaving my father with us to say good-bye. We were silent, in a numb trance, nothing to say. My whole body had that dead-weight, stinging feeling that you get when your arm falls asleep. I remember wishing I could see him again like he was on their second wedding day, but I thought I never would.

Until now.

"You got faith in your old pop? Tell me you got faith, and I'll stop."

"I got faith."

"I can't HEAR you," he said.

"I got faith!" I screamed. "I got faith!"

"Are you sure?"

"I'm sure!"

He rose quickly and sang at the top of his lungs the chorus of Buddy Holly's "That'll Be the Day." Just as I was catching my breath, he dropped to the floor, whipped up my shirt, and blew on my belly, making loud fart noises, like he used to do when I was little. Then he jumped up, rushed out the door, and stormed back in, loaded with shoeboxes and plastic sacks.

"Here," he said, throwing me a box and a large sack. "Open them."

There were black leather shoes, my size plus a half, two green and red dress shirts, and matching socks. And Hawaiian print bathing trunks!

"Well," he said, snapping his fingers. "Don't just sit there like a bump on a log. Get ready. It's about time you saw the Strip!"

While I showered I thought about what this could mean for me. Had my father really come through? Sure, all I'd seen so far were some new clothes and champagne, but who knew what else was in store? Las Vegas was turning out to be a paradise for me, an oasis in the middle of my desert of a life in Houston, and as I dismissed all thoughts of my father's dealings being less than honorable, I also dismissed any intentions I'd had of ever returning home.

After I put on my new dress slacks and red shirt, my father and I picked up Abbey and drove to the Strip. I sat in the front passenger seat so I could see everything. It wasn't dark yet, so it didn't look that impressive at first, although everything seemed new and large and windowed. My father took me from one end, near the airport, to the other shabby end, where there were dozens of little motels and wedding chapels on each corner. Then he circled back toward the newly rebuilt MGM Grand, the largest hotel in the world, he said. Thousands of people roamed the blackjack, craps, and roulette tables. When I went to the bathroom, a black man in a tuxedo offered me cologne and a shoeshine.

We went into a spacious room with red drapes, hundred-foot paintings, and no clocks. My father plucked a rubber-banded wad of bills from his pocket and slipped the maître d' a twenty. In the middle of the room was a buffet as long as a football field. I'd been sustaining myself at my father's house on rainbow sherbet, pineapples, and taco salads, but that night I gorged myself on prime rib, lamb, roasted brisket, duck, and several desserts. I couldn't stop. I ate twice what my father and Abbey ate.

Abbey said, "I told you, Neil. You've been starving him."

Outside, the Strip was brighter than the daylight, though it was dark in the rest of Las Vegas. We walked a long way, past the Barbary Coast, where we stared at a million dollars encased in high-security glass. My father thought it was the greatest thing in the world, and I suppose it was, except the bills didn't look real enough, spread out in ten-foot paper sheets, with red, white, and blue chaser lights framing the case. A bored guard was perched on a stool beside the case, eating a huge pastry.

We circled back to the Desert Inn and took the elevator to the lounge at the top, where a blue eye-shadowed hypnotist convinced my father, Abbey, and thirteen other volunteers to sing "God Bless America" as they held hands and swayed in a circle, and where one woman took off her bra and twirled it above her head like a lasso.

At the Imperial Palace we watched one hundred high-stepping showgirls, wearing gold tassels on their nipples, purple-glittered G-strings, and high-feathered headdresses. Their tassels moved in two hundred synchronized circles, and the glitter from their pelvises reflected off the glasses at our table. Midway through the show my father wiped imaginary drool off my chin with his napkin.

Finally they took me to Caesar's Palace, an enormously beautiful fortress bathed in green lights, gold and red and blue-green fountains rising a mile in the air like Texas gushers. My father spoke to a Keno girl, then we made our way, me in a half-hazy tingle, through the casinos and the lounges, under the chandeliers, past the white marble urns and cherubs and naked gods and goddesses, to one of the pools outside, where my father pointed out the pool boys. They were all older than me, maybe twenty, wearing Hawaiian trunks and white Caesar's T-shirts, laughing raunchily at the bar with a pretty red-headed bartender.

My father ordered cocktails for all of us, then on a napkin he drew a picture for us of an underground house he'd seen in a magazine. I stared at Abbey. Her expression was both wary and incredulous, like she had listened to his promises and schemes before and wasn't sure whether or not to take him seriously this time. I felt strange watching her, partly because she seemed sexy in her fancy blackjack dealer dress. After gulping down my drink, I went to the pool and lay down beside it. The bottom was clear, deep, clean, and brilliantly lighted. I lay there, half-drunk, and studied my reflection in the water cast against the reflections of the stars and the marbled pillars behind me, until Abbey bent down and splashed some water in my face, then pulled me up and kissed me full on the mouth.

"You're all right, kid," she said.

My father laughed. "Be careful," he said. "You don't want to overstimulate his hormones." She flicked water at him as he continued to cackle.

As soon as we went inside, two men, one wearing a three-piece blue suit, the other a sports jacket, beckoned to my father. My father didn't introduce us; instead, he said he would catch up with us in the casino. When I looked back at them, they were arguing in hushed tones against a wall and the shorter, stockier of the two thumped my father hard in the chest. I thought suddenly about the mysterious package, about the phone calls, the champagne, even my clothes. Were these men on the other end of all those calls? Did these men have the package? Then I realized that maybe I needed to help my father, but Abbey, reading my mind, pulled me over to a row of quarter slots.

"Who were they?" I asked when my father rejoined us, laughing as if nothing had happened.

"Just some amigos," he said lightly, then grabbed me in a playful headlock. "Abbey, let's show this boy what a lucky sonuvabitch he has for a father."

In three rolls at a craps table, he won two hundred dollars, and we left Caesar's Palace singing "Happy Trails." Then he pulled me up on the ledge of the biggest fountain, and we leaned over, almost falling in, and let the water spray our faces and clothes and douse his cigarette. As we made our way back to the MGM Grand, Abbey walked ahead of us, suddenly closed mouthed, a little upset it seemed. But my father was unfazed. She drove us home, then headed back to work, and my father and I drank the other bottle of champagne.

While I got ready for bed, he made a telephone call from the other room. Then he opened the door quietly, as if he was afraid he'd wake me. "Did you have a good time tonight?"

"You bet!" I said. Yet, despite all the excitement, I had some misgivings. By now all the champagne and food were cramping my stomach. I still wondered about the men who hassled my father at Caesar's Palace and about Abbey, who was still perturbed when she dropped us off.

"*Muy bueno*," my father said, "*muy bueno!*"

He sat on the edge of the bed, lit up a cigarette, then smiled at the ceiling. I couldn't see anything up there, except a brown water spot. He blew out a couple of smoke rings.

"You have a girlfriend in Houston?"

"No, not really," I said. I'd gone out on a few dates and had a frustrating, two-year crush on Susan Gloyna, but nothing serious enough to keep me there.

"When I was your age, I was hornier than a toad." He slapped the covers where my leg was and leaned forward. "But you got it right, boy. No sense in getting lashed to the mast, tied to a lot of responsibilities before you even know what in the hell you want from life." The smoke from his cigarette snaked up beside his face. "Let me tell you, it takes time to figure out the difference between your asshole and a hole in the ground. I know from experience."

He cackled, and I smiled back at him. Then he just sat there a few minutes, thinking, and I wondered how drunk he was. "So, why'd your mother and Marty split up?"

This was the first time he'd asked for any details about my mother's marriage, but now I figured, from the false casual tone of his question, that he'd been thinking about it a lot. I wanted to tell him how she'd pulled me into the middle of their fights, and how that last night she had screamed for me to kill Marty when I found him drunkenly hitting her. And how I had been the hero, broken his nose, but didn't feel like a hero at all, but rather sick and sad and somehow implicated. It seemed much too complex. Besides, I had promised my mother I wouldn't say anything, and that promise still seemed important.

"They just didn't get along," I said.

"He was younger than her, wasn't he?"

"Yes," I said.

He nodded as if that explained things. Then, sensing my reluctance to elaborate, he said, "Me and your mother came to Vegas on our honeymoon. Did she ever tell you that story?"

"No," I said.

"I was barely twenty-one, and shit, your mother was still only a girl. I was so excited about being here, and being married, I could've crapped my pants. I lost all the money we had that first night at the MGM. The old one, before the fire. Five hundred dollars her father gave us. It was a lot then. All we had." He took another slow drag off his cigarette and grinned. "Your mother was so goddamned furious. We left that night because we didn't have any more money. And she didn't talk to me for two weeks. Not an auspicious beginning to a marriage, huh?"

"I guess not," I said, not quite sure what "auspicious" meant.

"One of many mistakes," he continued. "But that's water under the bridge, as they say. Your mother's a good woman. They broke the mold with her. Remember that."

He lit another cigarette and smoked it in silence. His smoke rings jiggled up between us and dissolved. I closed my eyes, sleepy now and somehow comforted by my father's calmer mood, his memories of my mother and their life together.

"Do you like the school you're going to?" he asked me.

"It's all right."

"They got a pretty good high school right around the corner. Supposed to be one of the best in the nation. Pretty good university here too. UNLV."

"They've got a good basketball team," I offered.

"Helluva good basketball team," he said. "Helluva good team." He ran his free hand through the back of his hair and twisted it into knots. My mother swore she could hear him doing that from another room. I listened but didn't hear a sound except for the air conditioning unit outside the window. "You planning to go to college?"

I hadn't given it much thought. Neither of my parents had been to college, and though I did well in school, I'd always been a little bored. But it didn't seem like such a bad idea now. If it meant being here with him on nights like this, then I certainly wasn't opposed to it. I imagined myself living with him, both of us starting out fresh, moving into an underground house, daily trips to the Strip, me at Caesar's, poolside in my own white T-shirt, laughing with pretty blonde bartenders.

"Well, college isn't everything," my father said before I could answer his question. "You don't see many pointy-headed professors driving Mercedes, now do you?" He slapped his knee and stood up, then leaned over as if to kiss me, but wiped my chin instead. "Oops," he said. "You must still be thinking about those titty-tasseled showgirls. Or that million dollars you saw tonight!"

He turned out the light and shut the door. Falling asleep, I heard him in the other room, singing in a soft, twangy voice that sounded like the old folk records I remembered him playing before he and my mother broke up:

> Good night, Irene.
> Good night, Irene.
> I'll see you in my dreams.

I woke up at one o'clock the next afternoon. On the kitchen table, next to a legal pad with some numbers and names and two elaborate drawings of Caesar's Palace, was a note from my father. He said he'd be gone for the day and that I should "keep Abbey company." He had clipped two crisp one hundred-dollar bills to the note — "For groceries, etc."

I had barely dressed when the two men I'd seen at Caesar's Palace showed up at the door. I got a better look at them this time. One was much taller than the other and had a more intelligent face, a broad forehead and round, marbled eyes. The shorter one was stocky, with a harelipped grin and squinty eyes, which looked like raisins planted in the middle of his doughy face. They were both dressed in suits, but the suit seemed wrong, unnatural, on the shorter man.

"Is Neil here?" the taller one asked.

The stocky man tried to look beyond me into the living room, but I didn't move. Except for Abbey, nobody had ever come to visit my father, and I didn't think he'd let these men in, even though I'd seen him speak to them the night before.

"He won't be back for a while," I said. "I could take a message, if you'd like."

The short man turned to the tall one, and they looked at each other as if they were deciding something without actually speaking. Smiling, the tall man said, "You must be Lee."

"Yeah?"

"You planning to go to school in Las Vegas next year?"

"I don't know."

"There's a fine high school around the corner," he said. "I have a nephew who goes there."

"You play baseball?" the stocky one asked.

"Not really," I said.

"Huh." He tried to look beyond me again. "Too bad. They got a good team."

The tall man said politely, "Would you tell your father that Mr. Travolina and Mr. Watson came by? Please ask him to give us a call as soon as possible."

"Do you want me to take a phone number?"

"He has it," the stocky man said.

"As soon as possible," the tall man said again.

"I will."

"Thank you," he said and shook my hand. They drove off in a blue Pontiac.

I hadn't snooped around my father's apartment much, not even during all those nights he spent with Abbey. But now, though careful, I studied the notes on the kitchen table, rifled through his stash of used legal pads in a dresser drawer, inspected the top shelf of his closet, even looked under the bed. I didn't discover what I hoped to find: a secret notebook with Mr. Travolina's and Mr. Watson's phone numbers and job descriptions and dramatic details about my father's involvement with them and some clue as to the contents of the package from Colombia. Instead, as I explored every bit of that small, tacky apartment, I discovered that there was not one photograph, not even a snapshot or a school portrait, of my sister or of me. No trace of his life growing up in Oklahoma, or later with my mother and us before he moved to Las Vegas. I had never really wondered about this before, but now the absence of any evidence of his previous life stunned me. I went out on the hot balcony, listened to the traffic on the street nearby, and looked absently down on the sad little pool below, and it dawned on me that maybe my father, like me, had come to Las Vegas to escape.

I ate dinner with Abbey. She seemed hung over from the night before and still upset for some reason, but we went to a good Chinese place with the money my father left me, and once we ate, she felt better. All through dinner I kept thinking about the night before when she'd splashed water on my face and kissed me. She seemed prettier now.

Later that evening we sat at her dining room table, and she explained the different strategies she'd seen blackjack players use and the house rules she had to follow.

"Do you love my father?" I asked her.

"Yes," she answered, as if my question was the most natural extension of our conversation.

"Are you gonna marry him?"

"I doubt it," she said in the same matter-of-fact tone.

"Why not?"

My father's interest in my mother and his story about their first honeymoon, as sad as it was, had started me dreaming again about them getting back together, a dream I'd not put much faith in for a long time. Going through his things in the apartment, though, had doused that hope. I liked Abbey a lot, and if he was going to remarry, she seemed a better candidate than most.

"I'm not sure I can explain it," she said. "For starters, I don't think he's trying to strike it rich so he can marry a blackjack dealer." She sipped her soft drink. "Besides, your father lives too dangerously."

"What do you mean?" I asked.

She shook her head. "Look, no one should know too much about their parents. It only complicates things." She stood up, anxious for me to leave. "Off with you now. I've got to get to work."

She kissed me on the cheek, and I was disappointed that it wasn't on the mouth, like before. She shooed me out the door before I could ask more questions.

I was restless, so I went to the pool, ran my fingers over the sheared part of the fence, and carefully pulled all the prickles out of a cactus so that it looked pocked. Trying to recall everything that had happened in the last two days, particularly the night before on the Strip, I wished that I hadn't drunk anything so that I could remember more vividly. After Abbey left for work, I lay down on the still-warm cement, made circles in the dark water with my feet, and counted out the seconds until the pool light flipped on, at exactly nine-thirty, as usual.

On my way back upstairs, I noticed the blue Pontiac in the parking lot. My pulse quickened. I pretended I didn't see, went upstairs, bolted the door, shut the curtains, turned off the lights, and peeked out the window. The two men who had come by earlier were sitting in the car, eating sandwiches. I thought about calling the police, but I didn't know if my father would want me to, so I decided against it.

I sat by the window and waited.

About two in the morning I heard the familiar hum of my father's van. He pulled into his space, shut off the motor, and got out. He didn't seem to notice the Pontiac. He started toward the apartment, and the two men got out. I wondered if I should open the window and warn him, but when my father saw them, he walked toward them, friendly, then suddenly turned and ran toward the apartment. The two men chased him, the stocky, mean-eyed one carrying a bat, the taller one running behind. I ran to the door, fumbled with the lock for a moment, then stepped out onto the balcony. My father was inside the fenced-in area of the pool, the two men circling him.

"Get inside!" my father shouted when he saw me, and just as he did, the stocky man pinned him against the sheared fence and swung the bat hard against my father's right leg. I heard it hit, a loud thunk. My father yelled, a quick, incredibly painful cry, and I thought I would be sick. The man with the bat reared back again, and I was sure he was going to bring it down on my father's head.

"No!" I screamed, bolting down the steps barefoot. I didn't know if he had been hit again, but when I got close enough, I saw my father crumpled on the cement, clutching his leg.

"Go back inside," the taller man said.

"Do what he says, son," my father said hoarsely.

I didn't move. The short man said, "Goddamnit," dropped the bat, grabbed my father by his hair and the back of his slacks, dragged him over to the pool, and pitched him in. My father began to sink.

"Drown, you son of a bitch!" the short man said and spat into the water. Then they walked away, right past me, the short man brushing my shoulder with his.

The taller man stopped for a second and looked down at me. "Sorry you had to see this," he said, shook his head, then left.

My father wasn't coming up, so I ran to the pool, afraid he was unconscious, dove in, and swam to the bottom, where he lay.

The pool light cast blue shadows across his face, and his black hair wriggled above his head. His dark shirt billowed out so that he seemed, miraculously, to have regained all of the weight he'd lost. His eyes were wide open, and I thought for sure he was dead, the bubbles coming out of his nose a mere illusion, his last breaths. But then he blinked slowly a couple of times, involuntarily, as if I wasn't even there. When I grabbed for him, he resisted, shook his head and tried to push me away, but he was weak, and I easily strapped my arm across his body in the lifesaving procedure I'd learned and swam to the steps at the other end of the pool. He sputtered for a couple of seconds, then just lay there, his damaged leg floating in the water. Limp in my arms, he stared up at the desert sky, his eyes hollow, empty. I knew it wasn't from the pain in his leg. My father had lost faith.

The next few hours turned into a series of logistical maneuvers. My father refused to let me call either the police or an ambulance. At first, he could hobble on his good leg, so we made it to his van, where with great difficulty I lodged him in the back and then listened carefully to his confusing directions to the nearest hospital.

By the time we reached the emergency room, he couldn't move his leg at all, and I had to ask some orderlies to bring him in on a stretcher. As I walked by his side, he squeezed my hand so hard I thought he'd break my fingers, and I wondered if this accident would be the end of my father's skinny days. He'd never be able to run again, I was sure. I pictured him expanding to the size he was when he was married to my mother, to the size he was underwater, and thought for a crazy moment that if he gained his weight back, then he would be restored to our family, that what he'd shed was not only forty-five pounds but also his history, me and my sister and my mother, and that by some act of poetic justice, this event would bring him back, fat and ours.

But even then I knew better. He and my mother were not the same people they were when they were married. This idea of not being who you set out to be or even who you think you are startled me then, made me wonder if I had any inkling who I was, if in twenty years I would look back on this time and not recognize myself or, worse, not care. If, like a snake, or some molting insect, I would outgrow this person and become someone different.

Just before the orderlies wheeled him into a room, my father sent me to his van to retrieve a briefcase hidden under the passenger seat. I found it, and would have opened it, sure it held some answers to my unspoken questions, but it had a combination lock.

A few hours later my father seemed to be his old self. After the doctors finished setting his leg, he spent the rest of the morning on the phone in his hospital room. First, he called Abbey at work to explain, in minimal detail, that he'd had an accident, broken his leg, nothing to worry about, but he needed her to bring us some clothes, he'd explain later. Then he called my mother and told her that he had a lot of unexpected traveling to do, so, unfortunately, I wouldn't be able to stay in Las Vegas. Everything was fine, he said, nothing to be concerned about, just some business, but he'd make plane arrangements and call her back. He didn't offer to let me talk to her, just quickly hung up and, as he flipped through The Yellow Pages, told me she was very excited about my coming home.

The next hour he spent dickering with travel agents. He was intent on my leaving as soon as possible, but in absurd contrast to his lavish behavior two nights before, he was outraged at the ticket prices. Every few minutes he would look at me with his hand muffling the receiver and, in scowling asides, complain about the thievery of the airline industry, as if he'd actually consulted me about any of these plans. Finally, to get the price lowered, he explained to one of the airline supervisors, in compelling and mournful detail, that his son's mother was deathly ill and he had to get back to her "before it was too late." He held up his thumb and index finger and slowly closed the pinch space as he closed the deal.

"You look exhausted," he said as he hung up, though he was the one in bed, pale and gaunt, his leg lifted in a traction cast. "Why don't you go get yourself some breakfast."

I went down to the hospital deli and, even though I wasn't very hungry, ate some eggs and an English muffin while I stared out the window at the quickly forming rain clouds. It struck me that in the whole time I'd been in Las Vegas, it hadn't rained once.

When I returned, Abbey was listening to my father argue with a doctor who wanted to put a screw and two pins in his kneecap.

"Guess you don't want to walk again," the doctor said and then started out the door.

"Goddamn doctors," my father said, mostly for our benefit. "I'll be damned if they're going to put hardware in my leg."

"It might not be bad to have something stronger than bone in there for the next time," Abbey said.

My father scowled at her. "There isn't going to be a next time."

"I gotta go," she said and turned to me. "Want to walk me out?" The rain had started to fall, so we said good-bye in the foyer of the hospital. "Not fair, is it," she said, more a statement than a question.

"What are you going to do?" I asked.

"I don't have to do anything, except get back to work."

We hugged awkwardly and she kissed my cheek.

"I'll see you," I said.

"You bet," she answered lightly, but I didn't hold out much hope. She loved my father, but I knew she wouldn't stay with him. That seemed the saddest part, somehow. It was the same with Marty. You never see these people again. They just wander into your life for a moment and then they're gone, and after a while it's as if they never existed. My father's old girlfriend. My mother's second husband. Nothing more binding than that, no matter how much you hate them or like them.

But, for better or for worse, you're stuck with your family.

"I guess all this doesn't look too good from your perspective," my father said when I came back into the room. "It isn't what it seems, though."

I hoped that he wouldn't try to explain himself. That would only embarrass us both at this point. Besides, I'd rather not know than wonder forever if what he told me was a lie.

"You gotta trust me here, son," he said. "I wouldn't hurt anybody." I nodded, though I wasn't sure at what. Was he talking about those men, Abbey, me? It seemed he was the one who had been hurt. "I'll get you back out here next summer. You just have faith in your old pop."

He pulled his briefcase off the nightstand, unlocked it, took out an envelope with my name on it, and handed it to me. There was a wad of fifty-dollar bills inside.

"Your allowance," he said and winked. "Put it in a safe place." I folded the envelope and placed it carefully in my back pocket, then leaned over and hugged him. When I started to pull away, he held me there a few seconds longer. "Do me a favor. Don't tell your mother about this," he said, and I had the feeling that my trip had come full circle.

That afternoon I packed my suitcases. My father, who was still at the hospital, told me to take one of his to accommodate the clothes he'd bought me, but it was still a tight fit. I was surprised at how much I'd accumulated in the few weeks I'd been there. After I zipped up my bags, I sifted through his sketches and started to take the one of Caesar's Palace but at the last moment decided on the elaborate drawing of the Taj Mahal that he'd done the first week I was there. I also found the napkin sketch of the underground house and slipped both between the pages of a book I was reading, so they wouldn't get crinkled.

In the evening it was still raining, but I drove my father's van down past the Desert Inn and the Silver Slipper and Caesar's. Only a few people were out, running across the streets, covering their heads with newspapers, stepping in as many puddles as they tried to avoid. The Strip just didn't look as good as it had before. I tried to convince myself that it was because of the rain.

That night I dreamed I wasn't able to save my father. The little pool outside his apartment kept getting deeper and deeper, he kept sinking faster and faster, and I turned back before I reached him. I woke up sweating, afraid the dream would return if I fell back asleep.

I sat on the balcony and waited for the rain to stop, but there were still dark clouds until dawn, so dark I couldn't even make out the stars or the moon. When the sun shone silver along the edge of the mountains, it burned off the clouds, and the sky finally cleared. By the time my cab reached the airport, the sun had lifted high above the mountains. It was going to be a scorcher, I could tell, well over a hundred degrees. As hot as the day I'd arrived.

A few months later, right after Thanksgiving, Abbey called to tell us that my father had died in an accident. His van had gone over an embankment, near the California border, tearing through the guardrail and toppling a couple of hundred feet before landing in a rocky ravine. The impact drove the steering wheel practically through his body, and the gashes on his face and limbs were so terrible that he was, she said, unrecognizable. The coroner said he must have died instantly. There were no witnesses. Just the mangled van, my father's body, and the torn guardrail. The police suspected it was not an accident. They knew my father was on the fringe of organized crime in Las Vegas, but no evidence could be found to link that association with his death. Not long after, the police officially closed the case.

The dream I had that last night in Las Vegas returned to me then, more vivid and painful, and continues to haunt me now, except that now in the dream I do reach him. His eyes are open, and I can tell from the expression on his face, a sly grin edging up at the corners, that he wants me to stay down with him. I try to explain that we must go up, but the water garbles my words, turns them to bubbles. I wrap my arm around him, but he mistakes my efforts for an embrace. And as I struggle both to save him and to wake up, he pulls me tightly to him, his grip surprisingly strong — and loving.

IV Penance

Penance

1990

My sister, Gloria, said I needed to get out, try being a real person again, so she'd dragged me to this party with friends of hers one Sunday afternoon. "I don't want to go," I told her. I didn't want to be around people. I wasn't ready. I felt like I was about to be implicated in something that I would have no control over. I'd been in Amarillo only a couple of months, holed up in Gloria's house, sleeping, reading, walking, driving, hoping the phone wouldn't ring, hoping no letters would come. Sleeping some more. I didn't want anybody — not my brothers, not my son or daughter, definitely not Cooper — to know where I was. I finally agreed to go out, but only as long as we were with strangers. So she brought me to this barbecue, and I *didn't* know anybody, so I started to relax. I drank only ginger ale. And I sat in the corner of the garden and watched and listened, managing to eavesdrop on conversations without being pulled into any. People spoke of their children and grandchildren, of college, of the quality of local schools, of property taxes and city council proposals, of the pros and cons of the new prison being built in town. Normal life. Implicit in their conversation was their happiness, a contentedness that was palpable and light and enjoyable to be around, like sitting on a pile of feathers. I didn't resent them. For the first time in a long time, I felt good.

Then this man walked over. He looked older than me, maybe fifty. He wasn't handsome really, though interesting — tall and wiry, with deeply tanned skin and ropy muscles in his arms and neck, and a small tattoo on his forearm that said U.S. Navy. He had a thick salt-and-pepper mustache and gray hair, pulled back in a shoulder-length ponytail, which might have looked silly on another man his age but seemed right for him, not just something he did to be stylish. He wore a nice white cotton shirt, khakis, tennis shoes and no socks, and a bronze-plated bolo tie with a bright turquoise question mark in the middle of it. He had on dark sunglasses, so I couldn't see his eyes.

"Mind if I sit down?"

"Go ahead."

He pressed out the crease of his pants in a smooth, efficient stroke, relaxed down into the lounger on the patio, leaned back and gazed past the garden to the long, summery Panhandle plains, which we could see from where we were sitting. Neither of us said a word for about five minutes, which was both comforting and unsettling.

Then he took a drink and asked, "Do you know why Texas doesn't fall into the Gulf of Mexico?"

"What?"

"Do you know why Texas doesn't fall into the Gulf of Mexico?"

"No."

"Because Oklahoma sucks."

I smiled. My first husband, Neil, was from Oklahoma and

would've appreciated that joke. "Are you from Oklahoma?" I asked.

"Born in Tulsa, but I moved here when I was a little kid."

"You been here ever since?"

"Nope. Been all over, but I lived in Tucson for nearly twenty years. Just moved back here a year ago."

"Why?"

"Ha! Good question. Business. Plus my mother's getting old. And it was time for a change." I nodded. "What about you?" he asked.

I didn't want to get into it. "Tell me about Tucson," I said.

That got him going. He told me how it was founded, who were the first settlers, how the Indians were eventually moved out to the edges of town, then to the reservations, blah, blah, blah. It was a history lesson, but not too boring, and better than me talking, particularly about myself. He went on for about fifteen minutes straight, then stopped abruptly. "Is that your real hair?" he asked.

I'd been wearing a wig for about fourteen years, ever since Neil and I divorced for the second and last time, back in 1976. My own hair was thin and wispy, old biddyish. I hated it—though my children always preferred it to my wigs, and so did Gloria. They had a right to say something. This guy didn't. I thought, *What a bastard.* I didn't like the way his lip curled up under his mustache. That pissed me off.

"It's none of your business," I said. It was a lame comeback, but he caught me off guard. I'd zoned out during the history lesson.

"Well, it just looks fake," he said, fingering his mustache. "I think you'd look better without it. You're a pretty-enough woman. There's no need to conceal anything."

I got flustered, and by this time other people at the party were looking over. "I'll take it under advisement," I said and stood up.

"What are you trying to hide?" he asked, smiling conspiratorially.

"Well, if you have to know," I said, staring at him hard and cold, and pausing for effect, "it's the chemo and radiation." His face flattened out, and his mouth opened a little, as if I'd punched him in the nose. Before he could say anything else, I walked away, found Gloria inside, and told her I was ready to go.

"What's your hurry?" she said. "Did Tom upset you? Don't let him get to you. He's a joker."

The man — Tom — came over, serious faced. "I'm sorry," he said sincerely.

"What'd you do?" Gloria asked.

"I didn't mean to offend you." He took his sunglasses off. He had nice eyes, soft with wrinkles around the edges. He looked penitent. "You didn't seem to be really listening, so I thought I'd do something to surprise you." He sighed. "I'm a jackass."

"What did you *do* to my little sister?" Gloria asked again, more concerned.

"He asked me about my hair," I said.

"Huh?" she said, a puzzled look on her face. "What about it?"

"He wanted to know why I wear the wig. So I told him."

"I'm sorry," he said again. "I was way out of bounds."

"I don't get it," Gloria said.

"You know. The chemo. The hair in the sink. The cue ball under this wig."

Gloria smiled. "Oh, you told him. Oh, well, that's good, Laura. That's really good."

"I really don't know what to say," he said. "I'm an idiot."

"It doesn't really matter," I said. "I only have a couple of weeks left anyway."

Gloria couldn't contain herself. She burst out laughing. Tom looked like he'd been punched in the nose yet again.

"You've been had, buddy," she said and hooked her arm in mine.

"You mean . . ."

"Gotcha," I said, then smiled and left.

Gloria laughed the whole way home. "You're making jokes. You're flirting," she said. "This is a good sign. Maybe you can return to the land of the living."

Gloria understood about returning from the dead. Her husband and oldest son had died in a car accident a dozen years ago, and then her daughter had lost a baby on the same night she received the settlement from the insurance company. For a while she felt guilty about the money, and that seemed to drive a wedge between her and her youngest son, Travis. But in the last few years, she'd returned to her old self, or rather she had retained her old self but had also transformed into someone else, someone better, wiser. She seemed illuminated. She didn't have to work now because of the settlement money, so she'd gone back to school, earned her GED then her bachelor's degree, and was now working on a master's in art therapy and volunteering her time at the homeless shelter, the YMCA, and a women's shelter. I had always looked up to her. More than any of us kids, she had turned out the best. Maybe it was because she was older when my mother disappeared. Gloria already had a life, was already fully formed, so the hole that was left was not as large or as empty for her. Manny, my older brother, was the successful one in the family, but he'd gone bankrupt once, been divorced, and though he had supported most of us at one time or another, there was always something distant and lonely about him, like my father. My younger brothers, Gene and Rich, had always seemed like children to me, though in many ways they were no different than me — all of us trying, like our mother, to escape our lives. Unsuccessfully.

At any rate, I admired and loved Gloria, and whenever I got too down on my luck, I'd come stay with her for a while until I got my bearings straight.

Tom was a good man, she said, or as good as they come nowadays. A Catholic. Separated, though not divorced, from his wife eight years ago. Two kids, one of them in college in Colorado. Tom's mother lived in town, and he visited her a lot. He owned a business, Auto Buddy, like Triple-A rescue. He sold wholesale memberships to car dealerships. The car dealer then sold his cars with the Auto Buddy package. If your car broke down or had a flat, or if you locked your keys inside, you called Tom and he came out and towed you, or got your keys out of your car, or fixed your tire, whatever — twenty-four hours a day. He'd made a small fortune with this business.

"Enough to gamble with. His one vice," Gloria said. "He'd be a good catch, Laura."

Gloria had always been the matchmaker in the family. In fact, she had set me up with Cooper.

"I've caught my fair share already, don't you think?" I asked, a genuine question, since there had been one man or another in my life almost constantly from the time I began high school, and I'd already been married four times.

Gloria raised one eyebrow and said sharply, "Carp don't count."

About a week later I got a note in the mail along with a blue carnation. It said, "I hear you're looking for a job. Can you cook? Tom O'Connor." I liked the note. It was simple. To the point. No fancy bull. I'd been away from Cooper for a while now, and though we'd ruined ourselves for three years, screwing whoever we wished, trying to kill each other's spirit in methodical, insidious ways, I was getting lonely.

Plus, I needed the money. Since leaving Cooper, I'd rarely left Gloria's house. I'd applied for a few jobs, executive secretarial work mainly, but no luck. And I didn't want to work for Manny again. He seemed to think I brought bad luck on myself.

So I went to work for Tom. It was a good arrangement. I catered his poker parties twice a week. I'd been the caterer for Manny and for a restaurant in Houston years before, so the job was easy. He paid me two hundred dollars each time, and this was poker money, so all in cash. I did a wonderful job. Made extravagant meals. Pork bellies, steaks, spaghetti and lasagna with nine different types of cheese, Mexican banquets, exotic Greek dishes, cheesecake. I treated them like kings.

And I liked Tom. He was a neat and efficient man, self-disciplined from years in the navy. He was also intelligent in odd ways. He knew a lot about history, as I'd already figured out from the first meeting. But not just Tucson history. He would monologue about European kings and civil wars, or about the Japanese who stayed in the internment camps in California during World War II, even the Italian and Irish and Polish immigrants in New York. And he liked to tell jokes, often crude, but usually good spirited.

One day, a couple of months after I started working for him, he asked if I would go with him to visit his mother and then out to eat afterward. She lived downtown, not far from the railroad yards in a small old house that Tom said he'd lived in when he was a boy. It was surprisingly light inside the house, a cozy three-bedroom place, with flowers and pictures all over the walls. It smelled yeasty, like someone had been cooking bread. It was very different from where I had grown up, yet seemed the embodiment of the word *home*.

Tom's mother was a frail woman, close to eighty, planted in her bed. She had a slight palsy, but her face was remarkably free of wrinkles for a woman her age, and her hair was almost reddish brown and thick, like a young woman's. She didn't have her glasses on at first, but she put them on when she heard Tom's voice.

"Is she the one?" his mother asked when she saw me.

Tom blushed and laughed uncomfortably. "Yes, Mama, this is my friend, Laura."

"Hello, ma'am," I said and smiled. Despite her appearance, when I shook her hand, her grip was surprisingly strong and warm. She put her other hand on top of mine and held it there for a minute, not letting go, and I felt that she was trying to gauge me from my touch, figure me out.

I helped Tom fix a plate of food for her, and then we sat with her while she ate, and Tom asked questions about the nurse who visited her twice a day and about her friends. He told her some new jokes that he always seemed to have a fresh supply of, including some dirty ones, which she appreciated, and then later he helped her to the bathroom and got her ready for bed while I looked at the pictures around the house. There were photos of Tom and his brothers and sisters, a family as big as mine, when they were young, and several of Tom as a boy, then as a young man in the navy with his crew cut, smiling. He seemed so young and naive, more exposed and fragile as a young man with his life ahead of him. The photo reminded me in this way of how Neil was when we first met. There was a kind of pleasant ignorance, surrounded by another shell of intelligence and something harder, more cynical.

There were pictures of all the wives and grandchildren. I found a picture of Tom and his wife and their two boys, the older boy with his arm in a sling. They were all smiling, of course, but I could sense some sadness in them all — a hidden loneliness and frustration. Or perhaps that's just the way pictures are. If you know the people are destined to part, then you can see the seeds of that future in the snapshot from the past. You know what you're looking for. His wife was a tall, thin woman, with a vulnerability around her mouth that made her seem as if she might be timid or afraid of life.

I wondered what it was that Tom saw in me. Was I her opposite, or did I exude a vulnerability and timidity that attracted him to me, some connection like the one I could see between him and Neil?

Once she was back in bed, I went over and told her it was a pleasure to meet her.

"Be good to my Tommy," she said, and I wondered if the old woman knew who she was talking to, if the fifty-year-old man with the wrinkles around his eyes and the gray ponytail who was sitting beside her was again her little boy, her little Tommy.

I nodded and said, "Good-bye, Mrs. O'Connor."

Then Tom said, "I'll see you Friday, Mama," and kissed her, and it was at that moment, with the gentleness of his lips on his mother's old cheek, that I thought there could be something substantial between him and me. And I also think I knew even then that his mother's words, "Be good to my Tommy," would haunt me.

We went to Manny's restaurant, Steak 'n' Taters, and ordered some barbecue ribs. Manny came out, wearing a greasy apron and cleaning his hands with a wet rag. I introduced him to Tom, and they shook hands, and then we chatted for a few minutes.

"How's Gene?" I asked. Gloria said he'd gotten down on himself after he and his second wife divorced, and went into a minor tailspin, getting laid off from Santa Fe Railroad.

"I haven't seen him," Manny said, and I could tell there was something else there, but he didn't want to go into it. "He stopped working for me a while ago."

One of the cooks came out and called him back to the kitchen.

"Busy," he said. "Good to see you again. I'd hug you, but don't want to grease you up."

"That's okay."

He shook hands with Tom again and said to me, seriously, "Take care of yourself, Laura." Then he leaned over and kissed me.

"Will do," I said, and he left.

Tom and I ordered. Then we drank a couple of beers and started laughing, and he told me some funny story about a couple he knew who raised ostriches out near Palo Duro Canyon, and I wasn't really listening, just coasting on the good time, and the beer, which I'd not had in a while, like it was a flying carpet.

"You're a good son," I said.

"She's a good mother," he said. "When my father died, I was only a boy. She worked three jobs and kept the five of us alive and happy, and never complained a bit."

"Never? Oh, come on. No one's *that* good. You're being nostalgic."

"Well, almost never," he said. "How about your parents?"

"My father died several years ago. I don't know about my

mother. I haven't heard from her in over thirty years now."

"Wow! How come?"

"She left my father and us when I was fourteen. Just disappeared. We got a postcard once, I can't even remember from where, but nothing before or since."

"That's sad."

"Used to be. It's old news."

"Something like that is never old news. It's always with you."

"Ha! You sound like a man with secrets."

"It's just that we all carry the past with us. It's impossible to escape."

"So you're a philosopher as well as an historian," I said.

"Sort of. Just experience, really."

"What can't you escape?" I asked.

"There are things, things with my wife and kids, for instance. Regrets," he said and smiled, then started crooning, "I've had a few, but then again too few to mention."

I rewarded him with a smile.

"What are your regrets?" he asked. "From the very beginning, you've been mysterious."

"Does that bother you?"

"I don't know. I'm curious, I guess. I want to know about you."

"No, you don't," I said and smiled again. "I like being a mystery woman."

The waiter came by, and Tom ordered another couple of beers for us. I was feeling tipsy, though, a kind of downward plunge that I knew might take me a while to recover from. "Ginger ale," I corrected the waiter.

"I want to sleep with you tonight," Tom said as soon as the waiter left.

I coughed. "You can't say that."

"Well, I at least want to kiss you, but I thought I might as well go for broke."

I laughed. "You don't beat around the bush, do you?"

"So, what's it going to be?"

"You'll just have to wait and see, won't you?" I said.

I had not been with a man in four months, not since Cooper, and that was drunken and mean and didn't count really. Tom's skin was surprisingly soft, despite the ropy muscles, the tanned arms, neck, and face. The rest of his body was milky white, and there was an odd and very sexy combination of strength and frailty in his thin, muscled body. In bed, when he ran his hand over my stomach, he seemed to be shaking.

"Are you okay?"

"I'm Catholic. We don't do this sort of thing lightly."

"What sort of thing?"

"Sin."

"This was your idea, remember."

"Don't get me wrong," he said. "I just said we don't do these things lightly."

"Are you sure you know what you're doing?" Gloria asked me as I put my clothes in the suitcase and boxed up the few belongings I'd brought with me from Houston.

"Yes."

"Don't you think it's a little too soon? You can stay here as long as you like."

"I want to do this. Besides, you're the one who said he'd be a catch."

"It's not him that I'm worried about."

"I'll be okay. Don't worry. It's not that serious."

"Be careful, Laura," she said and hugged me tight. "Please, please be careful."

Everything went pretty well for a while. Tom made a bundle with Auto Buddy, and I soon learned the business, started keeping the books, even went out on calls with him. Before long I could jimmy a lock, fix a flat, jump a battery, open a carburetor valve, tape hoses. You name it. I continued to cater the poker parties.

Everything would have been okay, I thought, if he hadn't decided he needed to marry me.

I was skittish. As long as we were only living together, enjoying each other's company, with no stronger connection, we were fine. We lived as I knew animals did, in the here and now, without concern for the past or future. He knew very little about my past. I'd just gotten out of the mess with Cooper. But there had been Marty and Neil, and other men who had drifted in and out of my life. During a bad spell with Cooper, my son told me, "Mother, you've got the worst karma with husbands I've ever seen." And he was right. If you are forty-six, and you have been married four times; if your first husband (the love of your life, the father of your children, the man you once remarried) is dead; if your other two husbands are bad memories, laced with infidelities and humiliation; if you begin to believe what your friends and family have told you — that you have indeed screwed up your life and will more than likely never get it straight; if you have all that behind you, then you don't trust your own judgment anymore, and you most certainly don't trust any institution so seemingly rigged against human happiness.

When Tom asked me to marry him, I told myself, "Get out, get out, get out! Move away before you're in too deep."

But I couldn't leave him. I didn't think I was in love with him.

In fact, I wasn't sure I believed in love anymore, since I'd seen, from my own marriages, what could be done in the name of love. Love wasn't the right word for it. Regardless, old patterns are hard to break, and if you're used to being married, then you can be appealed to.

The issue of marriage formed a wedge between us over the next few months. That I wouldn't marry him, would not commit to him in any definite, permanent way, disturbed, angered, then finally unnerved him. He felt that he was making a huge sacrifice by finally divorcing his first wife so he would be free to be with me. "I'm no longer a good Catholic," he would tell me. The issue was made worse by his ex. Her lawyer sent a letter to Tom demanding half of Auto Buddy. He would come home angry and frustrated, unable to figure out why she'd do this to him.

Then other events conspired to aggravate the situation. Losing heavily in a poker game one night, Tom had to leave for an Auto Buddy call and hit a parked car but did not stick around. So he constantly feared the police would pick him up and that he would lose his business altogether. Then his mother fell ill with a stomach infection, and while she was in the hospital having that treated, the doctors discovered cancer in her digestive system. Her stomach and colon were practically eaten away. When she decided not to go through the cancer treatment, Tom moved her to a nursing home. The doctors didn't give her much time, a few months if she was lucky. I went with Tom to see her several times, and each time she wanted to know when her son was going to do me right (her words), make an honest woman of me. He was living in sin, and divorce or no divorce, she wanted her son conducting only sanctified conjugal relations.

Then Cooper tracked me down and began to call in the middle

of the night, harassing me. He called once when I was out and spewed his vomit at Tom, told him that I would leave him, that I was spiteful, that I would use him, screw his best friends, take his cash, and get the hell out of Dodge. I wasn't to be trusted. Tom told him to take a flying leap and reassured me that he didn't believe a word that goddamn fool told him. But he became even more adamant about marriage.

"Please, Laura," he said.

"I'm sorry," I answered. "Your marriage hasn't worked out. Mine haven't either. Marriage won't solve anything for us. We're happier the way we are now."

"I've got a mother who wonders every day when we'll stop living in sin," he said.

"Doesn't a divorce put you in sin anyway?"

"Laura, please."

"Don't push this, Tom."

"What do you mean, don't push? How can I not push? It's driving me crazy."

"If I marry you, will that fix anything?" I said. "It's just paper. Expensive paper. The only thing it does is put us both at a disadvantage. It's a business deal, a contract, and this isn't business."

"Do you love me?" he asked.

"That doesn't have anything to do with it."

"The hell it doesn't."

He wanted assurances I couldn't give.

About a week later I went with Tom to the nursing home. His mother had experienced a resurgence. The nurses had reduced her medication, and for the first time in a few weeks, she was lucid and relatively pain-free. Tom and I sat with her for a long time. I washed and then brushed her thick hair, splayed out so beautifully on the pillow behind her while Tom read to her, first from the Bible and then some letters from Tom's brothers and sisters, who lived all over the country with their families. Then he got paged for an Auto Buddy call and had to leave. I stayed with his mother. She slept for a half hour, then woke up and saw me there and seemed confused at first.

"Jill," she said. "What are you doing here?"

"It's Laura, Mrs. O'Connor. Tom's friend."

She blinked her eyes a few times, then shook her head, as if to shake the cobwebs out. "Can I have my glasses?" I put them on her, and at once she seemed to recognize me. "Oh, yes, Laura," she said. "I'm sorry. I thought you were Jill there for a moment."

"That's okay," I said. I brushed her hair again and straightened her pillow so she was more comfortable. We sat there for a few minutes in silence, and I thought she had gone back to sleep again, but then she suddenly opened her eyes and reached up and gingerly straightened her glasses.

"My Tommy, he's a good man," she said. "But when he gets confused, he gets angry, and he doesn't see straight. Ever since he was a little boy, he has been this way. Don't be afraid."

"I don't know what you mean, Mrs. O'Connor."

"There is something about you, dear, that is afraid. I don't know if it's because of Tom. It may be. I'm sorry if it is. Maybe it's something else. But you cannot be afraid of your own life."

"I'm not sure I understand."

"Yes, you do," she said. "I see it in you, and you know it's there. But I don't know if Tom knows it yet. But he senses it, I can tell, and it confuses him." I nodded, though I wasn't sure at what. "He loves you, dear. You know that."

"Yes," I said.

"Do you love him?"

"It's more complicated than that."

"No, it's not more complicated. It just seems so. Please do me a favor. I won't live much longer. You must find out and know one way or another. My son loves you very much, and he deserves to know."

"Yes, ma'am," I said, but I felt more confused than ever.

"You deserve it too," she said.

A few days later I got a call from my son in Nashville, inviting me to visit. I hadn't heard from Lee in almost a year, and we'd not been on good terms for a long time. We had moved a lot, and I had a pretty serious problem with alcohol for several years and had to commit myself to a place in Houston for a few months. Lee and Cindy had been drawn into pretty bad situations with Marty and Cooper, and other men. They resented me, I knew, and had for a long time. I couldn't really blame them.

The last time Lee and I talked in person, I was still married to Cooper. I was drunk at the time, and we had a terrible fight. I told him he was an ingrate, that he should have supported me through my troubled times. He called me a lush. He said I married for money. He said I was weak, and that I had jeopardized their safety to satisfy my desires. He said he couldn't forgive me for that.

How could I answer that? When the hurt is that deep, what do you say? And it was hard to dispute what he said. I had jeopardized their safety. And while he had been hurt, it was Cindy who had suffered the most. Like my mother, she had disappeared from me. Dropped out of school to get married. Had a baby, then left him with her husband. Was heavily involved in drugs for a long time. Then I lost her. No one seemed to know where she was (or is). Or if they did, they didn't tell me. For all I knew, she could be hurt or dead or maybe just hiding from me because I hadn't protected her. Just as my mother hadn't protected me.

After I left Cooper, I started writing letters to Lee again, keeping everything light and newsy. No angst, no hint of problems. I mentioned that I worked for Tom and was dating him, but I didn't say that I was living with him. I figured Lee wouldn't approve. He had never written me back, so for him to suddenly call and invite me to visit him was quite a surprise.

He told me that he and his wife, Hannah, now had a little girl named Yvonne. (I hadn't even known Hannah was pregnant!) He was a repertory actor, and he said he had a role in an old Cole Porter musical, *Anything Goes*, at a professional regional theater. He wanted me to come out and see the baby and the show. I told him I'd love to.

I didn't tell Tom about the invitation, though, and a week later, while he was on an Auto Buddy call, I packed my bags, called a taxi to take me to the airport, and flew to Nashville. I left no note, no telephone number, no explanation.

I had a good time in Nashville. Lee was very funny in the musical. He played an Englishman, and I told him how impressed I was with his accent, and with his singing and dancing, and with the cartwheel he did at the end of the first act.

"My monocle fell out of my eye."

"I didn't even notice," I said. "You were brilliant. I cried, I was so proud."

"My mother, the blubber butt," he said.

"I take it back. You were awful. You have no rhythm. You were constantly off-key. Your fly was open."

I could tell that my being there made him happy. But we talked cautiously, skirting taboo subjects. We didn't talk about Cindy.

We didn't talk about his childhood. We went to Opryland and visited some of the war memorials. I spent much of the week with Hannah because Lee rehearsed for another show during the day and had performances at night. They had been married for three years, and I had always found it impossible to carry on a conversation with her. She made me nervous. Hannah was a petite, quiet woman, plain looking and self-conscious, essentially good natured. Her parents were not divorced, so there was always an edge there, a disapproving judgment that she tried to mask but couldn't entirely, and I couldn't help but think that her disapproval had its sources in fear. In her most private thoughts, she had to wonder if Lee would turn out like me or Cindy or the rest of my family, for that matter. But we got along surprisingly well while I was there. The baby was gorgeous, just starting to crawl around, and she gave us plenty to talk about.

Near the end of the week, however, there were two bad moments. On Saturday we were sitting in the living room. Hannah sat in the rocker with Yvonne. I flipped through a photograph album. Lee lay on the couch, tossing a basketball in the air.

"So what about Tom?" he asked suddenly. "You haven't mentioned him since you've been here."

I told them about Auto Buddy and the catering and a few of the trips we'd taken, mostly a rehash of what I'd said in the letters. I showed them a sepia-tinted picture of Tom and me dressed up like frontier trappers, wearing deerskin jackets and squirrel-tailed hats, holding shotguns and jugs that read "Rot Gut."

"You're not going to marry him, are you?" he asked, and I saw Hannah shoot him a dirty look. A warning.

"I know what you think I should do," I said. "Or shouldn't do."

"It's your life," he said and shrugged his shoulders like he didn't give a damn.

"Yes, it is," I said and went back to the pictures.

Hannah saved us by asking Lee to run to the store while she put the baby down and I started supper.

A couple of days later, before I went home, I was playing with the baby and Hannah said, "You're wonderful with kids." She meant it as a compliment, but I took it the wrong way. I was sure Lee had told her horror stories. I doubted he remembered that I was a good mother when he was young.

"Even if I'm not always good with adults," I said. I smiled to take the heat out of what I said, and Hannah smiled back, then changed the subject.

At the airport I told them what a wonderful time I'd had and complimented Lee again on his performance. I made them promise to spend Christmas with me, though I knew even as I said it that it was an empty promise. I had no idea where I'd be.

On the plane, flying over Tennessee, Arkansas, and back down into Texas, I felt terribly depressed. Seeing Lee and Hannah with their new daughter made me think of when I was eighteen and married to Neil, Lee just a baby himself. Though it was terrible to admit, I was jealous of them, jealous of their youth and their lives, their hopeful future together. They trusted and were committed to each other.

It was hard to imagine Lee coming to see me every day when I was eighty, bedridden. Impossible to picture him or Cindy giving me baths, combing my old lady's hair, telling me dirty jokes. And there would be no mother for me to take care of, either. I had thought that I had let that go, but at times like these, she was always there, or rather the fact of her disappearance was always there, like an amputee's limb. A phantom.

I try, as a rule, not to succumb to self-pity, but black periods sometimes overwhelm me. My ears popping because of the cabin pressure, I stared out the window at the oppressive white clouds and considered how I'd systematically destroyed every relationship that mattered to me.

I'd not called Tom the entire time I was away. I had pushed him from my thoughts. Why hadn't I called? Why hadn't I left a number, at least? Why had I not told him beforehand where I was going? On the plane I tried to examine why I wanted to hurt him that way. Was it my own cowardice — not wanting to face anymore scenes, not wanting to explain that I wanted to be away from him? Or was I running away from myself, from the inevitable progression toward marriage and what that meant in my life? I felt myself weakening. That was clear. Did I want something to happen? Did I want to reveal my worst self to him, prove that Cooper was right — I could not be trusted? It dawned on me that I'd spent my whole life waiting for people to find out about me, for the Fraud Police to knock on my door and tell everyone I wasn't as good as I pretended to be. I started to cry then, knowing, with sudden clarity, that, yes, I did love Tom. Why then was I so determined to hurt him and myself? That wasn't love. It made no sense. I felt a rage swell in my chest. But who was I angry with? Tom? Lee and Hannah? Cooper, Marty, Neil? My mother? Cindy? Myself?

Flying above the earth, above everything, I thought it would probably be best if I went to a place where I didn't know anyone, where I could be totally anonymous, where I didn't matter. But I know it's impossible to escape your own life, and if you tried, as I had done so many times, then you wound up more lost than ever before. I wondered if my mother felt this way, wherever she was. If Cindy felt this way.

Still, at the airport, I stood in line at the ticket counter for a good ten minutes before I finally fought off the desire to catch a flight someplace else and forced myself to take a cab home.

Tom was not there. The place was a wreck: newspapers all over the house, ashtrays full of butts, dishes stacked in the sink and on the counter with food still on them. I went back to the bedroom, and that too was a mess. The bed unmade, Tom's clothes strewn all over. My dresses were on the floor of the closet, fingered and thrown about sloppily, my favorite blue and black-striped one ripped.

I started cleaning. I didn't even unpack, just left my suitcases by the front door, and then cleaned and cleaned — not just tidying up, but deep cleaning with Comet, bristle brushes, vacuum, dusters. When I finished with the kitchen, I was starving, so I decided to fix myself something to eat. I got out the skillet and put several slices of bacon in. I cracked two eggs in a plastic cup, whipped them hard with a fork.

About that time I heard Tom's truck pull up outside. I kept about my business. Didn't move, just stayed right in the kitchen and jostled the bacon with a spatula, watched the white strips of fat wrinkle, turn clear. Tom unlocked the front door. He didn't come into the kitchen immediately, though he must have known I was there. The house was clean. The lights were on. The smell of the bacon. I turned the burner on medium, then got some bread out and put it in the toaster.

After a couple of minutes he came into the kitchen, carrying the small suitcase I'd left in the hallway. He set it gently on the counter, leaned across, near the light, so that his face and gray hair were lit up brightly, strangely, by the fluorescence. I wondered if he'd been drinking. He was not much of a drinker, and I had been, so I would have known, would have smelled. But, still, there was an exhausted, coiled look about him, as if he'd not slept in several days.

"Did you have a good trip?" he asked. He did not mention the suitcase. I looked at it, then at him.

"Yes," I said and carefully flipped the bacon over with the fork.

"I called Gloria," he said. "She didn't know where you were, either."

"I didn't tell her," I said.

"Where did you go?"

"Nashville. To see my son."

"There's someone else, isn't there?"

"Don't be ridiculous," I said.

He raised an eyebrow, as if he'd caught me in a lie. "What does he do?"

"Tom, there's no one else."

"Does he live in Nashville? Don't tell me he's a goddamn country-western singer?"

"Tom —"

"Why didn't you tell me where you were going?" he asked. "That's not like you. Not that I know in the least bit what you're like."

That's when I wanted out of there. Not because I was afraid. I felt ashamed for both of us, here like this. The accuser. The accused. I'd been in this situation before, and this moment seemed both deserved and beneath us — humiliating. He looked at me. I turned away, my eyes on the suitcase. He kept staring at me, for the longest time, but I wouldn't meet his eyes. Finally, he looked at the suitcase too. It was between us. A symbol of something, but I wasn't sure what.

My toast sprang up and surprised us both. I took it out of the toaster, then got margarine from the fridge and knifed it on. I came back to the skillet and stirred my bacon until it hardened in the popping grease. The air conditioner clicked on suddenly, rattled, then settled into a purr.

I felt very odd then, both desperate and calm at the same time. When I was fourteen, the day before my mother left me and my brothers with our father, I stood at the window during a heavy storm. While I was looking out the window, lightning suddenly hit the tree in our front yard. Cut it right in two. I knew a split second before it hit what would happen, and there was a thrill in that moment, in the knowing what was unknowable. I felt that same sensation now. Something unforgettable was about to happen.

"Are you hungry?" I asked.

"No."

"Are you sure?"

"I'm not hungry," he said.

There was a long pause, and I didn't breathe. I could feel something dark and thick puddling inside me.

"Marry me," he said. I didn't respond. In fact, what he said hadn't even registered clearly with me. I heard what was underneath his voice, and what was underneath sliced through me. Despite his anger, there was a tenderness there, some vulnerable spot that made me want to hurt him. He seemed more fragile than I'd ever seen him. Something had happened to him while I was gone. Something significant. He seemed exposed. I knew what his next words would be. "I love you," he said.

I hated us being there, what we had been brought to, though

how we'd gotten here I didn't understand, and what it meant I did not know. All I knew was that I wanted to escape my life at that moment. I wanted it to change. Permanently.

"Did you hear me?" he said.

"Yes." I put the spatula to the side. I reached back, turned off the eye on the stove, and began to move the skillet to a cool eye.

"Answer me, goddamnit!"

What happened next must have taken only a few minutes. It seemed like hours, like a movie in slow motion, all without words.

He reached across the counter and grabbed my arm and jerked it. The skillet was in my hands, and then it was away from me — how did I let it get away? did I throw it? — in one snap-rapid moment, all of it flying toward his face, the skillet hitting the counter and clattering to the floor. The bacon slapped his forehead, stuck there for an almost funny moment, then dropped to the counter. The grease beaded up like sprinkles of water on his cheek, his neck, his forearm, then glazed over like candle wax before he even had time to jump back. He wiped frantically at himself for a moment or two before he lunged, his arms outstretched over the counter. My suitcase slid across and toppled the toaster, the toast, the margarine. He grabbed for me, but I jumped back, my blouse ripping in his hand. He reached out with his other hand, and I slapped it. I could see blisters already swelling on his arm, over the hairs, and I skirted around the counter.

I intended to run out the door. But, instead, I fled down the deep hallway, which was light and seemed to yawn for me, and circled through the bedroom, into the bathroom. I shut the door quickly, fumbled with the lock, which would not lock at all, not at all, until I turned it the right way and it finally clicked, leaving me standing there a moment, just a quiet split second, listening to my own rasping.

Then I felt the floor begin to shake under me. I could feel the heavy thud of him in the living room, the hallway, the bedroom. When he kicked the door the first time, it buckled, a quick bubble of wood, and I stepped back, startled, my heart an entire apple in my throat. He kicked again, and the lock splintered the wood, a chip catching miraculously in my bra. I stood there, frozen. He kicked again. The door swung open, off its hinges at the top. I lost my footing, fell back into and through the shower curtain, slipping over the bathtub, the dark blue plastic swallowing me like a shroud.

I couldn't see. I was tangled. Then I felt myself being lifted and turned, the word *levitate* suddenly in my mind, the *pop, pop, pop* of the plastic rings breaking before I fell back against the porcelain.

I could see above me suddenly. Tom there, his long gray hair loose and wild, a thin slab of red creases on his forehead, the curtain rod in his hands. His hands shook, his knuckles white white white. When you are in a moment like that, you do not have time to be afraid, and I wasn't. I waited for what was going to happen. In a way I wanted it to happen. I thought, *Come on. Let's make a clean break, not leave it messy and unresolved!* I didn't give a damn about myself at that moment. That is the truth.

I screamed, "Do it!"

I closed my eyes for just a second, and then I heard rather than felt the dull crack against my jaw, and when I opened my eyes again, Tom was standing there with the rod in his hand, his own eyes wide open and, I could see, afraid — mortified by what he'd done. I closed my eyes and waited for whatever was about to happen. I felt eerily calm. Then I heard another crack, but it wasn't me. When I opened my eyes again, bits of the ceiling from above the bathtub sprinkled down on me like soft snow. The curtain rod dangled there like somebody's silver arm.

I stayed where I was, watched the rod. The house, the whole night, was amazingly quiet. I'd been in this moment before—too often. Everything completely frozen. I thought, *Is this what I asked for?*

Finally, I worked my way out of the tangle, not really knowing what to expect next. What would he do? What *could* he do?

I brushed myself off. My jaw tingled. I tasted blood and rinsed cold water in my mouth. It burned. I wasn't sure where Tom was, but I thought I heard a ripple of sound. I went into the bedroom. He sat on the edge of the bed, away from me, his face in his hands, his back jerking up and down in little spasms. I went over, stood before him. When he finally looked at me, his face seemed—I'll never forget this—like a spider web of wrinkles, his tears wet in the creases. He was trying not to cry, but it was coming out now in choked sobs that sounded worse than any wailing I'd ever heard before, and I felt that this incident, this thing between us, had hurt him more than it had me. It struck me that maybe nothing like it had ever happened to him.

Neither of us spoke. Then I turned and walked out of the bedroom, slowly, deliberately, retraced my steps down the hallway, into the kitchen. I turned off the stove, picked up the margarine, the knife, and put them in the sink. I unspooled paper towels and wiped the grease from the stove, counter, and floor.

I picked up my suitcase and started toward the door. I thought, *I can go anywhere I want.* And I could have. Back to Gloria's, or to Manny's, or back to Houston where maybe I'd find Cindy, back to Tennessee with Lee and Hannah and the new baby, back to Cooper, who perhaps I did deserve after all. I could go someplace new, someplace where no one would know me, where no one could find me. This was not the life I had imagined for myself, and yet here I was. I was accountable. Not for all of it. But for enough. And I wondered, really wondered, *What do I want? What do I care about? What does it mean to be here?*

I put the suitcase by the door and went out back to the patio, sat down on the lawn chair, looked up at the night sky, which was bluish black, clear, and pocked with a million stars. I thought about what Tom had said to me once, about the stars, how far away they are, how old the universe is, billions of years, and made up of mostly cold, empty space. A great *indifference*, he said. "The universe can be malicious because it doesn't *care*," he had said. Was that true?

I closed my eyes. It smelled good and green, with a cool westerly breeze, and I just sat there for a while and smelled the night. The violence of what had just happened with Tom — and what had been happening for so long now, with Marty, with Cooper, within myself — seemed remote, far away, as if it had happened to someone else. I felt it had blasted not in me, like an implosion, but *through* me. And I felt strangely cleaned out, purified, not really damaged. Above all else, I felt quiet now.

I don't know how long I was there before I heard the sliding glass open and Tom's footsteps on the patio. He came over and sat on the grass a few feet away and said nothing for a while. Both of us just listened to the night. I could see his long gray hair, uncontained, shining in the moonlight.

"What happened in there?" he finally asked.

"I don't know," I said.

"I want to tell you how sorry I am, but that doesn't seem good enough."

"I know. Me too."

"I don't want to be that person, Laura."

I didn't say anything. He ran his hands through his hair, then spoke softly, almost to himself. "I want to tell you something. When my oldest son was about nine or ten," he said, "I was always so angry then. I didn't love my wife anymore but was afraid to admit that to myself, afraid of what it would mean. One night I came home from work, and we started arguing, and Tommy kept talking and getting under our feet. I told him to go in the other room, but he wouldn't do it. He knew, I guess, what was going on between us, and he was angry too, mad at both of us, and afraid. We kept arguing, then we started yelling, and there was a momentum there that had a life of its own. Tommy tried to push me away, then started hitting at me, and finally I grabbed him by the arms and shook him, hard. He cried out, and I let him go. And then he crumpled to the floor, sobbing. I looked down at him, so small and sad there, and I promised myself I'd never be that kind of person again, never get that overcome by my own anger."

"What happened?" I asked. "With your son, I mean."

"We took him to the hospital. His shoulder was dislocated. But that was the real end of my marriage. And Tommy never trusted me after that. I couldn't blame him. I had promised myself it wouldn't happen again, though. Ever. But tonight it happened."

"It wasn't just you," I said.

"That doesn't matter." We were quiet again. Then he said, "My mother died."

"When?" I whispered.

"She slipped into a coma on Saturday, and I told them not to keep her on the respirator. She didn't want that. So they took her off, and then I sat there until she stopped breathing. It was quiet.

But I felt just . . . just empty. I didn't know where you had gone. I've been so angry, just simmering here, waiting for you to come back, sure you wouldn't, not sure what would happen if you did."

I wanted to say something, but I didn't know what to say. It seemed important to let him speak. I wanted him to go on, to tell me what he thought had happened.

"I knew I didn't want her to die, but when she did go, I wanted you here. And I could see you both slipping away, just like my boys."

He looked at me then, and I reached out and ran my hand through his hair, gently fingering his scalp, which seemed alive to my touch. I traced the red mark on his forehead, already a welt. I sat there by him, softly touching his head. Neither of us said a word for several minutes. He reached through the dark and touched my face.

I suddenly started crying. I didn't know why. It didn't hurt. And I wasn't sad. It was, in fact, one of the most remarkable moments of my life.

"I don't know what happens now," he said.

I ran my fingers through his hair, over the back of his neck.

At that point I didn't know if I would stay or not, marry him or not, if I loved him or not, if there was a more precise word for what was between us. But I felt a shift in me, that I was on the verge of something important, and I knew that I didn't want to be anywhere else at that moment. I was suddenly aware that I no longer felt the need to escape my own life. This is where I was. This is who I was. And, for better or worse, it was this defenseless and penitent moment that would keep me in Amarillo, where I felt I might belong.

In the *Prairie Schooner*
Book Prize in Fiction series

Last Call
By K. L. Cook